Verge

Z Egloff

*Winner of the fourth annual
Bywater Prize for Fiction*

VERGE

Z Egloff

Bywater
BOOKS

Ann Arbor
2009

Bywater Books, Inc.
PO Box 3671
Ann Arbor MI 48106-3671
www.bywaterbooks.com

Printed in the United States of America on acid-free paper.

Bywater Books First Edition: February 2009

Cover designer: Bonnie Liss (Phoenix Graphics)
Author photo: Sassy Stafford

ISBN 978-1-932859-68-3

This novel is a work of fiction. All persons, places, and events were created by the imagination of the author.

Mixed Sources
Product group from well-managed
forests and other controlled sources
www.fsc.org Cert no. SW-COC-002283
© 1996 Forest Stewardship Council
FSC

To my parents

Acknowledgments

It takes a posse. I am beyond grateful to all of those who supported me through this process, starting with my draft readers Debra Avanche, Juan Gonzalez, Char Hall, Jennifer Jacobs, Kem Mahiri, Jayme Paine, Susan Meade, Carolina Portales, Wendy Righetti, Sylvia Saxon, and Jill Shinn. Your collective feedback improved the book immeasurably. Additional thanks to Lillian Howan, Jill Koenigsdorf, Karen Laws, and Becca Lawton for taking me into the fold and providing insight, inspiration, and community. To my teacher Anne Matlack Evans for her encouragement and astute instruction. To my brother Georg and his wife Laura for their enthusiasm from the start. To Pauline Richardson, for allowing me the time and space to pursue this work. To my prayer peeps Maggie Brown, Reed Dickinson, Jeremiah and Shoshana Love, Pat Marcelli, Linda McDonald, and Yvonne Rawhauser for your open-hearted persistence. To Donna Norton for helping me hold the vision. To Renee Owen for kicking my ass. To Karl and Rebecca and the Healdsburg sweat lodge community for their smokin' prayers. To my Lesbo Row girls—Lisa Barry, Sally Castleberry, Andria Duff, Cairyl Gardner, and Sallie Hasseltine—for your blessings of friendship and faith. To Linda Collett, Pat Jacobs, Marcy Roth, and Barbara Stafford for the same. To VB, my first reader. To everyone at the Center for Spiritual Living, for continually enriching my mind and my heart. To Angela Rinaldi for her enthusiasm and expertise. To Bywater Books, for taking a chance with a freshly hatched writer. And to my parents, David and Susan Egloff, for their immense capacity for loving and believing in me.

Slam Dance

Jack is storming, a heroic kind of madness Claire has seen only in the movies. In real life, it's worse. Louder.

"What in God's name were you thinking?" He slams a drawer into his desk, releasing a flock of papers to the floor. "Though I suspect thinking had nothing to do with it. Did you park your brain on the freeway? Did someone run over it with a truck?"

Claire bites her cheek, sucks the skin between her molars. "I don't know what you're talking about." She does, though. She has a real good idea.

"Bullshit! Why do you think lying will get you out of this, Claire? Haven't you done enough of that already? Or maybe you haven't. Lie your face off, it doesn't matter. If you have no morals, nothing matters."

"I'm not lying." She spots her name on one of the papers on the floor. Her first paper of her last class in her last semester at this crummy little school. He gave her an A.

"And you're also no longer in this class." Jack's wrath thins to a point. To this. "And you're also no longer my teaching assistant."

Everything up until now has been bad luck, misfired circumstances, but this, this is not funny.

"You can't. Jack, you can't. I need this."

"Apparently you don't. Apparently you don't need much of anything."

The window in Jack's office is open and Claire can see the

1

huge tree, the one that is always there, eavesdropping on their conversation. *Sucker,* it says. She leans over to pick up her paper off the pile on Jack's floor ("Excellent, your usual perverse commentary") and stuffs it into her backpack.

"This is so messed up," she says.

"Indeed. I'm glad you understand something. Remarkable, really." He points. "The door is behind you."

"And the window is in front of me."

"It's your choice." Jack is smiling. Strict and simmering. "I'll alert the custodial staff. They can scrape your body off the sidewalk."

He's obviously not serious. Who could be serious about something like that? But as Claire rechecks his features—proud eyes, stretched mouth, cheeks still thick with anger—she sees that whatever is there that was hers, whatever it was, is already gone. Hurled out the window with the rest of the big ideas and failed expectations.

"But—" She stops. There's nothing to say. He's right. It's all her fault.

"But—some people make mistakes and some make disasters. Welcome to disaster, Claire. You've earned it."

She nods. Then tightens the strap of her backpack and walks out the door.

It's a three-minute walk from Jack's office to the bicycle parked in front of the Humanities building, and Claire marches down the sidewalk, hollow in herself. Chatting students, a line of trees packed with spastic squirrels, the scent of dying leaves, sweet and futile. She ignores it all.

It used to be good, with Jack. Claire can still remember sitting with her fellow students in the back of room 32A, the click and blang of the old projector inciting their minds and hearts to greatness, while their noble instigator sat at his desk in the front of the classroom, visions of filmmakers living and dead plastered across his chubby arms and too-short legs. Welles, Eisenstein, Fassbinder, Truffaut—all the Greats in the room with Claire and the others, the future and oh-so-inevitably-to-be-also Greats. Living projectors, every one.

Hanging with Jack was like hanging with a sense of promise, a crisp veering from the meaningless activities that plagued Claire's life before she stepped into his classroom. Through Jack's eyes, Claire began to fashion herself into someone with a mission—an edict, really—to turn life into art, pain into pathos, cruelty into climax. She would make movies, is what she would do. And Jack would help her, Jack would be her muse: her patient champion of all things artful, inspired, and cinematic.

But that's over. Claire screwed it. She screwed it literally and in other ways, and the remains of her actions have gathered themselves together to return the favor. It's righteous, warranted. Beautiful, in a way. And there's nothing to be done.

She slows her steps, halting in front of her bicycle and popping her key into the indestructible bike lock she's had since forever. She's thought about getting a car, but the expenses of college and her devotion to the motion of wheel and pedal and push have prohibited such a purchase. Claire stashes her lock under the clip rack over the back tire and pats her seat, for luck. As she does so, she envisions a parallel gesture from above—an invisible hand nudging her shoulder blades, wishing her well. And though she laughs it off, the skin under her T-shirt stings with the notion. Justified or not, the thought of solace is something to allow.

The way back is mostly flat land and heat. It's a half-hour from the college to Bearley and Claire chugs along the frontage road, pedals whizzing, baked air snaking up the back of her shirt.

The territory she's traversing, the whole clutter of houses

and people that branch out from the interstate in every direction, is an anomaly to Claire. How is it, she wonders, that a crop of beings can live in such close proximity to San Francisco, the greatest city on earth (so she's heard; Claire rarely goes there), and still maintain such short-sighted existences? Trucks with gun racks. Bumper stickers extolling the virtues of hunting, fishing, breathing etc. over their wives. Folks who can yak for half an hour on the finer points of proper lawn maintenance or barbecue strategies, but not ten minutes on anything culturally significant or socially challenging. Claire's family among them.

And the heat. Always the heat. Farther west, closer to the city, they have nifty devices like fog and clouds to mute the mighty California sun. Yet in Bearley, Point Firth, and the host of other towns and cities east of Concord east of Walnut Creek east of Berkeley east of Manna, no such relief exists. There is simply hot rage, from dawn to dusk, dusk being the only part of the day that the residents of these Easternly East terrains dare to venture out of doors. Hyperactive dogs, land-locked kids, surly dads in low-rider lawn chairs—it's in the evenings that folks come out to play, reveling in the brief respite before the arrival of yet another morning and the blast of yet another sun.

Claire takes it like a man. She accommodates herself to the heat as if it's a bad relative, smiling and lying low, shifting into inconspicuous. She's had years of practice, having lived here since her family moved from the Central Valley to Point Firth when she was eight, thereafter skipping from town to town until Bearley—cheap, empty, dust-engorged Bearley with its name like a jest, a built-in joke against itself—emerged as the place they would call home. Claire loves Bearley in the way you love anything you hate: quietly, brushing it with affection only when heads are turned. She knows there will come a time, years off, when the distance between her and this place will enlarge them both. Bearley will become an amusing memory,

4

a tale to tell, a still-to-be-born function that allows Claire to inhabit it now, to stretch and run and find her way inside the town's cramped, cozy walls. What Is To Come peppers What Is with magic and fractured realism. With lies.

Kitty's Chevy is parked in the driveway when Claire gets home. Her mother's truck is at an angle, as usual, situated in such a way that no one else can place a vehicle next to, or even in the vicinity of, the battered blue pickup. Claire glides in on her bicycle and flips the latch to the gate on the side of the house. The noise coming from the kitchen—splices of rock 'n' roll and laughter, probably Kitty and the neighbor—inspires a series of fleeing motions in Claire: gate open, gate shut, a trek across the field of dried mud and weeds that constitutes the back-yard of her mother's home. Claire's smaller, satellite version of this home, tucked into the northeast corner of the lot, is the converted outbuilding she moved into seven years ago, the day she turned eighteen. Her friend Shelly likes to say that it looks like the house of a drug-dealing Oompa Loompa. Claire likes to remind Shelly that she sucks.

It's more than stuffy inside, compliments of the California fall and Claire's lack of air conditioning. She pulls off her shirt and hugs the refrigerator, arms straddling the freezer's bulk. She waits until the goosebumps on her arms are hard as pebbles and her breasts ache with chill, then steps back, pops open the door, and rummages for dinner. It's not until later, plastered on her bed, an ice cube disintegrating into her abdomen, that she notices the blinking red light.

Usually this would be first, the checking of messages, but today's combination of heat and harsh times have relegated this task to Not Happening. The little red light says eight. Eight calls. Claire rolls over and the cube of ice slides off her stomach and onto the bed.

It's all hang ups until the last call, which is something else altogether. At first, Claire thinks it's a prank—a garbled voice spewing hysteria and volume into her tiny machine. After the fourth playback, though, she realizes it's not a joke. She shuts off the answering machine and picks up the phone.

"Is Shelly there?" Claire pokes her finger into the coils of the phone line. It's Kenny. Kenny won't tell her crap.

"Who's this?"

"You know who it is. Where's Shelly?"

Kenny is silent. Claire can hear people in the background but can't tell if they're real or televised.

"Dude. Where is she? Is everything okay?"

He sighs. Apparently his level of inconvenience in having to talk to Claire is topped only by having to answer her questions. "She's fine. It's cool. Everything's cool."

Claire twists the coils until the tip of her finger turns blue. "If everything's so goddamn cool, then why am I not talking to your wife right now? Why am I still talking to you?"

The voices on Kenny's end cease abruptly—a mute button pressed, a Play pushed to Pause. "And you think I want to talk to you, you lesbo freak? Let me tell you something ..."

Claire plunks the receiver back on top of the phone, snuffing out the fizzle that is Kenny. "Let me tell you something" is, in her experience, the perfect time to end almost any exchange.

She grabs her T-shirt from its bunched state at the bottom of her bed and fits it back on her body. The trip to Shelly's should be a breeze: rush hour traffic off the freeway, her bicycle, the heat of the day absorbed in her legs; this precarious mix should get her to Point Firth in thirty minutes, tops. The blinking 8 on Claire's answering machine blends into her peripheral vision and she holds it there, the latest line in a conversation she's been having her entire life.

"Go Away," says the doormat on the step outside the house of Shelly's parents, and Claire knows they mean it. Shelly's dad

Skinny, who is anything but, has a habit of roughing up other people's edges, everyone from his wife to various personnel in the local law enforcement office. Going away is usually Claire's plan, as far as Skinny is concerned. She's pretty sure he's gone, though; his truck is not in any of its usual resting places, his favorite being a spot next to the bush on which he likes to relieve himself after rolling in from the bar.

The front door is open, but Claire stays on the mat. Skinny's absence notwithstanding, barging into the house is never the preferred option.

"If you're looking for my sister, she ain't here." The voice streams through the door and into Claire's ears. "So you can take that Speed Racer bike of yours and pedal on home."

Claire squints. Through the awning, past a layer of smoke and dust and faded light, a pair of tanned calf muscles knocks against the living room couch.

"Cut it out, Viv." Claire clutches the seat of her bike. "I know she's here. She called me and I already tried Kenny's. Where the hell else would she be?"

"Oh! The bitch speaks!" Viv cackles, her laughter pricking the room with delight.

"Why you got to make everything so hard? You want me to stand here for an hour, talking to you? I know you want me, but you don't have to be so goddamn coy about it. You can just—"

"Shelly!" Viv roars, sending the cat beside her scrambling under the couch. "Get your ass in here! Piss ant's come calling!"

"Score one for piss ant." Claire eases into the entryway, bicycle and all. "You ought to take a vacation from yourself, Viv. Really. It'll do you a load of good." She props her bike against the mattress hugging the wall next to the door and steps into the living room. Where Viv is.

"Shelly ain't yours, you know." Viv is cradling a pink plastic tumbler in one hand and a cigarette in the other. Her hair is pulled back in a tight ponytail behind the sly eyes and flippant

7

lips of what is surely, Claire can never deny this, an unusually gorgeous face. "Don't matter what happened before. That's past. That's what we call 'gone.' You should—"

"Like I said, Viv, that personality of yours has got to go. Maybe you can get it removed, somehow. I'd look into that if I were you." Claire walks back to her bike and snatches her water bottle from the pack strapped to the rear fender. She takes a slow swig. It tastes like rain.

"Someone's gotta break it to you. Might as well be me." The gravel in Viv's voice dips into Claire's joints. Claire tries to shake her off by finishing the water and shoving it back in the pack, but Viv won't stop. "Least I know what I'm talking about. You, on the other hand," the grating ceases as Viv takes a drink of her own, "don't know *shit.* Why you keep coming here is beyond me."

Claire smushes a bead of dirt into the tread of her tire. If she were talking, if she were acknowledging Viv's basic aliveness, she could point out the holographic brilliance of Viv's last remark, could take a gold highlighter and mark it up for all to see: the infinite and diverse elements that are beyond the scope of Viv's capacity to understand them. But Viv doesn't matter. No one matters. Just Shelly. Shelly who is now standing, tense and shaky, over to the left, next to the dining room.

"Hey Shel," Claire says. "I got your machine. I mean, your message. I just did. Just now, before I came."

The house is dark, the house is always dark, but not so much that Claire can't see the ripe bruise on Shelly's temple and another one, big as a plate, on her thigh. Shelly's arms, enclosed in a long-sleeved T-shirt, are the probable recipients of more of these angry lumps, though Claire wouldn't know this unless she were to take off the T-shirt, and this is not something she would do. Indeed, her first two impulses, one right after the other, are to flee and to flake, like old paint, off the side of the earth.

"Thanks for coming," Shelly says. "I didn't want to call but, you know, I did."

It's still Shelly, in the middle of all the spoilage and the spots, still the exact same friend Claire has always had. This just makes it worse and Claire grips the handlebars of her bike, wishing she had something to contribute.

"I thought you'd be pissed, maybe. That's why I wasn't going to call. But now," Shelly slips a hand inside the sleeve of her shirt, "I don't know."

It occurs to Claire that Viv's presence is downing her usually functional systems. "Can we go upstairs?" she says.

Shelly nods and drags herself over to the stairs, taking the worn planks one at a time. Claire whisks through the entryway and helps Shelly maneuver the steps, realizing that, in her request for privacy, she has inadvertently caused her friend more pain.

"Have you gone to the doctor? You need to see a doctor, Shel."

They lumber down the hall and into the room that used to be Shelly and Viv's when they were kids. Shelly veers away from the bed, piled high with her mother's sewing projects, and settles on the bar stool that currently serves as part of the sewing machine station. She flips the switch of the machine and, for several minutes, watches the needle float in and out of nothing.

"I'll kill him." Claire plops on the bed, dropping a bundle of corduroy on her lap. It smells like hamsters. "I've never killed anyone before, but I'll bet I could kill him."

Shelly fiddles with the spool of thread at the top of the machine.

"Shel?"

"What?" Shelly guns the pedal, one last race of thread into the metal plate between her fingers, then shuts it off and places both hands, in prayer formation, between her thighs.

"I think we need to go somewhere. To get you help or something."

9

"Or something." Shelly turns to face her friend. Her bad eye is partially closed by the bruise, folded inside a shell of skin. Her hair, the towhead blond of a child even years past childhood and into her twenties, rests against her shoulders with a quiet grace that makes Claire's chest hurt, just to look at it.

"I'm not going back. He blew it. The bastard."

Claire bolts off the bed, chucking the corduroy off her lap. "Can we get Viv's car?" She is airtight, pacing.

Shelly nods and tugs down on her T-shirt, revealing the beginnings of another bruise on the inlet to her collarbone. "I love you, Claire."

"I love you too, Shel."

The intake worker's name is Sister Maria. At first, Claire thought she meant this as a tag or something, or a joke. Sister Maria is black, an older woman with short, sculpted hair and a past-the-knees denim skirt, and Claire thought maybe "Sister" was an affirmation of African heritage.

Then she saw the cross. That was the first clue. It was just a regular cross, gold and steady, with inscriptions or some sort of curlicues inside its body, but the way it was lying on Sister Maria's shirt, when Claire first saw it, gave her a bit of a jolt. That, plus Shelly told her when Sister Maria was out of the room. ("She's a nun, stupid.")

Not like any nun Claire's ever seen before. Claire's version of "nun" comes mostly from her mother: tales of habit-clad monsters with cruel eyes and implements of whackage— rulers, paddles, sticks, Bibles. Sister Maria is nothing like this. Sister Maria is serene and forthright and, in a manner Claire finds widely appealing and is already coveting, she wields an essence as gentle as it is powerful.

"We've been full up since this OJ thing started. They say there's going to be a verdict soon." Sister Maria grimaces.

The dimples in her cheeks are like creases in dough. "I don't want to know what's going to happen when that goes down."

Shelly picks at the bandage strapped around her thigh. The doctor has treated her wounds and loaded her up with medication and taken down, word for word, everything she told him about the origin of her injuries. "I kept telling him I'd leave. He didn't listen, though. And he'd beg me, he'd always beg me. That he'd be good. All that crap."

Claire watches Sister Maria watch Shelly. Sister Maria nods when Shelly tells her about the multiple times, about how this has happened before. But how did she know? How did Sister Maria know and not Claire? For this to go on, and Shelly not to tell her, it's as though Claire has been thrashed in a similar fashion. Except she hasn't.

Sister Maria, radiating calm, talks about the shelter, how Shelly can stay there and all the ways they can help her, can keep her safe. And so Shelly will stay. She glances at Claire and back to Sister Maria and says, "Yes." Says, "Definitely, yes."

"And this must be your brother." Sister Maria beams at Claire.

"Uh. No." Claire steps into the viewfinder reserved for moments like this one, moments frequent in number since she first shaved her hair off a few years back. People see the deliberately ratty jeans, the suede skater shoes, the chipped front tooth, the roomy T-shirt propped over moderately muscled arms, the fingernails ridged with grease from working on her bike and they think what Claire thinks too sometimes, when she looks in the mirror. Boy.

"I'm her friend. Claire." She sits up straighter to allow her breasts entry into the room.

Most folks are apologetic, but Sister Maria skips this part. "You sure are. Shelly's lucky to have you."

"It's the hair." Claire, unready for the lack of ruffled expectations about her gender, lapses into an explanation nonetheless.

She runs a hand through sun-drenched spikes to prove her point.

Sister Maria stands—she's been sitting next to Shelly this whole time, arm around her slight frame—and Claire sees that height is yet another one of her assets. "Why don't I show you your room, then. You can bring your belongings and we'll get you settled. And you," Sister Maria parks all that energy onto Claire, wraps it around her like a request had been made for such a thing, "are welcome to come back tomorrow. Anytime between ten and two. Just leave your name at the front desk before you go. Tell them Sister Maria said it was okay."

Shelly picks up a wilted purse—Claire wonders if there's even anything in it—and scoots closer to Sister Maria. She nods at Claire. "You'll come tomorrow?"

"Of course."

Shelly emits a noise like a gurgle, relief mixed with the pricks of terror that have been cruising there, almost hidden, since Claire first saw her this evening. "Thanks."

Claire shuffles around in place, her "time to go" dance. But she can't.

The nun steers Shelly down the hallway, magnificent composure shepherding waning fright, and Claire finds the way out with her eyes, the Connect The Dots course that ends with home and bed. Then returns to the pair trekking away from her, diminishing in proportion but not in stature, around a corner. She feels like she's missing something she didn't even know she had.

Mouth to Mouth

The next morning, she calls Max. She should have called him last night, but it was too late when she got home to do anything but eat half a bag of chips with questionable salsa and stare at the television. Then sleep.

"Sweetheart. I was wondering when I'd hear from you. I've been sitting by the phone this whole time, you know."

"I know. I like to keep you guessing."

"That's my girl."

"We got trouble, though. A bunch of it." Claire drags herself off the bed and over to the table full of papers that functions as headquarters for her crowded little house. She begins the process, more out of habit than necessity, of rearranging the papers in their various piles, sorted by subject and importance. She brushes them off, squares them, rubs the dust off the table with her fist, then onto her shorts.

"Shelly's in the muck. Bad." Claire lifts the pile of film school applications from the edge of the table and taps them against the surface.

"You got her pregnant, didn't you? I told you kids to use protection. When are you going to start listening to me?" Max sighs.

"Shut up. Her husband beat her up. It's not funny."

Max is silent.

"Max?"

"I'm sorry. That's not good."

Claire sets the applications back in the center of the table.

13

She smoothes their ragged sides with her pinky, tweaks the corner with her thumb. "No, it's not. I took her to the shelter in Point Firth. She says she's going to leave him."

"Good."

"Yeah. You should have seen her, though. She was a wreck. It felt like someone had eaten my heart out of my body and was poking around inside for the leftovers. She was trying so hard to keep it together, but she *so* wasn't. I mean, she was totally falling apart, I could see it. Kenny's such a loser. He's never deserved someone as excellent as Shelly. Not even for a second." Claire abandons her papers and settles underneath the table.

They breathe together for a minute or two. Finally, Max says, "Are you going to the meeting tonight?"

Claire nudges the table leg with her toe. "Probably."

"Claire?" Max injects the tiniest touch of authority into his voice.

"Yes." She nods at her toe. "Yes, I'm going to the meeting. There's another thing, though. Max?"

He waits. He's used to this.

"I sorta got fired. I sorta got fired and kicked out of my class. Jack's class. You remember that guy Jack I told you about?"

"Unfortunately I do, yes."

"Well, I guess he knows. About Rita. I guess he figured it out. Though I don't know how, exactly. And I sorta lied. That was probably the worst part. I said I didn't know what he was talking about. Even though I did. Although I sorta didn't—I mean, I didn't know *exactly* why he was so mad. Though it's probably about the sex." Claire rams her toe against the table leg so forcefully that the entire piece of furniture lurches forward several inches. She scoots forward to chase it down.

"It was bullshit, though. My lying. And now I don't know what the hell I'm going to do. I totally need that job. I totally need that class. And I totally need Jack's recommendation for film school. I blew it."

14

"You did."

"Thanks, Max. I can tell you're going to be a big help. Maybe you should call Jack. Exchange strategies."

"Oh, boo hoo. Look, pumpkin. The operative word here is 'did.' You can't control what Claire of a year ago, Claire who was blasted out of her mind twenty-six hours a day—correct me if I'm wrong here—was doing with her time and her amorous inclinations. For whatever reason, now is the moment the Universe has decided to deposit this little goody into your lap and you, my friend, are just going to have to deal. May I also point out that you, Claire in the present tense, Claire in the absence of false fortification, are much better able to deal with this situation now than, say, a year ago when you probably would have responded by getting tanked out of your mind. Am I not right about every single thing I'm saying here?"

Claire sighs. The table, powered by her toe, has now moved clear across the room and lodged itself against the kitchen counter. "It doesn't really feel like a little goody in my lap, though. More like a dump on my head."

"Whatever analogy works for you, my dear. My point is, you'll get through this. One glorious day at a time."

Claire grunts and slips a hand under her foot, testing for solidity. Still there. She rewinds, reviewing the events of the previous day in all their Technicolor splendor, replete with damaged affections, tragic betrayals, scattered remorse. Max waits patiently while she struggles through the rubble to arrive in a place vaguely resembling the present. Or as close as she can get to such a spot.

"Max?"

"Yes?"

"Like, thanks."

"Like, don't mention it. I'll see you tonight."

Claire is unable to hang up the phone, being so far from base camp, so she simply sets the receiver on the floor next to her. Her trip across the room has surely generated a revolution above her: applications cavorting with unpaid bills, junk mail terrorizing Twelve Step literature. She can almost hear them—hooting, hollering, roaring out the truth that order is dead, that only chaos stands a chance on this mossy green planet. She jiggles the table leg to make them stop.

When they do, and it's only a matter of seconds before they do, it occurs to Claire that the mayhem above her is the least of her problems. A thud of dread implodes in her stomach. She remembers Jack's face, the words that came out of it. What is she supposed to do about that? Losing the TA job is one thing—she's got enough money in savings to last her a little while. But Jack's class, Jack's affection? The loss is much deeper than Claire can comprehend, a chasm that overwhelms any optimism she could hope to muster. She is, indeed, so fundamentally fucked—and has only herself to blame for this posture—that the only viable solution is either to remain in denial or accept defeat. Given Claire's vast experience with the former, and her aversion to the finality of the latter, it's not a difficult decision.

She crawls out from under the table and peeks out the window over the kitchen sink. The bottom half of the pane is filled with fence, the top half with sky. It's so clear, the delineation between the two—no question which is air and which is wood. Claire blinks. Maybe that's true for her as well. After all, she's not the only one in trouble. Shelly's got it worse. Much worse.

Claire stands, wiping the dust off her shorts. How silly of her, to see herself stuck. Where else would she go but to see her friend? What else would she do?

Shelly is fresh out of her counseling session when Claire arrives. Her eyes are smaller than usual, hiding under flushed, swollen lids.

16

"The cops came and got him," she says. "They arrested him and took him to jail. His mom wouldn't bail him out, so he got his brother to do it."

They're sitting side by side on an incredibly uncomfortable couch in the main living room of the center. Claire can feel the springs of the couch becoming one with her thighs. "Too bad. He should have rotted in there a little longer."

"Yeah." Shelly is wearing a T-shirt Claire has never seen before. It informs the viewer that California is the "Happening State." Shelly's arms, instead of being coated with bruises like Claire imagined, are merely Shelly's regular old arms, attached to her regular old hands with the funny flat-shaped thumbs.

"The cop I talked to said Kenny's going to have to go to court and get sentenced and all that. Maybe do more time. Maybe just community service or some sorta crap like that. I felt bad for him for about a second, but I just can't anymore. Claire," Shelly runs one of her funny thumbs up and around her ear, bringing a swatch of hair with it, "I need a place to stay."

Claire bounces on the couch. She wonders what the back of her legs will look like when she finally stands up. "Unh hunh."

"Just for a while. I usually go to my mom's when this happens." Shelly steers around this like it's no big deal, though they both know that this piece of information is yet more late-breaking news as far as Claire is concerned. "But I can't do that anymore. I need to stay with you. They said I can stay here as long as I need to, until I find somewhere to get settled, but I already know where that is. I've got a restraining order out on Kenny, so he'll leave us alone. And besides, you're right next door to his mother and everyone knows that she's the only person Kenny's afraid of."

"Boy, this couch really sucks, doesn't it?" Claire studies the framed photograph of an elderly man in white—could it be the Pope?—over the television set on the opposing wall. This is dumb, sure, but responding to Shelly's request is even dumber. "Probably the suckiest couch I ever sat on. You'd think they'd work more on comfort at a place like this."

Shelly, who could make things easier by getting angry, or cranking up the waterworks, only makes things worse by saying nothing.

Claire bears this for a moment, then wanders into a view of her friend. The thick blond lashes, the nose brushed with freckles. The face that always looks like it's about to crack a joke but is holding back, for your own good. Shelly has always been beautiful, a defiant and nonchalant sort of gorgeous that outstrips even her sister, Viv, but now, with her crazy T-shirt and the patches on her skin spoiled by Kenny's stupid fists, she is somehow even more beautiful, more radiant for facing—for surviving—this.

"Yeah, of course," Claire says. "Goes without saying. You'll stay with me."

Shelly grins, then leans over and kisses Claire on the neck. Her lips smell like coconuts. "Thanks. It'll just be for a bit. Really. Till I can save up for my own place. Now," she turns her impossible face toward Claire, "what's wrong with you?"

"What do you mean?"

"I mean, what else is wrong besides all this crap with me?"

Rita's breath—panting, liquid—pounds through the synapses of Claire's brain. She can deny the dread, she can deny Jack's wrath, but how can she deny what happened? "It's nothing," she says.

Shelly fits her fingers, which could go on Claire's neck or her leg or anywhere else, around the bar at the bottom of the couch. "Dude. Why do you even try?"

"It's just some stupid trouble at school. I'm going to find a way around it, though. I have to get my hands on a video camera so I can do this documentary thing for Jack's class. It's still the beginning of the semester—I've got time. I'll turn it in and he'll have to grade it, right?"

"Right." Shelly looks skeptical.

"I should have taken that old one of Jack's when I had the chance. I always figured I'd wait till next year, after I transfer ..."

"Good morning, ladies." Sister Maria rounds the corner of the couch. She locks in on Claire at the "ladies" part, and Claire wonders if this is meant as a joke. Nun humor.

"Sister." Claire fights off a splash of shyness.

"There's someone on the phone for you, Shelly. A police officer. She has a few more questions. There's a private room over here, where you can take the call."

Shelly is already up, glued onto Sister Maria like a newborn duck.

"Claire, I heard you mention something about needing a video camera. Is that right?"

Claire bows her head, allowing the shower of love flowing off Sister Maria's shoulders to puddle in her lap. Then seep into her spring-embedded thighs. "Yeah," she says. "I sorta lost possession of the other one."

"I know someone who might be able to help." The love drips down Claire's knees, in between her toes.

"Does his name start with a J and end with an S?" Claire winces. "Sorry. That was dumb."

Sister Maria places her hand around Shelly's. "You're close. It's Sister Hilary. At our outpost in Bearley. Ever heard of Bearley?"

Claire tips her palm over her eyes and squints upward. "I live in Bearley."

"Then you've heard of it," Sister Maria says.

The nun's eyes are so kind, her tone of voice so generous, that Claire can pretend, watching her, that life is this way. She can pretend she's not a screw-up, or that's not all she is.

If truth is a feeling, then the benevolence jumping from Sister Maria's eyes to the pit of Claire's heart must account for something. It's probably an illusion, a corporeal sleight of hand that allows Claire to borrow the traits of entitlement and grace. But for this moment, at least, it's hers.

Mr. Film

Jack's office looks the same, only completely different. For starters, it's been three days since she was last here, and Claire is now fired and expelled. In theory only, though. That's the way she's decided to look at it. Who's to say that someone—Claire, for example—couldn't mosey back on into Jack's office and set things right. Who's to say that an intrepid young individual couldn't use her abundantly endowed powers of persuasion to convince Professor Jack Baines that all is well with Claire McMinn—that she meant no harm, really. That no harm was, in fact, done.

That was the plan. It's not really working.

"Refresh my memory. Why have you slithered back into my office?" Jack is facing away from her, sorting videos on a cart. His usual uniform—khaki on the bottom, oxford blue on top—seems especially formal today. Today being a pocket of time in which he hates her.

It's hard, being hated by Jack. It was so much better, when it was otherwise. When they were bonded and yet free—easy with each other like air is easy, invisible and pervasive and elementally kind. The last fun thing they did together was a couple weeks ago, a Friday matinee of *Jules and Jim*. The movie was Jack's idea, and Claire trotted along eagerly, always ready to spend another day in the dark with her favorite teacher. How many times had they done this, lured by the call of the marquee and the imperative to do anything but the tasks before them? And it wasn't just the classics that called. Many a film succeeded in prying them away from their books and into the chilled comfort of seats before a screen. Jack and Claire's shared taste in cinema ran wide and rapacious: old, new, highbrow, gutterbrow, foreign-born, L.A.-bred—they embraced it all. Though (and Claire is sure they would both admit this, even now) some films were more easily embraced than others, and *Jules and Jim,* with its sublime mix of story and stars and cinematography, was one of them. Jack and Claire couldn't help but poke each other in the elbows throughout the screening, in awe and exhilaration.

So, what happened? It's all vanished somehow (Claire is pretending, in this second, that it had nothing to do with her), and she is left with rusty parts unhinging a mouth that squeaks and pops with words that make no sense. He's saying so many things, so loudly. What is he saying?

"You fucked my wife, Claire. You fucked my wife and you chose, in a fit of logic that escapes me, to capture this unholy coupling on film and then stash the evidence, unmarked, in the bottom drawer of my," here the clacking mouth grows louder, the hinges straining, "collection of Buster Keaton shorts." Jack's shirt has come untucked, flapping over his belt. He pushes the video cart against the sea of books lining the far wall of his office and begins a slow march to his desk. He will not look her in the eye.

"It confounds me that you would do this, that you would betray my trust in such an obscene manner. With my wife, my Rita." Jack sits down at his desk. "She tried to deny it, at first. But confronted with your handiwork ... Well, she had no choice. Though she said it was all your doing. That you forced her into it."

"I don't ..." Claire lines up the toe of her shoe with the fringe of Jack's Oriental rug. The truth? Is she supposed to tell the truth? It's so lame, so inexcusable. "I don't remember."

"You don't remember." He opens the top drawer of his

desk, closes it. "You don't remember having sex with my wife."

"No. I remember ... that. I just don't remember filming it."

Jack scratches the side of his neck with his thumb. It is the only sound in the room. "I see. I feel so much better now."

"I was drunk. I was always drunk back then. Yes, it was stupid, but she ..." Maybe this wouldn't be the best time to mention that Rita started it, that she seduced Claire. "I honestly don't remember making that movie. And it's over. It's been over for a year. I don't want anything from you, Jack. I don't expect you to let me back in your class. I just want the chance to complete the work, outside of class, and turn it in."

"And the benefit to me would be ..."

"The benefit to you would be that you would never have to see me again. I'll turn in all my projects to the main office. I won't come in here and bug you anymore. I'll be dead to your world. Alive only in paper and cinematic form. And out of here at the end of the semester. Without this class, I can't leave. It's a way to get me gone." Claire dares to emphasize this last part with a dash of zing, a shot of fervor. What a snow job.

Jack opens the top desk drawer once again and stares inside. He doesn't shut it this time, only stays, transfixed by its contents. He's a prince of a man, Jack. Claire could see this even with her eyes closed. Sure, he has a taste for the sauce, for low goals and empty horizons, but these he fixes only for himself, not his students. For them, and for his solipsistic and under-appreciative wife, Jack offers the gifts of attention and belief—gifts that, time and again, bring out the best in their recipients and leave Jack with little more than pride of assist. He is, at the base and root and very bottom of it all, a fair and undeniably kindhearted man, and it hurts Claire to the bone to see what she has done to him. And to know that he will give in, that he will give her this.

"I don't know." He closes the drawer. "There's only one

23

way I'd do it. And that's if I never have to see your shameless face again. And you can't use my equipment. You'll have to find your own."

"Yes. Yes." Claire bounces on the balls of her feet. He's doing it again, unfurling the map, the intricate series of gestures and maneuvers through which she can make her escape. "Not a problem," she says. "Already taken care of."

Jack picks a book off his desk and begins to read. Only he's not really reading, because his eyes are shut and he's talking instead. "I thought you were someone else," he says. "Someone better."

Claire closes her eyes, joining him in the dark. "So did I."

She's still three miles from home and getting winded. The lip of Claire's bicycle seat snaps against her shorts as her legs pump the pedals, a rhythm of effort and exhaustion. There's plenty to think about, when it's just her hands on the bars and the swish of wheels to keep her company. She manages to sail through a wad of subjects, irrelevant all, until she lands on the only one worth considering.

Rita.

It was a Sunday afternoon, when they started up. Jack was out of town at a film conference and Claire was in his office, grading papers. She'd been his teaching assistant for a couple of months at that point, plenty of time for Rita to get a whiff. They'd see each other at the class parties at Jack's house, long liquid nights in which Claire was the recipient of Rita's remote and persistent interest, hanging glances ripe with questions and not-so-saintly possibilities. The few aborted attempts at connection—a brush of hands while pouring drinks in the kitchen, a protracted exchange on the dance floor in which they were supposedly dancing with other people but really with each other—only confirmed what Claire already knew. In the circus of life, Rita was the ravenous lion and Claire the T-bone steak. It was only a matter of time before appetites were answered.

So it was no surprise, the day Rita showed up in Jack's office. She opened with a fib, claiming that her husband had asked her to stop by and water his plants while he was out of town. Claire's observation that there were, in fact, no plants in Jack's office was then buried in the thunder of Rita's next gesture, which was to lift her fingers to her chest and slowly, methodically—like she was being paid by the minute—take off her blouse.

"You're straight," Claire said, dropping her pen to the floor.

"Not anymore, I'm not."

"Well. Then. You're married."

"Now, Claire," Rita clucked. "Is this any time to be discussing my marriage? Hmm?" She swayed to one side, then the other. A fluttering sound—was it a slip?—whistled out from under her skirt. "I think we have more important things to talk about."

At this, Rita released the front snaps of her black lace underwire bra and permitted her breasts—full, ready, at attention—to introduce themselves to her husband's TA.

The three beers Claire had had for breakfast, combined with the amount of time since she had last gotten laid (five weeks—a record), proceeded to work themselves on her better judgment until it was reduced to a soup of hormones and rationalizations. Who was she to determine the best time to discuss the state of Jack and Rita's marriage? Who was she to determine the best time for *anything*? She was merely a teenage boy with a huge boner saluting the thighs of this fetching neighbor lady not three feet away and she knew only one thing. That taking her, placing a mouth on that small pink waiting nipple seemed suddenly just the thing to do.

And so she did. Not only then, but many times thereafter.

She was a pip, Rita. A thoroughbred. She was almost fifty when they got together but still had the body of a woman half her age. It was the dancing, she said, that kept her in shape, but Claire knew it was probably more the students like her, all men until now, that Rita ingested like so many sticks of gum, chewing them until the flavor ran dry. What better way to stay young than to continually handle the flesh of said young?

Claire didn't mind. She'd had sex with a fair number of people at that point, but Rita was a newer model, despite her age. With her, Claire could be hungry and eager, or passive and withdrawn; however Claire was, it was all right with Rita. And the orgasms, they were the best. Rita, in a lucky draw of genetics or possibly karma, could climax in a wide variety of situations and scenarios, including little to no direct stimulation. Claire could simply look at her, and she'd come. It made her feel like Liberace, with his piano.

As for filming the two of them in the act, this is not a stunt Claire can track down in any of the back rooms of her memory. She's not surprised she did it—it certainly sounds like something she would have done back then—but the particulars of the act, the shapes and sounds of that catalogued moment of betrayal, those are lost to her, vanished along with the lack of discretion that pulled her into the whole mess to begin with. It kills her now, the damage she's caused.

She pounds on the pedals, increasing her speed. How fortunate that she doesn't drink anymore. How marvelous, how miraculous. Of course, her shorts still mash into her bicycle seat in a manner that keeps her rolling down the road; the hairs of her arms still catch fire when she imagines Rita's breath—anyone's breath—settling there.

Claire shifts from fifth speed to sixth, then eighth. Clouds fly by, then lifetimes. She'll be fine as long as she keeps her pants on.

Boss

"That was a good meeting." Claire rips open two packs of sugar and sifts them into her coffee. "I always love it when Audrey speaks."

Max grins. "Yeah, Audrey's great. You start to think your life is so hard, so much toil and struggle, and then old Audrey gets up there with her heroin and booze and her life on the streets and the molester boyfriend and the kids that got taken away and the cancer and the jail time and all that trouble with the IRS and you just say, 'Well now, what was the problem again?'"

"Exactly."

Claire and Max are snagging a post-meeting cup of coffee at the Starbuck's on Ashbrook in Point Firth. They used to join Peter and Dell and the rest of the gang at the diner on the corner of Third and Holton, but Max's newly acquired taste for designer caffeine has prompted this latest veering off course. It's fine with Claire. She likes having her sponsor all to herself and, given her recent brush with self-inflicted melodrama, she needs all the Max time she can get.

"Did I tell you about Esther's latest scheme?" Max chews on a toothpick, a perpetual appendage since he stopped smoking a few weeks back. "It's one of those pyramid thingies. You fork over your precious cash to people higher up on the ladder, and then money's supposed to come pouring back to you from the hapless minions you con into following you down the road to Stoogeville. My mother is so gullible."

"Sounds dangerous."

"She's driving me crazy, Claire. My days there are *so* numbered. It's like I look at her face and see a little calendar: boxes and check marks. And where the hell is Bert?"

Claire and Max take a synchronized sip. They both know where Bert is.

"How about getting your own place somewhere nearby?" Claire says. This is a crucial piece of advice. She can't have him moving back to San Francisco and leaving her alone in the wasteland. "There are all kinds of groovy pads just waiting for your sexy paws to caress them into sophistication. Why not give it a go?" Claire picks up a foot and slams it down on the other as penance. It wasn't a come-on, exactly. But still. She was going to stop doing this.

Max's looks are something that get him noticed by everyone—men, women, pets. Tall and slender like a colt. Or perhaps a filly. Black hair combed back off sweet wide eyes. A beak of a nose that might look obscene on anyone else but on him seems noble, elemental. Clothes cultivated in his previous career (as the owner of an art gallery two blocks from the San Francisco MOMA) to appear casual yet elegant, insouciant yet refined.

When he first took her on as his sponsee, there was an almost audible tension between them. This was odd, considering that both of them tend to prefer the ministrations of their own gender. Still, it made sense in a way. Claire was hard up, having quit sex at the same time she quit drinking. Max was similarly dispossessed, having lost his lover Bert four years prior, a bundle of time that should have lent itself to healing, but hadn't. The charge between them is mostly gone at this point, evaporated off the ruts and grooves of friendship and familiarity. When it reappears in a moment such as this one, Claire's throbbing foot the bearer of its impact, she finds it best to treat the intruder like an unexpected

FedEx delivery: sign your name, accept the parcel, and let the man go.

"Really," she says. "You need a space of your own. Somewhere to stretch out those long legs of yours. I'm surprised you didn't do it sooner."

"I have my reasons," he says. "Most of which rhyme with 'Esther.' I'm seriously considering it, though. I could break it to her gradually. So she doesn't do something sneaky like fall and crack her other hip to get me to stay. I have to watch out for that woman. She's got more than a few tricks up those polyester sleeves of hers."

"And you'd be in ..."

"Point Firth, probably. So I can keep an eye on Esther and still stay close to work." Work being the no-brainer job his sister got him at her insurance company. "It's a tad bit depressing. But I can't make friends with any other options just yet."

Claire dips a finger into the coffee-stained sugar at the bottom of her cup and licks off the remains with her tongue. It tastes like victory. "Point Firth. Boss!"

Max scowls. "Sweetie, I wish you knew how antiquated that expression is. It makes you sound like a gangster in a Blaxsploitation flick."

"And the problem with that would be ..."

"It's all Shelly's fault. Ever since she moved in, you're full of jive talk and giddiness. If I didn't know better, I'd say you two are licking the lesbian candle at both ends." He feigns embarrassment. "Oh, did I say *licking*?"

"Max. She's just staying with me till she can get back on her feet. No big whoop."

Max's eyes shrink to slivers.

"Okay, Mr. Smarty." Claire scoots her coffee toward the middle of the table, toward Max and his squinty gaze. "Maybe it's a medium-sized whoop, but nothing I can't handle."

"Are you sure you want to use the word 'handle'?"

"What? So I can't have friends? That ain't right, Maxie."

Max tilts sideways to extract a fresh toothpick from his pocket and pops it in his mouth. "All I'm asking is that you think this through a bit. What's your intention?" He leans in. "Why Shelly? Why now?"

"I told you. It's her husband. She has nowhere else to go."

Max blinks. His expression is blank, retracted. "Remember what I told you? About Bert?"

Claire nods.

"I'd been sober over three years when I met him. And I'm not saying you have to wait that long, though it wouldn't hurt. It's hard enough to walk this road without a drink in your hand. Try adding sex to that, especially when you're not even—what is it now? Ten months?"

Claire inspects her fingers, then the window behind Max's head. A young mother pushing a baby stroller cruises by, looking depleted but buoyant. Claire imagines crawling into the stroller, being pushed. "Yeah," she says. "Ten months. Almost eleven."

"That's what I mean. Ten months is nothing. You're nowhere near ready for this, Claire. You need to—"

"I need to convince my sponsor that I know what I'm doing." Claire's voice surprises her. It sounds not only confident, but reassuring, as if Max is the one with the problem. "I need him to understand that I'm not going to blow it."

"Lamb chop. You're not hearing me, are you?" Max drops his head, picks it back up. "It's a different ball of wax when you're sober. Especially sex."

"Ball of wax? Is that what you boys use? Isn't that a bit ... sticky?"

"Fine. Ignore my advice. You'll see."

New Tune

When Claire first wakes up, she's still pressed flat against the palm of sleep. Deep in. It takes her a few minutes to extricate herself from her unconscious, then Shelly's arms.

Since Shelly moved in, they've been sleeping together, but not in a romantic way. More like friends who were once lovers and then downshifted back to friends, never losing the easy physical intimacy that drew them together in the first place. Kenny doesn't know about this history, doesn't know that Claire and Shelly crept back over the sexual boundary even when Shelly was first living with Kenny, and he doesn't need to. Besides, even though the women at the domestic violence shelter warned that this was the most dangerous time, that leaving Kenny placed Shelly at greater risk for abuse, this has not been the case. Kenny, it seems, has got himself another girl. Rhonda, from the bowling alley.

"Shelly? Are you awake?" Claire flips around and butts her knees against her friend's, then sweeps the back of her wrist against the place where Shelly's shorts meet the pale flesh of her belly. The bruises are almost gone, faded back into Shelly's clear and perfect skin and the satisfied expression she wears while she's sleeping. Like she's guarding hard-earned spoils.

"Shel? You asked me to wake you up." This is a lie. Claire just wants the company.

"Mmmmrph." Shelly's stomach curls inward at Claire's touch, pokes out of reach. "Rrrrmrrm."

"I agree."

Claire swings her legs over the side of the mattress and heaves herself into her day. Only after an hour of various early morning activities, including the construction-level noise of the coffee grinder and a furious sorting of her video collection, does her friend stir, then wake.

"Where are you going?" Shelly, haloed by bedhead, props herself into a sitting position.

"To that Center place. Down the street. To talk to that nun lady."

"I'm going with you." Shelly kicks off the covers, pulls on one of Claire's T-shirts, and scarfs down a candy bar. Chocolate stains seep into the corners of her mouth.

For as long as Claire has known her, Shelly has been an equal opportunity candy inhaler. Some prefer their sugar in fruity form, some chocolate. Shelly's preferences in this area, however, know no bounds. The only exception to this is black licorice, which is, as Shelly likes to say, "of the devil."

"How is it that you never exercise and all you eat is candy and you still have such a great body?"

"It's my secret work out. I do it when I'm sleeping." Shelly drifts over to Claire and lays a finger on her arm. "Feel that?"

Claire closes her eyes. Traces of delight shift against her awareness. "Nope. I don't feel a thing."

Claire steps outside. It's early enough, but the sun is already fully charged, baking the yard full of weeds and the Pepto-Bismol-colored exterior of her house. She painted it herself a few years back, after Shelly teased her one too many times about not being girly enough. Though the shade is so bright, it's more a "Fuck you" to the confines of the color wheel than a statement of femininity. Claire refuses to repaint it. Besides, her foray into bad taste gives her mother's home—a prefab ranch house erected quickly and cheaply in the early '60s and deteriorating just as rapidly—something to compete with. The big house may be shabby, with its moss-covered roof, screenless screen doors, front yard patched with grass, but at least the place is painted white. It's a tired white, surrendering here and there to the materials—clapboard, aluminum—it was intended to hide, but the house doesn't bark at the world like Claire's does. Poor is one thing. Tacky and poor is something else altogether.

Shelly emerges from the house, candy bar in hand. "Dude. Who cranked up the heat?"

"Look out," Claire says. "I hear your hubby's mom out front. My sister too, I think. Don't let them snag us, okay? They're marathon talkers, both of them."

"So are you, Claire." Shelly steps around a toppled swing set, its rusted legs saluting the sun. "We would have been out of here a lot sooner if you didn't have to show me those new videos you got. And you couldn't just show me. You had to give me a lecture about how the action films have to go on *this* part of the shelf, and the comedies have to go over *here*, like if they got mixed up the movies would all switch around or something. Like the car crashes would slide into the kissy face scenes, or the guy in the action flick would blow up the chick in the romance movie."

"No. That's not true. I'm not—"

"And don't worry about Donna. It's just family. No sweat." Shelly finishes off her chocolate bar and chucks the wrapper on the ground. "Yo Donna, yo Angie." She sweeps open the gate and ambles into the driveway. "What's going on?"

"Just remember. We're in a hurry." Claire stoops behind Shelly to retrieve the candy wrapper, then trails behind her like the wife of royalty.

"Shel, Shel. Look at you. They don't make them as pretty as you anymore. My boy leaving you alone?" Kenny's mother Donna thomps a roll of newspaper against her thigh. She's a short woman, ornery—a cross between a pit bull and a tank. No one messes with Donna.

"You better believe it." Shelly leans into her mother-in-law's airspace like she's tracking her scent. "Kenny and me are way over."

"Good. I don't know what I did wrong with that boy. He came out funny, you know. I still think there was a switch-up at the hospital and some bitch out there's got my real son."

"We have to go." Claire steps out from Shelly's shadow and into bright sun. She ignores Donna, who is bound to be giving her one of those scorched-earth glances of hers and addresses her sister—Angela, who looks nothing like Claire but instead like the father they don't have in common. She is ruddy to Claire's fair, thick to Claire's wiry, steady to Claire's not. More importantly, Angela is tough—bullshit-free, self-sustaining—in a way that Claire can only pretend to be. It is this quality, or lack thereof, that most distinguishes Claire from her two younger sisters. In this, Claire suspects she is more like their mutual mother than she cares to admit.

"What are you doing here?" Claire says.

"Oh. You know. Talking to Donna. Now to you. Did you hear about mom's accident?"

"Accident?" Claire eyes Shelly, who's howling at whatever stupid story is coming out of Donna's mouth. "What did she do now?"

Angela chuckles. "Crashed the truck. Backed it into the dumpster outside the Safeway. She said it was rolling toward her, but Bunny and Walt said it wasn't doing nothing but sitting there."

"Bunny and Walt?" Claire tries not to scream it. "You let them drive with her when she's drinking?"

Angela picks at the spoon-shaped scab on her forearm. "Not drinking. Just tired. It was in the morning. It's funny, Claire. Nothing to wig out about."

34

"If you don't mind dead kids. Kitty's, like, the last person you should leave them with."

"She raised us."

"Yup."

Angela rolls her eyes. "Kitty's fine with them. They have fun with her. They're in there painting her toenails right now."

Kitty wasn't always a fan. Bunny and Walt popped out of Angela when she was a mere sixteen, an act that got her thrown out of the house and elevated to Number One position on Kitty's shit list. Nothing made Kitty madder than to see one of her daughters make the same mistake she had, the "mistake" being Claire, to whom Kitty had given birth the summer after junior high. Claire was just glad it wasn't her— that she, the eldest, had managed to avoid the interrupted childhoods of both her younger half-sisters. She's also glad that Bunny and Walt, the hellions in question, are safely ensconced indoors, attending to the pedicurial needs of their once-estranged grandmother. The one and only time Claire babysat for her niece and nephew, she was overwhelmed by the sounds of shrieking and the stench of corn chip farts. It's not an experience she's in a hurry to replicate.

"You're right," Claire says. "Kitty's the perfect choice. I don't know what the hell I was talking about." She catches hold of Shelly's elbow and tugs her forward, off the driveway and onto the street.

Donna waves goodbye, but it's a Shelly-only sentiment. Angela hollers after Claire, her voice collapsing the space between them. "Mom wanted to know where you've been lately," she says.

"Tell her whatever you want," Claire says. The air around her smells wasted, like rotten time. She marches over it. "Tell her I joined the circus. The freak show. World's Smallest Conscience. She can relate to that."

✦✦✦

The Bearley Community Center is a posse of portables next to St. Bart's, Bearley's only church. Claire has passed by it millions of times—it's just a few blocks from her house—and never given it much thought. Churches creep her out.

To get to the Center itself, they have to trek through a wide hallway attached to the entry of the church. The hallway leads to a painted-brown door marked "Community Center," and over the door sits a plaque in a chunky gold frame. Shelly reads it out loud.

"When you fed the hungry, when you clothed the naked, when you gave drink to the thirsty, you did it to Me. Come, you blessed of my Father." Shelly genuflects and makes the sign of the cross, kissing her thumb against her fingers.

"You Catholics," Claire says. "Always gotta be dipping or kissing or crossing yourselves."

"You're Catholic too. Just because you don't go to church doesn't mean it's not in you."

"Don't remind me."

The last time Claire was in church, she was practically a baby. They still had the incense then, and the Latin. She sat in her grandmother's lap (her mother had already stopped going by then), saturated in the vestiges of the Old Church. They moved out of her grandma's house soon after, and Claire followed Kitty's lead of rebellion against the archaic institution. The inscription still gets to her, though: the tenor of rage and gift, the offer of solace. But those, she tells herself, are something else. Those are hers.

"This is never going to work." She stares at the door, instead of knocking or pulling or whatever she's supposed to do.

Shelly frisks the handle. "Let's just check it out. Don't be a fraidy cat."

The woman behind the desk doesn't look like a nun, in

36

Claire's limited experience of how a nun should look. She's about twenty years younger than Sister Maria, for starters, and white instead of black, with shoulder-length brown hair that flops off her head like water. Better, or maybe worse, is her level of attractiveness, which is somewhere in the neighborhood of striking. Individual components demand immediate attention—a quiet mouth that curves up at each end; a face that seems to gather, then redistribute, the light around it; arms and legs and head and torso situated in space with an intensity that is at once delicate and empowered. Yet Claire's awareness of these aspects is quickly commandeered by their overall effect, one that both defines loveliness and then tosses it aside. For she seems to have no idea how beautiful she is, this woman. Has no plans or traps or enticements to attach to her simple, unopposed essence.

"Uh." Claire is unsure how to act in the presence of such a sight. "I'm looking for Sister Hilary," she stammers.

The woman stands, extending a hand. "That's me."

"It is?" Claire shakes the cool soft hand for as long as she can bear it, then lets go. "This is my friend Shelly. She's, um ... She came with me."

Shelly, chocolate bar kicking in, bounces on her knees like she's getting ready to eject herself through the ceiling. "Nice to meet you." She waves.

Claire clears her throat. "Did Sister Maria tell you about me? That I'd be stopping by?"

"No. What should she have told me?"

"About the camera? About the video camera?"

There are a few things Claire can imagine doing with this woman, this Sister Hilary. One is playing cards at her kitchen table, a bottle of beer for Claire if she were still drinking, a glass of milk for the nun. Another is telling Sister Hilary everything—absolutely everything—about herself, including Rita and Jack and the mess she made there and how she got sober and how life can kick the shit out of you sometimes and then still be such a blessing. Another involves the two of them in a bedroom situation, but they're not having sex, exactly. They're naked, though, and no talking is involved.

"I, uh ..." Claire expels a bunch of breath and snags some new air. "I have this project for school. And I need a camera. Sister Maria said you might have one. That I could maybe borrow it."

"She didn't mention it." Sister Hilary waves as someone behind them, Claire doesn't look to see who, passes by. "Are you interested in filming the Center?"

"No." Claire stutters. "I need it for school. For my project for school. Sister Maria said I could maybe borrow it."

"Oh dear. That's not quite accurate." Sister Hilary's peaceful demeanor ripples apart, pieces itself back together. "Sister Maria wasn't aware of the circumstances."

"The circumstances?" *What the hell?* Claire sneaks a peek at Shelly to trade cards of affront, but Shelly appears to be lost in the aftermath of her candy bar and a view of Sister Hilary. Shelly loves nuns.

"We purchased the camera last year with a grant from a local foundation," Sister Hilary says. "We were going to do a promotional video about the Center. Then our funding got cut and we weren't able to complete the project. Now all we have is the equipment."

"I see." Claire is still trying to line up all of her reactions to this woman in a comprehensible order. If only they didn't keep jumping out of place, boxing her ears, curling the edges of her expectations.

"But maybe that could still work," she says. "If I could just borrow the equipment for a little bit. I'm going to do a documentary about this place in Concord. A community center type place, like this one. It's gonna be awesome. I'm getting my AA at the community college and then I'm going to film school next year. So it's not like I'm an amateur or something. I've been doing this for a while. Your equipment would be in good hands. Totally. I'd bring it back in better shape than it started." She rides a palm over the vast improvements she would make, ruffles their bellies while they writhe in gratitude.

"That's the problem. Sister Maria wasn't involved in the project, so she didn't know." Sister Hilary frowns. "It's very expensive equipment, you see. We can't just loan it out. It needs to stay on the premises. You understand, of course."

"Of course." Claire watches her film on the AIDS hospice in Concord crash against the rocks. Then float about in the water, dreamlike.

"I'm really sorry for all the confusion," Sister Hilary says. "Maybe we can figure out a compromise."

Claire forces a reply. "A compromise? Like what?"

"Like having you film your documentary here. We have several projects you might find interesting. The food bank or the immigration support services. Or the after-school program for at-risk youth. Hey," Sister Hilary's sublime features ignite with what Claire knows is another horrible idea, "there's a thought. I just lost my volunteer who was working with the kids. Maybe in exchange for using the equipment, you could donate some time to the Center. You mentioned you're a student. Students have flexible schedules, don't they? Maybe you could help us out."

Shelly halts her leg-wagging to pitch a final mound of dirt on Claire's already well-marked grave. "She's got plenty of time. She's only taking one class right now and she's not even in it. I could help you, Claire. That'd be boss. I love kids."

Shelly flexes into Sister Hilary's aura and the two of them launch into a chatter fest about the activities of the Center. Claire stews in her own juices long enough to come up with a reasonable counter-argument, the "No" to Shelly's "Yes."

"I may have to get another job, though. Because I lost my job recently. At the college."

Shelly and Sister Hilary turn toward Claire in a sweep of resonance and positive vibes. They are both grinning maniacally, as if a family of boll weevils has just burst into song on top of Claire's head.

"What did you say, Claire?"

"Never mind."

Volunteers

Potholders. Shelly has decided that their first activity with the swarming mass of children in the "Rec Room" portion of the Center's largest portable will be the making of potholders. Apparently Shelly did this once in Home Ec class in high school and still remembers how. Plus, she found some material stuffed in a box (labeled "Supplies. Keep out!!!"), which she says will work just fine.

"Are you a man or woman?" A boy about half the height of Claire shatters the invisible shield she has erected around herself. She's in the back corner of the room, searching for the video camera.

"Both," she says, not looking at him.

"Dude. You can't be both. You ain't both." He waits. "Are you?"

Claire jams her fist into the darkest reaches of a cabinet and encounters not the camera but something sticky. She retrieves her hand to find it coated in bright red goo.

"That's from the Fourth of July," the kid says. "I remember. We put the leftover paint under there."

Claire takes a sniff. It smells sweet, like Halloween. "I don't think this is paint."

The kid shrugs. "We made it out of jellybeans and oil. When we ran out of the regular stuff. So what are you, anyway? A girl, right?"

Claire studies her inquisitor. He's chubby, like he should be taller but someone smushed him to this height and the weight spilled over the edges. His skin is the color of her backpack—a lush brown weathered by sun and handling.

"Right. A girl. Why don't you go back over there?" She points a gooey finger toward the table where Shelly, in a pair of shorts that displays the effortless way in which her thighs connect to her kneecaps, is demonstrating the initial stages of potholder construction. The gray-white wall behind Shelly and the children is covered with drawings: rainbows and houses and approximations of people.

"What are you looking for?" The kid scoots closer.

Claire finds an already partially dirty paper towel and begins to mop off her hand. "The video camera. Sister Hilary said it was over here, by the cabinets."

"Just wait a minute." A voice from the table area plants itself inside the conversation. Its origin, a puny-sized girl by the name of Lupe (Claire knows this only because there is a paper plate and yarn contraption around the girl's neck announcing this fact), nods at Claire. "You have to be quiet."

"Hunh?" Claire turns to the boy beside her.

"Don't look at me," he says. "Lupe's crazy. She ain't even Mexican."

"She's not?"

"Hell no. She's from El Salvador. Everyone from there is crazy. My brother said so."

"Your brother said that every single person from El Salvador is crazy? That's intelligent."

"Smarter than you." The boy peers at her with the intensity of a jeweler assessing an inadequate gem.

"If you say so." Claire finishes wiping off her hand and hurls the paper towel in the trash.

"He'd pound your ass. If he was here. He would."

"Look, kid. You gotta leave me alone now, okay? I got stuff to do. Important stuff."

He squints. "It's probably stupid. What you're doing. It's probably stupid, anyhow." He shuffles away and Claire

42

notices, though she tries not to, that his pants are shredded at the cuffs. She is washed with the image of all the children in the room as orphans, somehow. Her and Shelly too. It makes her almost unbearably sad.

"I knew it was right to bring you here." Sister Hilary saunters into the Rec Room and five kids instantly latch onto her skirt. "Look at the marvelous mess you're making."

Sister Hilary's oversized blouse is tucked into a denim skirt much like the one Sister Maria was wearing the first night at the shelter. There must be a code, Claire thinks, an agreement with God to wear only dowdy clothing in service of a holy war against fashion. How was it that she imagined, just yesterday, the removal of this clothing, a trespass into uncharted waters? Where's the decency in *that?*

"You look a bit lost." Sister Hilary scoops a lock of wayward hair behind her ear. Two short people remain at her hem. "I take it you and the camera are not yet one."

"You take it right." Claire attempts to eradicate any part of her expression that could be categorized as "lost."

"I should have explained better. It's over here, in the storage closet."

Claire trots behind Sister Hilary and watches while the nun reveals the contents of the storage unit at the far end of the room. There, behind a dust-encrusted broom and a stack of primary-colored cartoon renditions of the birth of Christ, lies a brand new video camera. Claire can tell just by looking that it's a high-end model, probably worth at least two grand. Beside the camera sits a tripod she recognizes as one of the fancier kinds, with the fluid-filled heads. She bends past Sister Hilary and rummages through the camcorder's carrier to find tapes, batteries, filters, cables, fuses, lens tissues, headphones. And the microphone, a Lavalier— one of the little clip-on numbers that are so great for recording interviews. *It's too much,* she thinks. *I don't deserve it.*

"Will this work?" Sister Hilary drops a hand and smoothes the head of one of the children at her side.

Claire fingers the Lavalier in its bag, hears its joyous song through the plastic folds. "It'll do."

Sister Hilary takes her around the Center to show her what she can and cannot film. The immigration clients are off-limits, as are the recipients of the Center's counseling services. Pretty much anything else in the Bearley Community Center is fair game, including all employees and clients of the food bank or GED or job training facilities who give their okay. The kids in the after-school program are fine as well, their parents having relinquished them to the care of the Center with requisite media releases.

Sisters Maria and Hilary, it turns out, are co-directors of the Center. They toil through perpetual funding cycles in an attempt to stay afloat; the church provides some financing, but they're dependent mostly on the low, steady drip of state and federal grants and United Way drives, just like any other nonprofit social service agency. They started out with the domestic violence and food bank work, then grew frustrated with this band-aid-only approach and instituted the training and after-school programs in an effort to hack away social injustice closer to the root. They feel marginally successful with these newer programs. Feel that they are, indeed, making a difference.

"No offense or anything, but you don't really look like a nun," Claire says. They're standing in the nave of the church, behind the last row of pews. Sister Hilary has been talking about waning church attendance, but Claire has had more than her fill of Catholic facts. "Not like how they always look in the movies, at least. Aren't you supposed to be wearing one of those black thingies?"

"Woman religious," Sister Hilary says.

44

"What?"

Sister Hilary rolls her shirtsleeves above her elbows and props her arms on the pew in front of her. "It's the preferred term now. Instead of 'nun.' We're not all cloistered women in convents anymore. We're in the world, part of it."

"Oh." Claire considers leaning into the pew as well, but decides against it. Is this how it was for her mother? Always being corrected, never measuring up?

"And the 'black thingies,' as you say, they went out in the late '60s. After Vatican II. Though some women religious still wear them. I was in elementary school when our teachers made the switch. Some of the older Sisters refused—they'd show up for class in full habit. It was a bit of a scandal, I suppose. Back then."

"Where was that?" Claire asks. "It couldn't have been around here."

"Why not?"

"Hard to explain. I can just tell you're not pulled from these parts."

"These parts, no." Sister Hilary dips her head into the space beneath her chin. "More like Beckett City, Iowa. Worlds away from here. You've probably never heard of it."

Claire waits to answer. Sister Hilary's eyes are too big for her face, giving her the appearance of someone who has absorbed all potential visual information and is now straining for the rest. Claire fetches yesterday's reel, her imagined activities with this woman: games, confession, possible sex. These three then explode in her brain with such enthusiasm (she can see it so clearly, her asking and Sister Hilary saying yes and it all going smoothly) that Claire finds herself struggling for posture. She imitates her instigator—shirt shoved over elbows, arms perched on pew, breath and sanity restored.

"Nope," she says. "Never heard of it. Must have been one of those picket fence deals—chickens in the yard, fresh cow on the table, all that."

"Sort of." Sister Hilary retracts her hands from the pew and stashes them in the pockets of her skirt. "And you?"

"And me what?"

"You're pulled from these parts?"

"Yes."

The sound of the air in the church is like a thousand people waving, pushing around the oxygen to make room for their blessings, their disappointments. Claire can hear this in her fingers, in the soles of her feet.

"It would be hard to film in here," she says.

"Why is that?" Sister Hilary has shifted several yards away from Claire, toward the stained glass baby Jesus above her head. She looks as though something has frightened her, as if she is no longer inhabiting herself but is residing somewhere else—up in front of the church, perhaps. Or maybe Beckett City.

"It's too hard a sound, in a place like this." Claire says. "Too many echoes. Best is a padded room—dead response. You don't want too much stuff you can't take out later."

"Later?"

"Like, when you're editing. You get all the stuff on film and then you get to fool around with it afterwards. It's the best part. Putting it all together. Once you get into it, it's like a puzzle. Like, there really is one right way it's supposed to go and it's up to you to figure it out. It's kinda like magic. Like there's this force arranging the whole thing and if you can relax enough, if you can calm down and let it happen, then it will. It's—" Claire stops, embarrassed. What is she doing? Sister Hilary's reticence must have caused her own to recede. It's as though she just stripped off all her skin and handed it over to the woman religious. "It's, um … It's kinda cool. That's all."

"It shows," Sister Hilary says. "In your eyes."

Claire wobbles in place. "What does?"

"How much you enjoy it. To make these films. It's nice.

46

It's …" Sister Hilary assembles an expression that is half smile, half sob, "it's sweet." Then pivots and strolls away before Claire has time to reply.

"Do you think Sister Hilary is, like, that way?"

Claire and Shelly are taking the shortcut home, tromping through the vacant lot next to the middle school. Tumbleweeds as big as cattle guard the corners of the field.

"Your gaydar blipped on a nun?" Shelly bangs into Claire on an inside step, causing her friend to stumble. "It's crack, right? You're addicted to crack now?"

"No. It's just …" Claire clops her shoes into a puff of dust. "Isn't that kinda weird, to give up sex? How can that be a good thing?"

"Duh. She's a nun. That's what they do. Give up sex for God. God tells them to do it."

"Yeah, I guess …"

"Claire, don't let the drugs take a hold of your mind. I'm telling you, it's not too late to get help." Shelly clamps her hands in a gesture of mock pity.

Claire slaps them away. "I was just messing around. I know what she is. I just think it's weird, that's all."

Shelly slows to a stop. The sun is behind her, making it hard to see the particulars of her face. "It's because you're such a horndog. You want to get your clammy hands into every woman who walks by."

"Shel …" Claire loops a thumb onto Shelly's shorts, where the belt should be. "That's not it." Then stays there until her expression exactly matches Shelly's—what she can make of it, at least. Glazed. Cocky. Aimless.

There are some things, she thinks, you shouldn't even try to change.

Too Much Fun

"See that guy over there next to the cantaloupes?"

"The one with the toupee that looks like it's been regurgitated by a yak?"

"Yeah, him. I say kidnapping. No, wait. Kidnapping and murder."

Claire and Max are loitering in the deli section of Jerry's Supermarket, playing "America's Most Wanted." Claire initiated this game after Max complained one too many times about being "forced" to watch the show with his mother. He now throws himself into these sessions with the same gusto she suspects he brings to the television-saturated living room of Mrs. Esther Kamminsky.

"Probably his wife," Max says. "No, wait—his wife and his brother. They were having an affair, and he snatched both of them. Took them off to a deserted hotel, tied them up, and tortured them with his heartfelt rendition of 'Tiny Bubbles.'"

"Perhaps." Claire wraps her fist around the ball of wax paper that once housed her sandwich. They finished eating ages ago. "But what about her?" She points to an older woman sporting a wool skirt and a receding hairline. "I'd say she tops him. I'd say she's one of those teachers who takes the concept of 'under her wing' just a little too far."

"Ewww." Max shields his eyes. "No sex with older women today, please. I just had tuna."

"Fool." Claire's wax paper ball bounces between her hands,

48

then ricochets off Max's shoulder. "Not sex. Cannibalism. She stores them in her attic. Catalogs them by breakfast, lunch, and dinner. Dewey decimal. She's old school."

Max jabs a straw into soda-faded water. "You know who that is, don't you?"

"Who?"

"Your eater. She was at the meeting this afternoon. Don't you remember? In the back by the coffee machine."

Claire squints at the ample, wool-ensconced rear currently making its way to the register, a sack of ripe tomatoes bumping off its side. "Whoa. She looks totally different in this light. I was even checking her out at the meeting. Thinking there's some dyke potential there. Along with the cannibalism, of course."

"You and your Everyone's A Homo nonsense. Next thing you know, you'll be telling me *I'm* gay."

"Not you, Maxie. You're as straight as they come."

"Nice. Speaking of straight, how's Shelly?" He chases away a grin.

"Ah. Shelly, she be fine. It's all good in the Shelly arena."

Max shoots over one of his "soul on a platter" glances. Meaning Claire's. Meaning sand-sifting inspection of all the pockmarked sectors of her interior life, holding them up for appraisal and possible removal. Loving her no matter what.

"Max." She squirms against the strict plastic of her deli chair. Her sponsor has unknowingly unearthed not Shelly, but a certain woman religious. Claire would prefer to leave this cranny of her consciousness unexplored. "No nookie. I promise."

"And how's the meditation coming?"

"Oh, you know. I try, I really do. It's just so hard to sit still. And my mind doesn't like me very much. There's just so much gunk in there. The second I start to pay attention to it, all the bad stuff I ever did comes flying at me like a pack of rabid monkeys. I'm telling you, Max, it doesn't really work for me."

He ferries aside his glass, better to impart his next morsel of wisdom, which is, "You need some way to connect, Claire. Some way to keep things right with your Higher Power. Nothing's better than meditation, that's all."

"I know. I'm okay with that, though. I'm cool with my Higher Power. Like at meetings, or with you. I feel it there."

"Sure, but—"

"Or after I've just finished watching a really intense movie, and I walk outside and everything still looks like a movie, except it's God that's directing it. And there's nothing that can happen that's out of place, nothing's wrong, because there's this huge energy behind it all, behind everything, and all I have to do is walk through it. Like that."

Claire waits. Voicing the experience has made it true, her skin and sensations charged with life. Max can feel it too, she can tell. It's not until she remembers the detritus, the facts and fictions she's failed to bring to the table, that the spell is broken.

"That is good." Max tips his glass back between them. "That's something. And I'm not knocking those experiences. It's just that, with meditation, you have a structured time, you know? A way to touch in that's part of your day, every day. So you never get too far off track."

"But I kinda have that. I mean, in my way." Claire tilts her chair back, knowing what she should say next, but won't. The episode that brought her to sobriety—its grace, its violence, its always-present impact—is something she's never shared with anyone. If she told Max he'd surely laugh—or he might, and she can't risk it.

She drops her chair forward. "I stay in touch," she says. "You know that. I keep it going, keep it real." She finds the portion of his face where she can deposit this information, can show him that the wires are connected without having to reveal their Source. "Seriously. Don't fret."

"Fret I must. Especially where you're concerned. If I didn't—"

"How about that guy?" Claire motions toward the frozen food section, where a cane-enhanced gentleman is filling his cart with bags of mixed vegetables. "What a weirdo. Extortion, for sure. Arson too, I'll bet."

Max stares her down, but only for a second. He turns toward the object of distraction, his eyes pinching with suspicion.

"And the cane," he says. "I'll bet he does something really funky with that cane."

When Claire gets home, her mother's boyfriend is under the hood of the Toyota, changing the battery.

She clicks by him with her bike. "Hey there, Tex. How's it hanging?"

"Low to the ground and choking on the fumes. How about yourself?" He's still under the hood.

"Can't complain."

Tex isn't from Texas. He's never even been there. He's simply someone who rolled into Kitty's life with all the force of the eighteen-wheelers he drives for a living. That, plus he's Donna's baby brother, though at 320 pounds and pushing forty years of age, he's not such a baby anymore.

"You should drop by sometime," Tex says. He emerges from the hood, socket wrench in hand. A week-old beard is gaining ground, giving him the countenance of a blond bear. "Kitty's starting to worry you've expired back in that little house of yours. I know I'd love to see you some."

Claire loves Tex. He smokes enough weed to keep him in a constant state of No Worries but, Claire supposes, being married to Kitty has its price. Not that they're even married, exactly. Kitty claims she's been down that godforsaken path too many times now (three) to try her luck again and besides,

51

Tex is on the road so much she hasn't had a chance to get sick of him yet. Not like a husband.

"Sure," Claire says. "Maybe I'll stop by later." She wheels over to the gate and thumps her bike tire against the chipped blue of the fence. "After I'm done with my gig at the Community Center."

"Awesome," Tex says.

They both know she's lying.

Hieroglyphics

"This sucks," the kid says. His arms swing around like a broken scarecrow, then droop at his sides. "Are you gonna to have anything blow up or explode? Because if you're not, it's gonna suck."

Every day of the five days so far that Claire has been at the Center, this kid has been there to remind her she looks like a boy or to point out the stupidity of whatever it is she's doing. His name, she's pretty sure, is Enrique, but Claire won't call him that. It would only encourage him.

"If it sucks so bad, why are you here?" She shuffles around the preproduction papers on the counter in front of her, hoping that this will convince him to leave.

"Because." He stomps his feet against the floor, a well-worn carpet the shade and consistency of dirt. "They ain't doing shit over there."

"Hey, hey. Language. We're in the vicinity of a church here, bucko."

"Okay. They ain't doing crap over there." He flops an arm in the direction of Shelly and the rest of the children, who do, indeed, seem to be doing absolutely nothing.

"Yo, Shel." Claire bellows over to her friend. "Maybe you should whip out something from the old 4-H handbook. Teach these kids a few new tricks."

Shelly is slumped on a fold-out chair, the little girl Lupe in her lap. "I told you to stay away from the crack, Claire. Just say 'No.'" She blushes.

4-H is code for Claire and Shelly's old high school club. It stood for Hedonism, Heresy, Hieroglyphics, and Homosexuality and was created by the two of them as a cover for their extracurricular sexual activity. They first met in World History class junior year, paired together to do a report comparing the Egyptian dynasties to the societies of ancient Greece. This prompted Claire's hand-drawn renditions of Greeks and Egyptians in compromising positions (passed to Shelly during class time), which led to after-school study sessions having less and less to do with Greeks or Egyptians, which led, eventually, to a kiss in front of the television in Claire's bedroom.

Shelly hides her thumbs in Lupe's night-black hair. Someone gave Lupe a haircut since they were here last, hacking her bangs to an inch of their life. The stubbed strands hang over a face as round as it is content.

"You're a singer," Lupe says to Shelly. "You can sing us something." She wriggles off Shelly's lap and drops to the floor, hands clapping.

"How did you … ? All right," Shelly says.

"There's a guitar." A boy with a slit-thin braid points to the corner of the Rec Room. "In that closet."

A parade of children passes behind her—scuffling feet, spastic shouts—and Claire fastens her attention back on her papers. Shelly may be copasetic with Lupe's fine-tuned perceptions, but Claire would rather stay off the radar. ("You're an alcoholic," Lupe would say, palms clasped together, eyes bright. "You slept with someone else's wife.")

The brood crowds around Shelly, guitar on her lap, and they attempt to find an overlap of musical tastes. This is harder than it seems. A bunch of songs, all in Spanish, are discarded as unintelligible (by Shelly), as are all the songs from Shelly's childhood the kids have never heard of. They settle, finally, on that most banal of intersections: Madonna. Shelly switches the lyrics around, removing the naughty stuff, and the kids switch over into hyper mode, flailing around the room like they're at their first rock concert.

It's in all the commotion—Shelly's lucid voice and crummy guitar playing, along with the roomful of youthful enthusiasm—that Claire is kept from noticing anything but a tugging on her T-shirt. The origin of the interruption is Enrique (*he's still here! what is he still doing here?*), but not the cause. That would be Sister Hilary.

She's standing behind and slightly to the right of Claire with another woman that Claire can't place at first, but then does. It's the lady from the other day, from the meeting and the store. The eater.

"Claire, this is Sister Frances. She's on sabbatical from her position in Southern California. I was just showing her around. She's interested in your video project."

Claire turns too quickly, spattering a clump of papers onto the floor. Enrique, in a gesture that physically hurts her in its attentive sweetness, rounds them up and plants them back in her hands.

"It's nice to meet you," she says.

"And you." Sister Frances does not appear to be happy to be meeting anyone. She practically growls the words. Enrique scurries away.

"How *is* your project coming along?" Sister Hilary is inhabiting a high range of hopeful. She is, now that Claire stops to notice, more than a little nervous. "It seems like you've been hard at work back here."

"It's coming along great. I scouted out all my options already, where I'm gonna film. Then I did an outline and a treatment. And I did a bunch of research, on Catholic social services agencies and stuff. I'm gonna use some of that. And I read your mission statement. Sister Maria showed it to me, when she was here the other day."

"She did?" Sister Hilary chirps, nodding at Sister Frances. "How nice of her."

"So, yeah. I'm building the video around that. Your mission

and all the stuff you do to make that happen. It's impressive, I gotta say. You're actually doing what you set out to do."

"Claire's a film student," Sister Hilary says. "Like I was telling you."

"Yes." Sister Frances' face appears to be set at scowl. "You were."

"I'm working on the shot list now," Claire says. "I should be able to start filming soon."

Sister Hilary grins, her nervousness flicking into the corners of her mouth. "That's super, Claire. If there's anything I can do to help, just let me know. It's fun to have a project like this going on. An influx of creativity. It's neat to see."

"Thanks." Claire clutches her shot list and tries not to look at Sister Frances. The receding hairline, the one Claire spotted from clear across the produce aisle, appears to be not so much receding as set back extra far off her brow. As if all the electric worry vibes and negative ions emanating from her skull have relegated her hair to an afterthought, a middle-of-the-scalp affair. She must remember Claire from the meeting; that must be why she's acting so strange.

"There is," she says to Sister Hilary, "the church to see yet. Why don't we do that now?"

As they coast away, Claire blames herself. It's that stupid game she plays with Max, the plastering of sinister secrets onto otherwise ordinary citizens. That's what drove Sister Frances off. Claire settles back into her preproduction process, reminding herself to be nice from now on.

Mama

She's fast asleep when the trouble begins. It's nighttime in her dream, and Claire is at the bar. She visits here often, a little field trip to the local pub, where the drinks are perpetually free of charge and the buzz is always just kicking in. There are no penalties here, no unforeseen consequences along with the harmless, endless drinking.

These excursions terrify her upon waking, though Max insists that they are merely warnings, meant to keep her humble. That the difference between sober Claire and Claire in the dream is only a decision away, and in spite of the fact that her impulse to imbibe has all but evaporated in her waking life, these dreams serve to put her on notice. On alert.

It would be easier if they weren't so much fun. Tonight, for example, is Hula Night, and the thing she's missing by being asleep—namely, an incessant pounding on her front door— is incorporated into her dream as drums, backbeat to all the fun she's having. There's a contest too—limbo, is it? No, it's drinking. A hearty drinking challenge. She's good at that, count her in. Except someone's yelling now. Two someones. They're pissed and it might be at her, at Claire who is simply shining in the breeze of a delightful buzz, stationed as she is at this outpost of mirth and merry.

"I'm not here," Shelly says. "Why don't you just fucking go away?"

Claire is awake. Awake and sitting up in bed, the bar scene lapping off the edges of her consciousness.

57

The banging starts again. Not drums, not fun, but this. This ruckus at her door. Kenny.

"Just let me in. C'mon. I have something to tell you."

Claire rubs her dream off her face. Shelly is standing in the corner, broom in hand.

"What are you going to do," Claire says, "sweep him to death?"

"Shut up. You got any better ideas?"

Claire flaps back onto the bed, eyes closed. "Is he threatening you?"

"No. He says he just wants to talk."

Claire yanks the phone off the nightstand and onto the bed, her thumb on the square blue Nine. "Let him in, then. If you want. He knows better than to try anything with me here."

She smells him first, before she sees him. Kenny's trademark scent. Grass stains and dried sweat and metal.

"They changed the court date," he's saying. "That's all. I thought you'd want to know."

"Duh. Of course I know, Kenny. I'm part of the case too."

"I know."

"So? So why else are you here?"

"No reason."

"Yeah?"

"Yeah."

Claire sits up, hand still wrapped around the phone. "Kenwad. I haven't seen you since you beat up my best friend."

"Claire ..." Shelly and her broom take a step toward the bed.

"It's not true," Kenny says. "We just got in an argument. I never touched her."

Claire thrashes her legs under the covers and glares at her nemesis. He's dressed for work, which these days is a construction gig. Dirty jeans house extra-long legs attached to a torso squeezed into a bright white T-shirt. Even his body is stupid, Claire thinks. And mean.

When Claire was twelve, Donna and her boys, Kenny included, moved in next door. They brought with them a cat named Buster, who would swallow anything you put in front of him. Once, when Claire wouldn't give Kenny a coin she'd won at the County Fair, he snatched it and fed it to Buster. Claire had to lock that damn cat in her room and wait for her coin to come out its other end. She's hated Kenny ever since.

"If you never touched her, then where the hell did her bruises come from? The *air?* The air from your mouth maybe slapped her around a little bit?"

Kenny picks a penny off Claire's headquarters table and pinches it between two fingers. "Did you guys hear the news? OJ's innocent. They said so this morning. He's free to go." Kenny flips the penny above his head and holds out his hand. It lands with a light smack.

"Out." Shelly's broom is engaged, aimed at Kenny's groin. "Get out. I still have a restraining order, you know. We'll call the cops and they'll bust your ass. You can take OJ's spot." She jabs the broom into the air several times before placing it at her feet where, somehow, it looks even more dangerous.

"Shel." Kenny strokes his chest. "Let's just—"

"You're free to go."

The second he leaves, Claire tears out of bed and over to her headquarters table. She tidies up by splashing the dust off each pile, then ruffles their edges with her palms and pats the tops of their heads.

"Sorry," Shelly says. "I thought he forgot who I was."

"No one could ever forget who you are, Shel."

Shelly's cheeks are flushed from the encounter and her posture is hunched, like her spine just lost a few of its key vertebrae. She trots over to her candy sack and pulls a fresh bar off the top. "Right after my news, too."

Claire finishes with her table and sinks onto a chair hovering along the outskirts. "What do you mean?"

"Didn't you hear the phone ring?" Shelly pops on top of the counter, legs swinging against the recently painted orange cabinets. "I thought you might have heard me talking."

"I was busy sleeping, remember?"

"Yeah, well, you missed me getting a job."

Claire's foot jerks involuntarily, crashing her ankle into the chair's leg. "A what?"

"A job." Shelly wrestles her candy bar out of its wrapper. "You know, one of those things where you show up every now and then and they give you money? One of those."

Claire abandons her chair for a vertical position, then thinks better of it and takes another seat. "But why? I mean, how come?"

"My counselor said it would be a good idea. So I can save up and get my own place. Otherwise I'm just mooching off you and I'm still not, you know, standing on my own." Shelly's heels thump against the cabinets, one at a time.

"But when did you—"

"It's at the bank. Right downtown here." Shelly's fists pump into the space in front of her. "The new Wells Fargo Branch."

"I didn't—"

"It'll be great, Claire Bear. It's all gonna work out great." Shelly raises her arms in what looks like a gesture of appeasement. Or is it liberation?

Claire crunches her other ankle into the chair, voluntarily this time. "Don't call me that."

"Why not?"

"Shelly." Claire tips a penny, Kenny's penny, off the table and buries it under her foot. She sort of wants to cry. "Why the hell didn't you tell me about this? And what about the

Center? We've barely been there two weeks. You're gonna leave me alone with all those attention-starved munchkins? I was just about to get going on my movie." A fly lights on one of Claire's papers and starts shitting or barfing or whatever it is flies do when they land. She shoos it away. "You always do this, Shel. You always leave me stuck with the beginnings of your schemes. 'Volunteer at the Center.'" She imitates a high-pitched voice that sounds nothing like Shelly's. "'Sure, Sister Hilary, we'd *love* to volunteer at the Center.'"

"Hey," Shelly bends down and, without leaving the counter, swipes another candy bar out of her bag, "you wouldn't even be there if it wasn't for me. Taking those volunteer jobs got you hooked up with your precious la-dee-da camera in the first place. And you haven't been doing crap with the kids anyway. That was all me."

"All you?" Claire stops. The insufferableness of Shelly's logic leaves little satisfaction in defending against it. Better to barge in at a different point of entry altogether. "Shel. We didn't have to volunteer, you know. That Sister Hilary would have let me use the camera even without any sort of volunteering action. I could tell. But now I'm stuck. See," she scrunches her thumb into the pads of her fingers and twists her hand upward, as if protecting the truth from Shelly's harmful influence, "this is like the fifteenth time you've done something like this. Remember when we were seniors, and you ditched me at the Garlic Festival? Or after the earthquake when you said it was God's intervention and you couldn't see me anymore? Or Kenny? What about Kenny?" She lets the name fester, the sleazy syllables speaking for themselves.

Shelly polishes off her candy bar casually, like she's digesting Claire's little speech along with the chocolate. Claire waits for it all to congeal: her words in Shelly's stomach, the weight of reason and guilt parked heavy against her friend's interior. Except it's not working. Claire inspects the package of tanned limbs and hard eyes that is Shelly, the old friend whom Claire

61

has hurt just as much—with booze, with language—as Shelly has ever hurt her. She's huddled inside herself with all of Claire's foibles, all of her mistakes, and she's not letting go.

The knock on the door saves them, in a way. Claire knows exactly who it is, too. The way each knock is padded with silence, so the knocker has time to inhale the sound, ingest it, remember what she's done. Then knock again.

"We heard you the first time. Just come on in."

It's not an easy entrance, though. Never is, with Kitty. She jiggles the handle like she's never worked one before, finally figuring it out and guiding the door into open. Once inside, she shields a hand against the light even though, from what Claire can tell, it's brighter outdoors.

"Kitty." Claire finds this is all she can manage.

She's called her mother Kitty since she was twelve, since it started to dawn on her that "mom" was something Kitty was not all that good at. Today, straddling an early morning hangover inside an early morning pick-me-up cocktail, Kitty is already chomping at the bit, amped and belligerent. Claire can practically see the outline of an invisible knife in her mother's grip, ready to poke.

Claire strikes first. "Sinatra pooped in the driveway again. You have to do something about him. He's got no conscience, that dog."

Kitty staggers sideways and peers back toward the doorway, as if Claire were addressing someone else. Perhaps Ol' Blue Eyes himself. When she realizes that this is not the case, when she homes in on herself as the object of accusal, she slides a hand across the belly of her bony body and chuckles. "That's not Frank's. Frank's shit *sings*." She chuckles again. Her hair, like red straw, pricks against her shoulders. It's a new shade, this red. Deep and blistered, like fried blood.

"It is too Frank's." Claire will never be old enough not to get riled up by her mother. "I can totally tell. It's his signature shit. He's had years of practice."

Kitty flicks her gaze at her daughter. "Wrongo."

The thing of it is, Kitty adores Sinatra. Ever since he got carted home from the pound as Angela's dog, everyone knew that Kitty had dibs. The feeling is mutual. Even though he's ancient and arthritic and can barely eek out a proper woof anymore, Sinatra still follows her around like a lovesick fan. She'd be a fool not to reciprocate.

As if on cue, waiting until enough controversy has been stirred up on his behalf, Sinatra toddles into the room like the legend he is and collapses at Kitty's feet. He sighs heavily.

"He better not deposit any goodies in here." Claire rearranges her T-shirt and herself. It must be—what?—nine a.m. and it's already hot as hell in here. There's a speck of orange paint on the hem of her shirt, a souvenir from the recent kitchen makeover, and she tries to peel it off, though it seems to want to stay. Five seconds into this project, she realizes her mistake.

Kitty clears her throat—an epic sound in Claire's auditory awareness. "Thought I heard a fight back here. Some sorta banging and carrying on. That better not have been Kenny I saw. Donna'll pinch his grits if she sees him around here."

"I got a job, Kitty." Shelly bounces off the counter and sidles over to Sinatra, roughing up his ears and palming his belly. "Just now, over the phone. I'm gonna work at the bank downtown and get my own apartment. Isn't that boss?"

Kitty nods, but it's a gesture of frustration as much as acquiescence. Not only is she knocked off her scouting mission, she's confused to boot. Claire can tell—by the way her mother peeks at Shelly, then away, gathering evidence one button at a time—that Kitty is unclear as to where, exactly, Shelly is staying. How this could have possibly escaped her is baffling. Then again, Claire's drinking days saw a rack of revolving overnight guests (mostly girls, sometimes boys) ferried through her house with such speed that one would have thought Kitty would have coughed up an opinion or, at the very least, an observation as to the depth and breadth of her daughter's nocturnal hospitality. But no. There was nothing. And then, like now, Claire is both amused and disappointed by Kitty's complete, multifaceted obliviousness.

"Where you been, though?" Her attention wobbles back to Claire. "Tex said he saw you, but I don't ever see you. You never come over to the house anymore, not like you used to. Like you're too good for us now, is what it's like. Isn't it?"

When Claire was little, she was given a toy that had belonged to Kitty's older brother Steve. (Who was gay. Who died of AIDS. Whom no one ever talks about.) It was a white cone with rainbow-colored rings stacked up its sides, biggest to smallest, purple to red. Claire loved its order, its predictability, the feel of the fat plastic rings inside her still-growing fingers. This is Kitty—in her bluster, in her accusations—resembling the purple-blue-green-yellow-orange-red sweep except for one thing. There's no center, no cone to make it stick.

"You've gotta keep a better eye on Bunny and Walt," Claire says, plastic flying. "They're always out there in the street, causing trouble. I never saw such unruly kids in my life."

Kitty scowls, battered but undeterred. "Better than Ronny and Dale," she says.

This is true. Claire's other half-sister Lisa, the one who skipped town and married a Marine, has two boys who, as Kitty likes to say, are the type of children who would be "best kept caged."

"Maybe," Claire says. "But the other day I saw them out there with a bunch of firecrackers. Walt was lighting them under the Henderson's truck, and then over in the bushes. It's a miracle nothing caught on fire. Could have had the whole neighborhood in flames. They need more supervision, Kitty. You can't just let them roam around."

"You were exactly the same when you were little." Kitty bends down to join Shelly in her adoration of Sinatra. The dog's plump black tail whaps against the floor. "Worse. You would get out of bed before the sun did and the cops would be at the house before breakfast. So don't tell me about wild. You did wild plenty." She massages Sinatra's eyebrows and he grins in response. "And how about your little stay in Juvenile Hall, you want to get into that?"

"No." Claire attends to her speck of orange paint. Perhaps she was wrong about the cone.

"Yeah, you have to tell me about that." Shelly unfolds herself onto the floor. "She never talks about it."

Claire, disgusted with her ineffective efforts in paint- and Kitty-removal, kicks her chair out from under her. She watches her mother and her best friend fawning over the dog and a crappy chapter out of her childhood and wonders what Max would say. He'd say, "You can only control yourself." He'd say, "Live and let live." He'd say, "Head for the hills, Claire. Your mind is a toxic waste dump and you better not get caught in it alone."

"Thanks, buddy," she says aloud, and goes outside to check on the sun.

Chaperone

Sister Hilary is not at her desk when Claire passes by, which is weird. Usually she's there and Claire can wave, casual-like, on her way to the Rec Room. But today of all days, Claire's first day there without the protective influence of Shelly, Sister Hilary is strikingly absent.

No worries. Claire is armed with both a plan for the short people (Hide and Go Seek!) and a comprehensive shot list that will enable her to start filming. Today. She's already a third of the way into the semester and, so far, has nothing to show for it. If she were still in Jack's class, like a regular person, she'd have help with the process—motivation, encouragement. But she's not, so she doesn't. Motivation and encouragement are commodities she has to manufacture for herself.

She shoves the door into the Rec Room and notes with a slice of regret that Sister Hilary is not here either. But Sister Frances is. The older woman, clothed in a gray suit and an air of condescension, stands in front of the room next to a chalkboard. The kids are scattered around the tables, looking like POWs. Or no, Claire thinks—worse. These kids are soldiers who have been promised reprieve—given it, even (Shelly's songs, Shelly's face)—and are now sentenced to this. Catechism.

"Let's look at the next passage." Sister Frances is saying. "Share with your neighbor."

Shiny black catechisms flutter at the tables like so many

caged birds. Only Lupe is attentive, hands planted in her lap, paper-plated moniker still yoked around her neck. Claire looks away.

"Hey." Enrique trails behind her so close she can smell his breath. A brew of onions and soda. "Bet you need some help *today.*"

"Bet I don't."

Claire rifles through the closet until she finds the camera. Her camera. She pops off the lens cap and frames his spiky hair (like hers, almost) inside the viewfinder. "You know, actually, you're right. You can help me by leaving me alone. A-l-o-n-e. Bye bye, now. B-y-e B-"

"I can spell. Jeez." His shoulders nip inward and he drags himself back to his spot at the table, though not before turning around several times to test Claire's resolve.

She feigns obtuse, digging in the camera bag to double-check her tape supply and tinkering with the tripod until she understands its mechanics. The camera is raring to go—she can feel it whirring beneath her fingers—and she aims it toward the far wall to set the white balance. The camera does this automatically, but she prefers the precision and pretension of manual setting.

The light in the room is all wrong—she needs cellophane on the windows and reflectors in the corners—but for now she'll take this, what she has, and go for a little spin. She starts with some long shots of the classroom, some mid shots of kids and catechisms, a close-up on Sister Frances. It's at the end of this last shot that the subject of Claire's attention sniffs out the camera like a chimp with a new nit.

"What are we doing?" she says, camera rolling.

Claire punches Pause. "It's my movie, remember?"

Sister Frances seems to remember only how much she distrusts and dislikes Claire. It's odd, really. Claire has spied her at a few more meetings now—always in the background, always silent—and at the Center with Sister Hilary, who continues to treat her like royalty. With all the adulation, Claire is surprised Sister Frances has time to notice her, let alone detest her. But she does. Perhaps it's exposure she fears, Claire outing her as a Twelve Stepper. Or perhaps she perceives Claire as a threat to the symbiosis between Sisters, though the latter makes no sense. There's nothing about Claire that interrupts that bond, the worship and allowing of such worship. Either way, Claire is hated, and senses herself as such. All this from the soaring forehead and pinched gawps of a woman who, from what Claire can tell, is in need of a stiff drink.

"I was supposed to ask for permission first," Claire says. "Sorry about that. Maybe I'll go film somewhere else for a while." She packs up her camera and, without a backward glance, scuttles out of the Rec Room.

The hallway is empty, just Claire and an old wheelchair stashed under a portrait of a solicitous-looking man in a red dress. It's like he's blessing it, sparking the wheels with sanctity. Which gives her an idea.

"Enrique." She pokes her head back into the Rec Room. "Come here a sec."

He looks to Sister Frances (he is, at heart, a good boy), who nods him away with all the precision and authority of a drill sergeant.

In the hallway, breathless, he scouts Claire's hands and face for clues. "What?"

"Here's the plan. I'm going to do a tracking shot of this hallway leading down into the church. And it needs to be smooth, which I can't do just me and what I got here. I need this wheelchair," she unfolds it into the beam of the red-dressed man, "and I need you to drive me so we can get the shot. You dig?"

He scratches his neck. "This makes me your assistant, right? Like, your special assistant?"

"Yeah, yeah. Special."

She plunks herself in the chair, sets up her camera, and instructs Enrique to push her—not too fast, not too slow—down the hallway. They make it to the nave of the church and Claire sails into the end of her shot, stained glass guarding vacant pews and a figure in the corner kneeling in prayer.

"Perfect," she says. She sets the camera in her lap.

"Claire?" The figure, who is Sister Hilary, who is alarmed, scurries toward them. "Are you all right? You hurt yourself?"

"Big time," Claire says. "Fell down and cracked my leg in two and Doctor Enrique here had to stitch me up with spit and sales tax. Isn't that right, Enrique?"

"Right." His voice echoes against the walls of the church. "She's hurt real bad."

"I see." Sister Hilary crosses her arms, dividing her body into two parts—the slacks-clad bottom and the head-shaking top. "Glad you're so well tended, Claire. We wouldn't want you wandering around wounded. Without a chaperone."

Claire flips a tape out of the camera, hoping this makes her look professional. "Everyone needs a chaperone."

"Indeed. Speaking of which, I sent in Sister Frances to help with the kids program. I assume that's going well?"

"Sister Frances sucks." Enrique baps one of the handles of the wheelchair, inching it toward Sister Hilary. "Shelly's way better. How come she can't come back?"

"Shelly had something else to do." Claire and Sister Hilary say this together, the language blending into one sound. Sister Hilary laughs.

"How about you, Claire?" Enrique says. "Why don't you be Shelly from now on?"

Claire nudges the wheelchair backward, away from Sister Hilary's jovial face. "I can't," she says. "Gotta make my movie. I mean, I assume ..."

"You assume it's all right even though you promised to help out at the Center as a condition of using the camera?"

Sister Hilary's glee shoots forward, cuffing Claire's ears, her suppositions.

"Kinda."

"That's fine." Sister Hilary unlocks her arms and tugs at the length of her sleeves. "We have Sister Frances now, and despite your initial assessment, Enrique, we expect she'll work out just fine. She was a teacher, you know. At a college."

"You don't say." Claire swallows into a dry throat. She wonders what else Sister Hilary knows about the venerable Sister Frances.

"You have some input, Claire? About our new teacher?"

"No," Claire says. *Only you, Sister Hilary. Only the way your aura is pooled, like a cup. Round and steady so I can sit inside, toes dangling, and wonder how I got here. Wonder if you allowed it.*

"We'd better go," she says. "Let you get back to your prayers."

Lounge

Max's mother is devoted to plastic. As such, the couch upon which Claire is planted is coated in the stuff. So, too, is the recliner where Max is splayed out, flat as a foot.

"This is Esther's throne," he says. "I never get to sit here."

"What time will she resurface?"

"That's anyone's guess." He taps his heels together like he's making a wish. "This is her night to play cards over at Myrtle Silverstein's. Those old broads are ruthless, I'm telling you. Money is involved and, well," he retrieves a second piece of quitting-smoking-gum out of his shirt pocket and slips it in his mouth, "wills have been changed over this thing. I'm not kidding." He munches thoughtfully. "Remind me why I'm quitting smoking?"

"So you won't die."

"But I will. Shouldn't I be happy until then? Shouldn't I be smoky and stinky and have limited lung power and a compromised immune system? Who says I can't have that?"

Claire creaks forward, unpeeling one of her legs from a resistant cushion. "You told me if you started talking like this to slap you. You want me to come over there?"

"I never said that. You're hallucinating again, Claire. Maybe you should take up smoking. To calm your nerves."

Claire releases her torso back to the plastic. "Max, do you think there's something wrong with me? Like, really wrong? Like, rotting-turd-at-the-core kinda wrong?"

Max flicks a shoe off his foot. It falls onto Esther's whorled

71

wool carpet without a sound. "Of course, lamb chop. That's why you're here. That's why we're all here. So God can fix us."

"Well, God's sure got a shitload of work to do on me. I think God gets worn out just *looking* at me."

"Whoah, precious. Let's not play Sicker Than Thou. You know where that leads."

Claire closes her eyes, settles into the soup she's got brewing. Shelly's in there, along with two Sisters who shall remain nameless. They're scouring her insides, paddling around each other with suspicion and hazy motives. She can't tell Max about this yet, it's too raw, too ridiculous. Though that's exactly why she should be telling him.

"Why are we here?" she says. "Shouldn't we be at your new place?"

Max's eyebrows slump toward his eyes. He sighs. "I'm not moving. That place I liked fell through. Besides, it's not the right time yet. Esther started hyperventilating at the very idea. Truly. I had to get a bag and everything. You know," he stretches his lanky body into a sideways position, offering him a full view of Claire, "you could always talk to … someone. About your family, your childhood—the sewage of your youth. It couldn't hurt."

"I thought you Big Book thumpers didn't go for therapy. Throws you off your program. Isn't that right?" Claire is setting fires. She knows his answer to this, knows he spent a few years in counseling after Bert died, after he moved here. "Besides, I'll be out of here soon enough. Once I clear up this school stuff, once I get everything settled with Jack—"

"Jack who hates you? That Jack?"

"He doesn't have to like me. He just has to pass me. That's all I need."

"So you say."

"It's true. Once I get that and a few other things taken care of, I'm good to go. SFSU or UCLA—one of them has to let me in. This time next year, I'll be there, not here. Out of the muck."

Max chuckles. "Muck is portable, my dear."

"Not if I can help it."

"But it is," he says. "Believe me." He props himself up taller, elbow wedged in plastic. "Why do you think you're an addict? Why do you think you're still trying to control all this shit that's out of your control? Talking to a therapist wouldn't kill you, Claire. It might even help."

Claire groans. "Max, you don't get it. You had the intact family—screwed up, maybe, but intact—with the mom and the dad and your sisters and you were the baby and the only boy and adored by your mother as the possibly risen Christ, except you were Jewish, so she probably wouldn't say that, but you were *valued*, at least. Me, I never even had a dad, though I had to hear all the time how I look just like him, bum that he was. And then my mom actually comes from a semi-regular kind of family, but she skipped out on all that on the backs of a bunch of losers, starting with my dad. And she's never really liked me much, I was always getting in the way of her next husband or her next party or her next drink. Why the hell would I want to talk about *that?* I already lived it, I don't need to talk about it."

Claire sloshes around for a bit, the well-padded couch barely able to contain the cache that is her sorrow, her carefully constructed grief. When she tires of this, though, there is Max, who is bound to supply just the right potion of advice, that specialized shot of spiritual sanity to make it all come clear. She only needs to ask.

"So?" she says.

Max flips the lever that transforms his recliner back into a regular chair. He finds her with eyes both patient and inexhaustibly wise. "You think your life is hard? When I was a kid, I had to walk to school with no legs."

The Great Outdoors

The church is silent, as if God is taking a nap. Claire is perched in a middle pew, over on the side where the pearl gray shadow from the post in front of her creates the illusion, for someone peering in from the outside, that she is not here.

She's got her reasons, though. For being here. The last week has been a blessing, of sorts; Sister Frances' reign in the afternoon classes and Sister Hilary's acknowledgement of Claire's non-participation in these classes have released her into a film-only existence. It's an existence, she has found, that's best spent far away from Sister Frances. A research trip to the Point Firth Center was one remedy for this. The other has been to do all her filming between the hours of noon and two p.m. when, for whatever reason, Sister Frances seems to disappear. (Claire suspects a noon meeting, but won't investigate. She's happy for the reprieve.)

Sister Frances, however, is not the only recipient of Claire's all-purpose avoidance skills; Sister Hilary is the one who has been giving these skills their greatest workouts. Staying away from her, she who seems to never leave the Center or any inch of its hallowed ground, has proven to Claire to be a challenge of epic proportions: like trying to lift fifty-pound weights with her eyelashes.

The camera, in its buffering potential, has shown itself to be a huge help, along with Claire's legs and their ability, on command, to walk away from the source of distraction. But the biggest problem is Sister Hilary herself. She is, Claire can no longer deny this, an extremely compelling individual, packaged inside herself in such a manner that Claire cannot help but peek around the corner of her own awareness and wonder—hope, marvel—at what lies within those long limbs and pensive, pent-up features. The fact that this is all insane—on account of Hilary being a nun and Claire being an unreformed pervert (in a good way) of the highest order—only compounds the issue.

And so she is here, in the church.

She was late getting started today, for a number of reasons too stupid to review, and it is after four p.m.—after the point at which she could have returned the camera to the Rec Room free of the high-gloss glare of Sister Frances. She was on her way to do just that, a good five minutes before Sister Frances usually makes her appearance, when Sister Hilary, ubiquitous as always, materialized at the end of the hallway. Sister Hilary has a beauty mark above the curve of her mouth on her right side, and it was Claire's conjecturing of how it would feel to place her thumb upon this mark, a mark which called out, bold and elusive, even across the thirty-foot expanse of the hallway, that prompted her legs to shuttle her into the relative safety of the church.

She takes a breath now, all the air she can handle, and blows it into her lap. Christ is up front, a sliver of a man on a gold cross, high above Claire and anyone else who would ever be here with her. To her left, embedded in stained glass, are Saint Philip and Saint Simon. And who the hell are they? Claire should know these things, she should know a lot of things, but she doesn't. The parameters of the church—its ceiling like a ski lodge, its rules and rosaries, its forever-held breath—are such that she has no choice but to shrink inside them.

Something happened to her, this is true, an experience that some would categorize as religious. It brought her to sobriety and altered her life. But it's not here, it has nothing

75

to do with this place. This place offers only the cross, and the saints, and the air so tall it chokes her. What is it, she wonders, that Sister Hilary extracts from these walls that infuses her with such certainty, such grace in the face of a world that so often veers in the wrong direction? Is it something more than what Claire has, the source that has kept her sober? Or is it altogether different, as similar to Claire's version of a Higher Power as a light bulb is to the sun?

Claire squirms against the pew, against the hollow gaze of the bleeding man at the front of the church. She needs to leave, needs to slip out of the deafening quiet of this intersection between heaven and earth, this church she does not understand and in which she does not belong. Sister Hilary can have it, all of it. There is no room for Claire here, no room for the Truth she has yet to talk about. To anyone. She is happy for Sister Hilary, sorry for herself. There's no other way to hold this and yet, as she rises from the pew, camera in hand, she finds herself embodying a third possibility. One in which she is straddling the two poles, arms wrecked and refashioned by the distance spanned, then broken.

She blinks against it and closes the door to the church.

Two minutes later, Enrique tackles her outside the door to the Rec Room. "Claire! Where'd you go? I thought you left maybe, but Sister Hilary said you didn't. Look," he says, "come see."

He takes her wrist and pulls her into the room. The stifling regime of Sister Frances is apparently over. The tables are covered with pencils and papers and laughter.

"We're drawing today, see?" Enrique says. "It was Lupe's idea."

Lupe's hand is stretched around a fat yellow crayon. She's pushing it across her paper as though tracing a pattern hidden inside the page. "Hola, Sister Claire," she says.

Claire blanches. "Not me. You got the wrong girl."

"Didn't I tell you, Enrique?" Sister Hilary, seated on the far side of the table next to twin girls in dark braids, salutes Claire with a crayon. "Didn't I tell you she'd show up?"

"Uh," Claire says. She marches over to the cabinet and puts her camera away. Then takes it out again. Fear, like a razor, zips through her knees. Sister Hilary is here because of her, she can feel it.

"How's the movie going?" Sister Hilary asks.

Claire jams her palm against the top of the tripod and spins herself around to face the table. "It's going really well. Great, in fact. I've got almost all the footage already. It's been a breeze, filming here."

"Glad to hear it. It's been a breeze having you here."

"Really?" The fear has reached Claire's stomach, rendering it weightless. "So yeah, when I'm finished with all that, then I just have to edit the little sucker and I'm done. Finito."

Claire wipes her hands together in a gesture of complete and total finality. Then searches Sister Hilary's face for the reverberations of this act. Nothing. Sister Hilary is glowing like a campfire scene—like she's the embers, the marshmallows, the tunes on the periphery, the whole bit. Claire understands. Sister Hilary's presence here is about her, but only one of them knows this.

"What happened to Sister Frances?" Claire says.

"We decided to switch. Give me a little break from the office. It's only for a while, though. Till we get someone else in here." The children moan at this and Sister Hilary tips into a nervous smile. Perhaps she does understand, after all.

"I could shoot you," Claire says. "I mean, in the room. You and the kids." She pats her camera. "If that's okay."

"Shoot away." Sister Hilary picks up a new crayon, a black one, and restarts her drawing. She looks like the children around her: their full-throttle enthusiasm, hearts spilling onto their pages. It is on the edge, Claire thinks, that one may best enjoy a fire—its rage, its depth, its unpredictability. Only on the edge that potential and actual remain separate states. She leans in, tapping her warming kneecaps with her fingertips. She is so screwed.

"You never told me why you and Enrique hung that sheet in the corner." Sister Hilary is finishing her drawing. All the kids have gone and only she and Claire remain. "I assume you weren't doing laundry."

"No laundry." Claire is sitting across from Sister Hilary, sketching a stick figure movie set. She is attempting to draw a horse—it's a Western, her film—but it looks more like a rodent on steroids. "It was for the light, for the filming. It redirects it, evens it out."

"And the cellophane on the windows?"

"Outdoor light is blue. The cellophane tricks it into becoming yellow, for inside. Nifty, eh?"

Sister Hilary trades her red crayon for a green one. Claire can't see much of the picture, but it's thick with slashes of shape and radiance. She seems to know her way around a page, this Hilary. "Yes," she says. "Strange how light can have a color, isn't it? We think of it as light. No agenda."

"Hmm," Claire says. *Why "agenda," Hilary? Why pick that word?* "You look like you've done this before."

"What's that?"

"Drawing. You look like you love it. Like it's all that matters." Claire inches onto the platform of familiarity—smooth, shaded. Light breezes brush against her ears.

"It was Lupe's idea." Sister Hilary, seemingly oblivious to the shift, leans over her drawing. "We couldn't say no. She's a wonder, that girl."

"Lupe scares me." Claire shivers. "She knows too much."

"She knows where she came from, that's for sure."

"You mean El Salvador?"

Sister Hilary sets down her crayon. "No. That's not what I meant."

"Then what did you—"

"How did you know she was from El Salvador?"

"She told me," Claire stammers. Something's gone wrong. She's just not sure what it is. "Are you all right?"

Sister Hilary studies Claire as if she doesn't know her. And doesn't care to. Like Claire was just plunked in front of her from the army of a warring nation and it's Sister Hilary's task to avoid interrogation. "Of course," she says. "I'm fine. Why do you ask?"

"You don't look fine. You look upset. Or mad. Is it me? Did I do something wrong?"

"You? No." Sister Hilary returns to herself. Slivers of light dash out of her eyes. "Of course not."

"Because you look like you—"

"In fact, your presence here has been something of an inspiration to me. I thought maybe you knew that."

"An inspiration? Me?" Claire waits, then picks an orange crayon out of the pile. Her rodent needs a saddle. "You shouldn't say stuff like that. I mean, I know you're just trying to be nice and all, but you don't have to make stuff up just to—"

"You have no idea how you come across, do you?" Sister Hilary's fingers twitch as though they're considering reaching out to Claire, but they tap the edge of her drawing instead. "The effect you have on others?"

Claire shrugs. "I have a bit of an idea. It's usually not so great, my effect on others."

"Stop it. That's exactly what I'm talking about. However it is you see yourself, it's wrong. You have an assuredness about you that's ..." Sister Hilary stares into her drawing as if the right words are contained there, sits up as she pulls them out. "It's interesting, is what it is. I don't know that I've ever seen such a total lack of self-consciousness. It's a gift, whether you know it or not."

79

Claire stops drawing. The grip on her emotions, the one she didn't even know she had, starts to loosen. "A gift?"

"Sure. Look at Enrique. He can't help but follow you everywhere you go. He sees it. He knows it's worth following. You'll make a great director, I'll bet. People will want to work with you and you won't even know why. Charisma can't be manufactured, Claire. It's just there. Which is probably why you don't notice its effect on others. You're not trying to impress or persuade anyone. You're just being yourself."

Claire wants to shake Sister Hilary's hand. Or hug her or kiss her, but not in a naughty way. What she wants is to thank her. Thank her for saying such wonderful things.

"I dream about that sort of stuff," she says. "About being a director and stuff. But I don't know about the charisma part. That's not usually how things work for me. People don't usually see me like that."

"Well, I do. And I'm always right." Sister Hilary chuckles, her hair grazing her cheek. "So you'd better get used to being the center of attention, because that's what's going to happen. Maybe not yet, but eventually. It will. A lot of avenues are going to open up for you."

"I don't know." The language feels slippery, out of Claire's mouth. She fights an urge to crawl under the table. Or into Sister Hilary's lap.

"Believe me. Nothing's more appealing than someone who's just being herself. It's what everyone wants. That kind of freedom."

Claire presses her thumb against the clump of orange in the middle of her drawing, obliterating her rodent horse. "Being myself isn't always such a good thing. It's gotten me in lots of trouble." *Could get me in trouble again.*

"Well, sometimes trouble is necessary. It makes things happen. I've seen my share of it, in this life." A wave of anxiety revisits Sister Hilary's face.

"You mean your life in the Church?" Claire can't stand it,

80

to see Sister Hilary hurt. She speaks swiftly to sweep her out of it. "Working with people in the Church? Or other stuff?"

"In the Church." Sister Hilary is immune to help. She stumbles inside her words. "And other stuff. Like you said."

"So how did that work, anyway? The Church part. How did you—"

"How did I become a woman religious?"

"Yeah."

Sister Hilary nods. She appears to have tamped down her fright, latched onto a part of herself that is sure and unfettered. "It was Sister Frances, actually. I met her when I was in college. Before that, it never appealed to me, this life. I never thought about it. But I met Sister Frances and it all started to make sense. Not right away, of course. I fought it. But eventually it dawned on me. I'm a Sister. It's who I am. You can't fight that."

An entirely inappropriate scene flashes in Claire's mind: candles, chanting, a stern and stoic Sister Frances instructing a young Hilary to disrobe, convincing her that nakedness is next to godliness. "Uh. Where was that?"

"Iowa." Sister Hilary stares at Claire. "Holy Names College, outside of Des Moines."

Can she see it? Can she see the disrobing? "Uh," Claire says again. She nips a green crayon from the cluster between them. (*The one Sister Hilary was just using! What am I thinking?!*) "That's nice."

"It probably seems strange to you, I realize that. Not many women choose this life anymore. But it chose me. I guess that's the best way to explain it. Like you and your movies."

Sister Hilary's eyes, the ones that take up so much of her face, are focused on Claire. *She's gobbling me up*, Claire thinks. *She'll absorb all there is till I'm bone thin, dry, a stick figure like the director of my Western.*

"I'm an alcoholic," Claire says. "I don't drink anymore, but I used to. A lot. I'm in recovery now." She folds up her paper—cameramen, extras, rodent, director—and stuffs it into her pocket. "I guess you could say it kinda chose me too."

Sister Hilary smiles, a quiet shift that matches her eyes. "The drinking or the recovery?" she says.

"Both."

"It's all the same, though, isn't it? My vocation. Your movies. Your recovery. They're all part of a larger pattern. A blessing."

Claire blinks. Has she ever felt this way? So rushed and safe and scared and seen? It's too much, Sister Hilary's attention, her gentleness. It hurts.

"You really live this, don't you?" Claire says. "Like, you trust it. Just the way you talk about it. When you say things, it's there. In your voice. It's really … I don't know. It's weird to see that. To see someone who has that."

Sister Hilary slants forward, her gaze expanding with the erosion of distance. "But you do too, Claire. I can tell. You have it too."

Claire slides her fingers into the folds of her pocket. The figures inside jump and flip like bugs caught in a jar.

"Mmm," she says.

Action

Shelly and Claire are sitting inside a date. It's been nearly three weeks since Shelly started at the Wells Fargo and tonight, as a thank you for the shelter and support, she is treating Claire to dinner and the movies. The dinner part is already over (small portions and live music, real waiters), and the movie part (*Pulp Fiction,* Claire's choice) is about to begin.

"How about this one?" Shelly says. "I say itty-bitty. Three inches, probably. See his face? It's like he's apologizing already. His pants are still on and he's already sorry."

"I guess."

"Or *this* dude. He's in the Ten Plus club, I'll bet. Check out that walk, like he practically has to chain it to his thigh. No worries, see?" Shelly bashes Claire's elbow with a fistful of Gummi Bears. "It's all taken care of, as far as he's concerned. Set for life. Damn." She pops a pair of Bears in her mouth. "How come women can't have that? We gotta worry about our breasts and our faces and our hair and our butts. Guys get to hang it all on just that one thing."

Claire fumbles around their shared bucket of popcorn, snags a few kernels. "For someone who claims to have given up gardening, you sure talk an awful lot about hoses." She considers a bonk to Shelly's arm, but revokes this privilege prior to execution. She bears down on her popcorn instead, crunching the steam out of her system.

The easy physicality of a month ago—arms around waists

83

in the middle of the night, fingers on arms or thighs to enunciate a point, shoulders smashed together on the couch for a video—is over. Shelly's job at the bank, combined with Claire's newfound dedication to the Bearley Community Center, has wedged apart their peaceful physical niche, shocking it into something tense and unresolved. Their limited time together has become a grab bag of sexually tinged banter and libidinal near misses, endless in scope and severity. Claire's not sure if this mayhem is spillover from her continually charged and curious encounters with Sister Hilary, or if it's the other way around. Or if it's simply her year of sexless sobriety, spinning her in circles, chasing her own tail. In any case, Claire is a perpetual jumble of attraction and aversion— willing bait and wriggling free, all at once.

"It's a skill," Shelly says. "You're just jealous because I have such an amazing skill. I could start charging money, you know. Make big bucks."

"Yeah, Weenie Ranker, there's a job title for you."

Shelly splits open a pack of Junior Mints and offers them to Claire, who declines. "Jenny, that chick at work I was telling you about ..."

Claire plucks the mints off Shelly's lap, takes a handful, sets them back. "The one with the wigged-out sister, or the one that collects model cars?"

"The car chick. Her. I think she maybe plays on our side of the duckie pond, if you know what I mean."

Chocolate and a tang of mint bloom against the roof of Claire's mouth. "What do you—"

"And then Roy, the manager guy, the one who always wears those weird socks? He said today that, given my job performance so far, I could be eligible for a promotion in, like, two to three months. Isn't that awesome?" Shelly's legs kick forward, upsetting the equilibrium of the teenaged couple in front of them. "Sorry," she says.

"Yeah, that's—"

"And then Viv, she says I can just *have* her car for a long as I need it. So, trips to Point Firth, Concord, whatever, no problem. We can go anywhere, Claire. Hey hey hey, look." Shelly skims her fingers against the air above Claire's arm. "Movie's starting."

"It sure is," Claire says, then drops her arm into her lap, Shelly's non-touch seeping into her thighs.

Four hours later, they're in bed. The movie is over (they both loved it, though felt stained, in a way, by the violence), and Viv's cruddy old car has delivered them safely to Claire's hovel. And bed.

They've each staked out an edge, a sliver of Claire's already not so big mattress. It's as if they're making room for a soon-to-be-arriving guest, a portly soul who can't bear to sleep alone. This space between them cries out for mercy, for understanding, for something—anything—to assuage its lonely belly and aching ribs. And yet they remain firm, soldiers in their outposts of isolation. Claire, for her part, allows only an energetic exploration, fending off the force, like sideways gravity, that coaxes her toward Shelly. When this becomes too much, though, when she flaps her hand one too many times on the sheet that separates her from her friend, Claire gives in to sound.

"Shel?"

"Nnnnnnr." Shelly's pretending to be asleep, but Claire knows she's not.

"Do you remember the last time?"

Shelly yawns and flops onto her side, facing Claire. In the dark, her pale yellow hair looks like a napkin around her head. Her bedclothes, a black short-and-T-shirt combo, are indistinguishable from the darkness around her. "You mean that time we were on the washer-dryer, and Kenny came home with Duane?"

85

"Yeah."

"And you pulled out of me, and Kenny came back there, and you said you were just helping me separate the whites from the darks?"

"Yeah." Claire smushes her pillow into the wall behind her and props her head against it. "I was way trashed that day."

"You were always way trashed, Claire."

"Yeah."

Silence soaks up the rest of the conversation.

Claire thinks about how she should probably try to squeeze herself into sleep, about how that would be the best way to stay out of trouble, but she can't. All of her cells are standing at attention.

"Shel?"

Shelly curls into a fetal position, knees stabbing the dark. "What?"

"I was thinking about how it probably wouldn't be a good idea to do that again. I mean, not the washer-dryer thing, but just in general. The you and me thing. How we should probably stay away from that, still. I mean, like we have so far. Still."

"Right," Shelly says. Her breathing has picked up, like she's trying to grab more than her share of air. "I was thinking the same thing. How it's not a good idea and all. Of course, we *could*. But that might mess everything up. You know?" She shifts positions, feet dangling off the end of the bed. "I'm still married to stupid Kenny, technically at least, and me and him still need to get annulled and all that. And you, you got that thing where you're not supposed to get with anyone in the first year of being sober—"

"Well, it's almost a year now. It will be. In November. Which is soon."

"But—"

"But, no. You're right." Claire chucks her pillow onto the floor and slides back down onto the mattress. "You're totally right. We shouldn't. Of course we shouldn't. That's what I mean. We shouldn't."

Claire sighs. The chasm between her and Shelly, bloated and impudent, strains against her good intentions. It would be so easy to punch a fist through its weight and heft, to slip to the other side where Shelly's breasts and tongue and sex lie waiting. Claire, the seasoned initiator, could crack their fledgling pact in half like so many water-starved twigs, eager for the burn.

And yet she won't.

The texture of the space that separates her from Shelly is such that its very existence—its unyielding there-ness—prevents her from wandering anywhere but inside her own head. It is her devotion to this void, and to the person she can never have who hovers within it, that keeps Claire from the one person she could have, the warm shape stationed on the other side of the bed.

"It's good," Claire says, "that we talked. It's good we had this chat."

"So you're fine, then? With everything how it is?" Shelly's voice is pinched.

"Sure, yeah. You?"

"Sure."

"Good."

"Great."

Roger That

Claire is dubbing herself into the movie. She should have been done with this thing ages ago, but chance and circumstance keep pressing her into a future where she's still at the Center, still piddling away at her film. Her stalling has its limits: the deadline for Jack is a mere three weeks away. But three weeks is three weeks—twenty-one days of puttering is a feat for which Claire is extremely well suited.

The latest time-stretcher was her discovery of a sound mixer (brand new! still in the original box!) on the floor of the portable closet. This then facilitated a flurry of activity around sound and its components: the taping, then dubbing of a wide variety of noises and audial augmentations onto the now-edited documentary. The final addition, which she will start today, is the voice-over narration captured inside the tape player she holds in her hands. It's a tiny task, one from which she must find every possible distraction. For its completion will denote the end, the unthinkable: a segment of days, weeks, and years in which she has absolutely no reason to be at the Bearley Community Center.

Today, though, she is saved by Lupe. Claire is in her "studio" (the far edge of the Rec Room, shrouded by the same sheet that doubled as a reflector weeks ago), fiddling with the Pause button that will, eventually, flood her prerecorded narrative into the film, when she hears the suggestion.

"Let's play the story game," Lupe says.

"What story game?" Sister Hilary's voice leaks into Claire's headphones.

Claire considers the options—stopping or starting, forward or reverse—and gratefully chooses the one marked Delay. She peels off her headphones and peeks around the corner.

"The one where you make up a story," Lupe says.

"I'm not sure I know what you mean, Lupe."

Sister Hilary and a handful of children are wrapped around their usual afternoon activity—talking and drawing. Ever since the volunteer arrived earlier this month (a retired gym teacher who probably has the rest of the kids outside playing kickball), Hilary's dedication to drawing or the kids or the Rec Room has continued unabated.

"You know you know you know." Lupe bounces on her chair, bangs flapping. "You pick things and make up a story."

Sister Hilary sets down her brush. The children remain at crayon level, but Hilary has advanced to paints. "I haven't played that game in years," she says. "I forgot all about it." Her face is a mixture of shade and light, one part grief to two parts relief.

"Of course," she rallies. "We can play the story game. Why not? It's easy enough to learn." She lifts her brush off the table and jabs it into a glob of paint. "Here's how it works. You kids call out three things—people or objects or whatever you want—and then somebody, I can start, has to make up a story with those three things in it."

"What do we pick?" someone says.

"Anything you want."

"A frog," Lupe says, still bouncing.

Enrique glowers at Claire. He's camped out in a portion of the room farthest from her studio, his articulation of affront at not being included in her editing project. "A garbage can," he says. "A dirty one."

"Good," Sister Hilary says. "Now we only need one more thing."

Another boy says, "Moon. The light the moon makes."

"Perfect." Sister Hilary wipes her temple, leaving a deep blue over her eyebrow. "So it's a frog, a garbage can, and a beam of moonlight."

"A *dirty* garbage can," Enrique says.

"Yes. An extremely dirty garbage can. Filthy." Sister Hilary scans the room, collecting the attention of everyone around her, and begins.

"Once upon a time, there lived a frog named Roger. Roger was a particularly happy frog, because he had a whole world all to himself. Roger, you see, lived in a stinky smelly garbage can clear out in the middle of nowhere and, as far as he was concerned, it was heaven. He had lots of rotten trash to eat, and slimy sewage to slip around in, and strong metal walls to jump against to keep his legs nice and strong." Sister Hilary's voice soars with authority. Though she's looking only at the children around her, skimming from face to face, she seems to be reading pages from a hidden text.

"There was only one problem with Roger's wonderful existence, and that was the nighttime. For it was at night that a teeny weeny hole in the top of Roger's garbage can," Sister Hilary pinches her thumb and index finger to indicate just how small, "let in a moonbeam that scared him half to death. Every night. The moonbeam, sometimes bright, sometimes faded, would sneak into Roger's can and make shapes like monsters and goblins against his slimy metal walls. Every night, Roger was sure he would be eaten alive by these horrible beasts. But every morning he was still alive, still Roger, splashing happily in the piles of rubbish that, thanks to the light of the sun, he knew were really rubbish and not scary monsters."

"Why did the moonbeam make it look like monsters?" one of the kids says.

"Ssssh," says another.

"Then, one day, the impossible happened. Roger's world was forever changed. A new garbage man started on the

90

route that included Roger's can—his name was Frank, Frank the Forgetful—and this Frank made a crucial error. He forgot to put the lid back on Roger's can." Sister Hilary's mouth drops open like this is the worst thing she has heard in quite some time. The kids mirror her upset—gasping, squirming in their seats.

"In fact, Frank the Forgetful not only forgot to put the lid back on Roger's can, *he took it with him.* So the people who lived in the house that supplied Roger with his garbage, a nice elderly couple who only needed their trash picked up once a month, were unable to place the lid back on Roger's can and return him to his previous existence. So, what did Roger do?"

The kids look to each other, to Claire, back to Sister Hilary. They don't know.

"Roger sat in his can and listened. He listened to the birds and the sky and the wind and all the things he had never paid much attention to with that big fat lid over his head. He sat and listened until he started to get curious. You see, Roger could *hear* all the new noises and goings-on, but he didn't know what they were. Finally, he poked his little green head over the side of the can and looked around. Trees, grass, butterflies, a long paved road leading off to the edge of the earth, these were just a few of the many wonders Roger could see from the top of his can." Sister Hilary smiles. The road is on her face—twisting, ambling out of sight. She blinks.

"Our friend Roger stayed up on the rim of that garbage can until he couldn't stand it another minute. He had to take a chance. A leap. And so he did. He hopped right out of his can, out of everything he had ever known, and landed smack in the middle of a gorgeous mud pile full of bugs and crickets and all sorts of other things frogs love. What fun he had! What a happy little frog he was! What a glorious time for Roger!" Sister Hilary laughs.

"But the best part," her hands spread, fingers flying, "the

best part was at night. For nighttime was when the moon came out, and Roger got to see what magical tricks the moonlight played on the landscape. It was nothing like inside his can. It was lovely and amazing and filled Roger with a sense of wonder so immense that his little froggie toes jiggled with glee. He would never, ever be afraid of the moonlight again." Sister Hilary waits. "The end."

The kids clap and jump about on their chairs. "Tell another, tell another," they say.

Claire rouses herself from the stasis of interest and inactivity. "How'd you do that? You didn't really just make all that up, did you? It sounded like you knew it ahead of time. Like someone was whispering instructions in your ear or something."

"It's easier than it looks," Sister Hilary says. "You should try it."

"Oh, no. That's not a—"

The short people turn to Claire. "Yes!" they say. "Yesyesyes!"

"The Three Little Pigs," Enrique says. "That's a thing."

"That's three things," Claire says. "You already picked all three things."

Enrique scoops up a crayon, breaks it in half. "So?"

"So, how can I tell the story if it's a whole other story that already exists?"

"You can do it," says Sister Hilary. "Just try."

"This is silly." Claire checks her camera, the VCR. She could finish. She's almost done.

"Sure it is. That's why you should give it a try."

Claire wags her head. "All right," she says. "But then I gotta get back to my movie." She flicks the barrier sheet out of her way to make room for her story. "So it's the Three Little Pigs, eh?"

Enrique crushes his broken crayon into the tabletop. He won't look up.

Claire thinks for a second. "Okay. There's these three

pigs, little pigs, they are, and they live in these three little houses. The houses are of straw, wood, and—uh—bricks. Yeah. And they're happy, these pigs. They're happy with their little piggly existences in their little piggly houses and such. So it's all good." Claire surveys her audience. They look bored, unimpressed. Like they're stoned.

"But then," she scoots her chair forward for emphasis, "but then one day this *wolf* shows up. He's no good, this wolf. He's trouble. He likes pigs, but in the wrong kinda way. He likes to *eat* them, you see, and this is extremely bad news for the pigs. Extremely bad news indeed.

"This wolf, his name is Randolph. That's one of the reasons he's so mean, by the way. Because of his name. Because it's so dumb. So Randolph goes to the house of the first little pig, Miss, uh, Miss Portia Porkerhouse, and he calls out to her through her straw-built walls. He says, 'What's that smell? What could it be? Why, I do believe it's *bacon*. I do believe I smell me some greasy slices of Porkerhouse headed right for my hairy, growly belly. You better hold on to your walls, Miss Portia, because I'm blowing them *down!*'"

The mood in the room has improved. A wash of smiles flicker under wide eyes and bunched brows. Enrique is the sole holdout, though this is not unexpected. Sister Hilary, on the other hand, may be laughing, may be scowling; Claire wouldn't know. She can't bear to look.

"Now, Miss Portia, she's not one to get real rattled about stuff. Not even Randolph threatening to eat her up. Miss Portia, you see, has a nickname, and it's Portia the Pyro. Portia loves fire more than mud or pig chow or ribbons at the State Fair. So what does Miss Portia do? She grabs a thatch of straw from one of her straw-built walls, and she shoves it into the big old blaze of a fire she's got going in her fireplace. Then she opens her front door, fire-lit straw in hand, and says to Randolph, 'Special Delivery! Hot off the press!' And she chucks that fire onto Randolph's tail."

One of the smaller kids yelps in delight. Claire grins.

"Now, well, Randolph, he doesn't take too kindly to this. He runs off howling like his tail's on fire. Because it is. And it takes about two weeks or two months or something like that before he feels well enough to drag his crispy old self off the couch, but eventually that time rolls around and there he is, venturing out again.

"This time, it's another little pig he's decided to pick on. This time it's ... Johnny. Johnny Jowlface. He lives in a swanky wooden shack he built all by his piggly little self, the swankiest wooden shack you've ever seen. And Johnny, he's ready for Randolph, because he heard about the wolf's pathetic attempt to make bacon out of Miss Portia. So this time Randolph doesn't even have to say a word, he only needs to poke his sorry old fried-tail self onto Johnny's front lawn and Johnny, he plucks a board of wood off the side of his house and hurls it on over at Randolph. And a big old nail—wouldn't you know it, but there's a big old rusty nail sticking out of that board—a big old nail flies up and over and straight on into the slimy, wolfy eye of Randolph. Right in the middle, where the pupil is."

There are groans at this. Groans, and faces covered.

"And old Randolph, he takes off screaming like he's got a burned-up tail and a rusty nail sticking out of his eyeball. Because he does. And he has to go off and try to fix himself up all over again, which is getting harder and harder because now he's only got one eye and a toothpick for a tail. But that doesn't stop him. No siree. Once he feels good enough, which isn't too good, he hauls himself over to the home of Lucy Lardbutt, who's got the snazziest place in town. Brick and mortar and all that fancy stuff. And Lucy, she's not worried about Randolph at all, because she's got such a fort for a house. She thinks, Whacked-out bacon-sniffing wolf? No problem." Claire chortles.

"But Lucy, she's dead wrong. She didn't count on Randolph

being stupid enough to walk right up and knock on her front door. Which he does. And when Lucy opens the door, dazed and hopeful like she's about to get a package of truffles, Randolph snatches her up right then and there and eats her alive. Just like that."

Claire scans the room—the gaping mouths, the stunned expressions. "The end."

No one speaks. Then, "Gosh," says Sister Hilary, who appears neither battered nor transformed by the story but simply—now that Claire has the nerve to look—the same, "what was the moral of *that* story?"

"The moral of the story is … that things don't always turn out like you think?" Claire shrugs, then snaps the sheet in front of her face, evaporating into the blank, buzzing white of the editing room.

"You have to mix up the shots, see?" Claire chops her palm in time with the next frame flashing on the screen in front of them. The sound is turned down, camouflaging the film's finished condition. "Each one is from a different angle and distance. So it's seamless."

Sister Hilary frowns. She is settled beside Claire on one of the kids' chairs, arms latched around denim-skirted knees. After Class has become a territory, a place they both inhabit.

"I don't understand," she says. "Not exactly. Why does that make it seamless?"

Claire pops up, grinds her thumb into Pause. "Two shots that are almost the same, like this one and," she skips ahead a few frames, "this one? If they were right next to each other, it would look like you messed up. Like you took your shot, and then took it again, but from maybe just a little closer, or a little to the side. You know?"

"I think so. Yes." Sister Hilary is removing the blue smudge above her eyebrow, scratching it off with her fingernails. "Angles and distance. Interesting."

"You think this is incredibly boring, don't you?" Claire winces. "You could be back at your desk or checking in with God or something. And instead you're stuck here, talking to me."

"Did I say that?"

"No, but—"

"I find it fascinating, actually. Mixing up the perspectives. It reminds me of one of the paintings I'm working on at home. I've been painting nonstop, you know. Ever since I started with the kids last month. And there's this piece—or, it's a series of pieces. And I've been stuck around precisely that issue. Perspective. What you said about mixing up the shots ... Maybe I can shift things, like you described. I don't know how I'd do it, but I'm sure there's a way. Anyhow. I'm babbling."

"No you're not."

"Yes I am. You see? You're not the only one who worries about being boring."

"You? Please." Claire fidgets with an extra tape stashed on top of the VCR. "There's nothing you could say that would ever be boring. You're totally smart and totally together and everything you say makes perfect sense."

Sister Hilary's placid expression fuses with concern. "That's a mighty shiny vision you have of me. I hope you don't really believe it. You don't, do you?"

"Well ... yeah."

"Then you shouldn't. My life isn't nearly as orderly as you might imagine. If anything, you're the one who has it all figured out. Though that probably doesn't make much sense to you, does it?"

Claire can't answer that. A majority of her interactions with Sister Hilary—even now, two months in—consist of agitated improvisation and furtive swooning. Times like these (her brain in pieces, her tongue a useless chunk), she's found it best to simply start over. Pick a topic, any topic, and jump back in.

"I haven't seen Sister Frances for a while," she says. "Not at the Center, at least."

"You mean, you've seen her somewhere else?"

"Yeah, I mean, no." The syllables ping at Claire's throat. "I mean, not really."

"Oh." Sister Hilary reorganizes her arms and her face. Then turns toward Claire. "Can I ask you something?"

Claire notches her wrists against the counter and leans in, offering the illusion of a regular person, having a regular conversation.

"You mentioned that you're sober. That you stopped drinking. I was thinking ... I was wondering what it's like. To not drink anymore. How that is for you. That is, if it's not too personal a question."

"Not too personal." Claire bumps against her wrists, against the counter. The casual pose seems to be working. She feels easy, harmless. "I've been luckier than most. In that it truly was taken from me. The urge to drink. That's probably what you saw, when we were talking before. That faith, or trust, or whatever you want to call it. I get that from program, and from the people there. Max, especially. He's my sponsor. He's awesome. You'd love him. He's like the smartest person I know. Other than you, of course."

Sister Hilary smiles. "Of course."

"And he quit drinking ages ago—like almost ten years. So he's got a really strong program. He knows everything, I swear. I can't get anything past him. I try, but it never works."

"He keeps you on track."

"Yeah. And going to meetings. That's another big part of it, for me." Claire stops bouncing, relaxes in place. "Sometimes, when we're all there, in the room together, and someone's telling their story—because that's what we do, we talk about all the trouble we caused and how we got out of it—you can just feel it, the ground that holds us all up. It's so huge. It's amazing. You know?"

Sister Hilary nods.

"It's the only reason I'm sober." Claire resumes her bouncing against the counter behind her, against the part of her story she's leaving out. "When I was drinking, there was nothing like that. No faith. No connection. Just me by myself and my fucked up life. Oops, sorry." She shakes her head, rubs her fist into her eyes. "I forgot."

"I've heard the word before, Claire. I think I'll live."

"Yeah, but still." Claire sustains the beginnings of a blush. "What if God comes down and sews my mouth together? I know you've got pull and all."

Sister Hilary chuckles. "Would you *like* God to come down and sew your mouth together?"

"Sometimes, yeah. Sometimes I think that might be a good idea."

Sister Hilary rustles in her child's seat, lifts herself up and into the chair where Claire was once sitting. This movement cracks open a space for her scent, a blend of cinnamon and soap, to filter in. "That's a blessing, then. That you were able to stop. I know it's not always that easy. Some folks struggle more at the beginning. At least, that's what I hear."

"They do. Yeah," Claire says, suddenly impatient. Who are they talking about here? Sister Frances and her fledgling sobriety? (She drank for years. Has been sober for three months. Is finally speaking in meetings.) "There's a lot I should do. Things. And such. Maybe I should go."

"Did you still want to look at my drawing?" Sister Hilary stands, hanging with an expression Claire recognizes from having produced it herself so many times: a brush of hope, cradled by low expectations.

"That would be—sure," Claire says. Where would they go? she wonders. They can't go anywhere, but if they could.

Maybe a flat place, a terrain marked by absence. Or maybe a guilt-riddled scar of a thing, chilly and insolent, like the moon of an abandoned planet.

Sister Hilary's drawing is on the art table, swirls of motion next to a heap of crayons and papers.

"It's a study," she says. "For a painting I'm working on."

Claire huddles above it. There's a man—or is it a woman?—in the center of the picture. Its eyes are like Sister Hilary's—enlarged by thirst and capacity for vision. Normally Claire would be on guard against these eyes, arming herself with avoidance and equivocation, but this, this collection of shapes and slashes patterned into open hands, solid robe, a scrap of a smile, eyes that ask for nothing (or is it everything?), this drawing leaves Claire devoted, wordless. She stifles a cry.

"I have you to thank," Sister Hilary is saying. "You're the one who got me painting again. It was Lupe's idea, of course, but it was your presence that got me charged up about the process. And now I can't stop."

Claire swallows into the swell of pressure that always accompanies tears. "Oh."

"And since you've been such an inspiration, I wanted you to have this. It's a drawing of Saint Matthew. I wasn't sure how you'd feel about a picture of a religious figure, but after what you said about your program, I thought you might like it."

Claire, having fired up a particularly humiliating memory (seventh grade gym class, in the showers), has managed to compose herself. "Sure."

"Are you all right?"

"Sure."

Sister Hilary rocks backward, like she can travel anywhere she wants, so why not back a little bit? "Something told me you might enjoy it. I don't know why, but I thought I should at least make the offer. That is, if you'd like it. You don't have to take it if it doesn't seem appropriate."

"No, it's cool. It's great." Claire snatches the picture, then decelerates the motion and slips it gently between the two textbooks inside her backpack. "Thanks."

"Are you coming tomorrow?" Sister Hilary is practically singing, rolling the vowels with her tongue.

"What's tomorrow?"

"Thanksgiving. Big feast here, remember?"

Claire's head shakes on its own. "That's right. I … I might. Dinner with the family, of course, but I'll try to stop by."

How can she say it? How can she tell her that this gift is too much?

It's not until she's almost home, sprinting through a mist of half-assed rain and streets that smell like washrags (*when did this change? when did winter arrive?*) that Claire remembers her movie. Remembers she left it ticking in the VCR, guileless, exposing itself, frame by frame, to the silent TV screen.

Supper

Night. Thanksgiving was a day of strain and release—strain being the effort expended in Claire's appearance at the family dinner; release being the Twelve Step meeting she attended after, shrinking her resentments to the size of holy molehills. The Bearley Community Center, as it turned out, was unable to insinuate itself into either side of this equation. Claire has yet to shake off the mortification of practically bawling in front of Sister Hilary and is vowing—on the hour, every hour—to steer clear of the place for at least a week.

The stars have made themselves scarce tonight; the sky is weighted with gray puffs and quick to deliver rain—all over Claire, in fact, as she pedals home from her meeting. She minds only at first, when dry meets damp and the notion of making it home rainless is still a possibility. Once this dream has been laid to rest, and Claire's resemblance to a drowned hamster has reached exact replica, she no longer cares. She comes to embrace her state of drench as a kind of freedom, an exemption from the tyranny of the dry.

Light blasts out of her mother's kitchen window as the click of Claire's bicycle wheels accompanies her into the driveway. The Stones are complaining about their lack of satisfaction inside the higher ethers of volume on Kitty's speakers; Claire wonders if the cops have already been called and this is round two. Kitty and Donna were pretty well tanked at four this afternoon when she ditched the festivities for the sanity of her meeting. Tex, padded with stuffing and cannabis, already crashed on the couch. It will, she suspects, be a long night.

"I'm gonna get it first!"

The front door shoots open and Claire is accosted by her niece and nephew—Bunny and Walt, both of them screaming and frisking Claire's pockets for change.

"Cut it out," she says. She shoos them off her. "It's pouring out here. You two should get back inside."

"Hey Claire, hey Claire." Bunny hops in place. She's kid skinny, with always-in-motion feet and a confusion of curls. "Guess what. Guess what Kenny did."

"Kenny? Kenny's in there?"

"He hid the turkey's brain in the bushes and we're gonna find it," Walt says. His face gleams with rain and the blush of the open front door.

"He did not," Claire says.

"Did too!" Walt shouts it out. Though Claire always denies it, everyone tells her that this child is the miniature, black-eyed version of her. Down to the chipped front tooth.

"Kenny's a liar," she says. "He just said that to get you to come out here. He's probably in there laughing about it right now."

"Help us, Claire." Bunny tugs on Claire's wrist, pulling her over to the row of cypress bushes on the side of the house. "Help us look."

"I'm telling you guys. There's nothing in there but dirt and bugs."

"Bugs!" Walt races past them and dives headfirst into the bushes. Only the soles of his sneakers remain. Keds.

"Mommy and Kenny got Kitty to put a dress on Sinatra and make him sing," Bunny says. "Then Kenny told us about the turkey brain. He said it's worth a lot of money. Like, twenty dollars."

"I think I found it!" Walt's feet wiggle in the air. "There's something squishy down here!"

102

Bunny shrieks and releases Claire's wrist. "Save some for me! Save some for me!"

"It's not turkey brains, you guys. You really should go back inside."

Bunny, scampering around the bushes, hair already a splotch of wet, ignores her aunt. "We'll fry it up," she says. "We'll fry it up and feed it to Sinatra."

Claire's room is dark and smells like sleep. She peels off her soggy clothes and finds dry ones, rubs the rain and the day off her skin. Then places her wet things in a pile on the floor beside the couch.

"I'm here," Shelly says. She flicks on the standing lamp next to the bed. Her hair is gathered back in a loose ponytail and she's wearing an expression of contentment and reserve. She pats down the sheet around her, draws the blanket up to her knees. "I just got back."

"What happened?"

"Oh, you know. The usual. Bobby and Jim tried to rob the 7-Eleven and got tossed in County. Other than that, it was pretty mellow. My mom says 'hi.'"

Shelly's brothers have a long-standing tradition of robbing convenience stores on holidays—all except for Easter, which is, according to them, "sacred."

"What? No 'hello' from your sis?"

"Viv hates you, you know that." Shelly's feet kick at the blanket. She watches them like they belong to somebody else.

Claire plops down on the couch. She's been sleeping here for about a month now, ever since the No Sex pact started shredding her slumber into nonexistence. "She just wants me, is all. She can't stand it that you've been where she's dying to go."

"Whatever. Viv is strictly dickly and you know it. The only place she's dying to go is deep inside the pants of the latest bozo she's brought home from the bar. I'll tell her you say 'hi,' though."

"You do that." Claire eyes her backpack, the one harboring Sister Hilary's drawing, on the other side of the couch. She's been trying to forget about it all day—the picture, Sister Hilary, the feelings she can't have. But here it is, stashed inside her pack, taunting her.

Pick me, it says. *Throw away the last vestiges of your morality—if you ever had any to begin with—and seduce the willing woman religious. You know you want to. You know you can. So what if you ruin her life? You're not going to let that stop you. Are you?*

Claire turns away from the pack and everything it implies. Lust. The chokehold of misplaced affections. Irreconcilable desires. She's been stuck inside the problem for so long she couldn't see the solution. But maybe there is one. Maybe it's closer than she thinks.

"We've been good, haven't we, Shel?" Claire bounces off the couch and over to the fridge. The eyes of her backpack bore into her bones, but she won't look, won't acknowledge its insistence.

"What do you mean?" Shelly's feet calm under the blanket.

"You know," Claire says. "Good. Like, we've been behaving and all."

No! cries the pack. *This will just make it worse! How stupid can you be?*

"Well," one of Shelly's eyebrows eases into her forehead, "that was the idea. Behaving."

"It was," Claire says. "It's just that—"

Stop it! It's the wrong person! The wrong time! Abort!

"It's just that … maybe behaving is a dumb idea. Maybe we should do something else."

"I don't know …"

Listen to her!

"C'mon."

104

"But we said we wouldn't." Shelly smoothes the blanket around her feet. "We'd be liars, then. Both of us."

Will you listen to her? She's giving you an out! Take it! Save yourself! Please!!

"No." Claire shakes her head. She knows whom she's saving. And it's not herself. "We're not liars. We just agreed to something we maybe can't stick to anymore. Something that needs to change. That's all. It happens all the time. People changing their minds and stuff. It's good. It's a good thing."

No!!

"Mmm." Shelly tips the blanket above, then off, her feet. "Get the hell over here."

Claire is chasing an elusive come. She and Shelly have been trading orgasms for nearly an hour now, but this one is different. Shelly's fingers are riding merrily along, deep in and back, deep in and back, and her tongue is exactly where it's supposed to be, inching Claire to the edge of that holiest of precipices. And yet. And yet there's a bug in the back of Claire's brain that yanks her out of it every few seconds, splatters her on the ceiling or the wall next to the kitchen counters. A bug, a pest that peers through Claire's consciousness, watches Shelly's mouth on Claire's fur and says: *I told you. I told you this was a bad idea.*

"No," she says, urging into Shelly's hand. Shelly, who's done this often enough to know that nothing Claire says matters at this point, meets Claire's urging with a bit of her own, tongue and fingers strumming hips, thighs, impatience.

"No," Claire says, climbing higher and deeper, palms burying Shelly's hair. She tightens, rushes, comes—all without her mind's involvement, jerking and ticking against the time spent getting there.

She waits a minute, chest cramped and caving, then "Whoah," she says. "That was … Whoah."

105

Shelly retrieves her hand and slides on top of Claire. She licks the skin above Claire's eyes, then kisses her forehead, her mouth. "You took a while that time. You getting tired?"

"Tired?" Claire sighs, the last traces of orgasm brushing her skin. So much trouble. She's in so much trouble.

"What makes you think I'd be tired?" she says.

Shelly rears up on her elbows and gazes down. Her breath, falling onto Claire's face, smells like sex and Skittles. "Your hair's getting long, Claire Bear. It almost hits the pillow."

"It's my inner femme. She's itching for release." Claire jerks upward, into Shelly's thigh. Her body against Shelly's feels numb, like a ghost. Like a traitor.

"You got another in there, Shel? I bet you do."

"Nah," Shelly says, hips twitching. "We should stop."

Claire presses harder into Shelly. Maybe more contact can stop the numbness. Can banish the traitor.

"One more, babe," she says. "Just one more. Then we'll stop."

Later, after Shelly has been asleep for several hours and her measured breathing has almost, but not quite, drowned out the whisper and hiss of the not-quite-asleep backpack across the room, Claire tells herself a story. A true one.

She was seven years old, maybe eight. Part of that pack of years before the full reach of life—what it could do, what it couldn't—had blasted apart the insularity of childhood. It was a few days before Christmas and Claire was in Kitty's bedroom closet, hunting for the presents she knew were hidden there. Every year she did this, rummaging through old dresses and piles of crap to score a hit of thrill off uncovering the Tonka truck, the Easy-Bake oven, the baseball bat awaiting wrappage and placement under the white-tinsel tree on the coffee table in the living room. It always wrecked things— padding into the room on Christmas morning, knowing precisely what you were going to get—but this didn't stop her from returning, year after year, to the busted boundaries and certain bliss of poking through waste in search of treasure.

This year, it was a model car set (Kitty had purchased it over the protests of Claire's stepfather, who had insisted that a miniature Corvette was no sort of present for a girl), and Claire had just fixed her mitts on the bright shiny box when she heard the sound: the click and bash of her mother at the front door. What was she doing home so soon? There was supposed to be so much more time. As Kitty approached the bedroom, muttering sharply, pissed about something, Claire knew there was no way to untangle herself—her arms, her feet, her steps to the door—and not get caught. A wiry pleasure, the ache and thrall of inevitable capture, clamped in on Claire's heart that day.

Same as now. As the backpack sings a quiet song from its place on the couch and Shelly sleeps tight beside her, Claire wonders who will catch her this time. And what she'll do when she's found.

Sketch

"So, does this place have a kitchen or what?" Claire thrumps her heels against the stack of packing boxes that constitutes her chair. "Not that you even need one, really. Just an IV coffee drip would do it for you. Whatever happened to your Gay Man Chef gene anyway?"

"Esther's got it. It's probably in that shoebox under her bed, where she keeps her old lottery tickets and victorious wishbones. Always has to save something for herself, that Esther."

Max and his mother are currently not on speaking terms. Thus his new place. The initiative to move was apparently born out of a scuffle involving Esther's post-bingo impudence, a remote control, and sparring episodes of "Melrose Place" and "Murder, She Wrote." Max refuses to discuss it.

"What's in here?" Claire jabs the box beside her with her toe. "Pictures. Hey *hey*. Pictures. Mind if I have a look?'"

"There's nothing pornographic in there, if that's what you're hoping for." Max is lying flat, stretched across carpet the brash blue of rocks on an aquarium floor. He says it makes him feel like a freshly paroled goldfish. "The porno shots are in the vault."

Claire plucks out a framed photo of Max on the beach with an older man—white blond, muddy eyes, his face wiped with restrained amusement. "Is this him?"

Max's head scrapes up, thumps down. "That's him," he says. "Taken about a year after we met. Right before we

108

started the gallery. He had his hand on my ass in that shot, I remember. His mother was taking the picture. She had no idea." He laughs. "Bert said it was a pincher crab, trolling for lunch. He thought it was so damn funny. It was, eventually. Just because he thought it was."

"He looks like me."

"What?" Max says, but Claire can tell he knows what she's talking about.

"Except for his hair is longer and he's got more going on in the eyebrow department. Other than that."

"Hmmm." Max heaves himself upright. He's wearing a bullet-gray T-shirt that matches his mood: wrinkled, aching to be pampered, but refusing to admit as much. "That explains it, then."

Now it's Claire's turn to play dumb. "What do you mean?"

"How it was," Max says. "At the beginning. With you and me. That little spark. You looked so much like a goddamned boy. I thought you were one, first time I saw you. I told you that, right?"

"I thought maybe it was just me." Claire sets the photo back in the box, next to another picture of Bert—later, thinner, sick. "Or, no. I guess I knew it was both of us. You gotta get a charge off someone, you know?"

"Indeed," Max sighs. The sun from the window lands in his eyes and he squints against it. "If it weren't for that new boy at Starbucks, I'd be bereft. Without a bottom upon which to lay my ... anchor." He smirks.

"No! You didn't."

"I didn't. I wanted to, but I didn't. He's confused. He's straight—or not. And I'm tired. Frankly, I don't know if it's possible for me again." He shakes his head, sun bouncing off his brow. "It's hard getting exactly what you want. Don't let anyone tell you otherwise."

Claire thinks of Shelly, how she tastes like Sweet Tarts, how her flat-shaped thumbs feel inside her, how they've packed the last week of nights with enough sex to birth an entire nation. And how wrong it all feels.

"I've been meaning to tell you something," she says. "I keep forgetting."

Max rolls onto an elbow, out of the sun. "Hit me."

"You know that lady at meetings, Frances? The one I pegged as a cannibal when we were playing Most Wanted that time?" Claire watches the relevant subject skitter to the left, off into a corner where it sits panting, ebullient.

"The one who always dresses like it's her first day of library school?"

"Yeah, her. I know her. Outside of meetings. She's a nun and she works at the Community Center where I've been making my movie. And she hates me for some reason. Really. There's a serious hater vibe emanating from her nunly self."

"Isn't she the one you thought was a dyke?"

Claire squirms on her cardboard throne. Her corner subject remains sweaty, elusive. "No, Max—that's part of it. There's another nun there, Sister Hilary, and the two of them, well, I don't know. I think that's maybe why Sister Frances hates me. Like she's worried I'll bust up whatever they've got going. Or something. It's weird."

"You Catholics," Max says. "Always stirring sex into your religion. Like it's part of what you're worshipping." He leans in, limp black hair obscuring an eye.

"Max. I'm not Catholic. Just my mom—"

"Sweetheart. It's nothing to be ashamed of." His hand dives into the carpet, thin fingers raking its bright blue plush. "Or maybe it is. Did you hear about that guy in the City? O'Shea, I think it was. Into boys. Talk about holy perversion—"

"But Max," Claire bops a heel against her box, "this is two grown women. It's not the same. Mutual, consensual sexual contact is way different than—"

"Mutual? Consensual? *Nuns?* What are you saying, Claire? Tell me you're not considering a foray into such godforsaken territory. 'Behind the rosary beads,'" he says in a hyped-up, game-show voice. "Because if you are—"

"I'm with Shelly." Claire nudges forward, shifts on her throne. "Since last week. We're back together." She nods into his baffled expression. "So you can get off the nun trip. It's not like that."

"I never said—"

"Whatever." Claire tries to gather herself up, pry her body off the box, but gets exhausted halfway through and slumps back onto the cardboard. "And don't tell me it's fucked up and wrong and all that crap because I already know that. It's just— it's just sex and a mess, but maybe we can make something of it this time. Maybe. Or not. I don't know."

Max stares at her out of the swamps of sadness that occasionally cruise through his otherwise calm demeanor. "Sweet pea. I want you to be happy. And sober. That's all I want. Are you … How was it?"

"It was okay." Claire looks at her lap. "And hard. And kinda strange. Probably because it's been a while. I guess," she says, finally rallying enough to coerce her knees upward and prod herself off the packing box, "I should get home. Before it gets too dark."

Max laughs. "Fine. Spare me the details. I'll live."

"I love you, Max," Claire says. "I know you just want what's best for me." She straps on her backpack and moseys over to the door, aware of the flush, like baking cinders, coursing through her system.

"Wait a minute, pumpkin. Something fell out of your pack. Something precious. My, my." Max clucks. "Look what you've been hiding in that nasty old sack of yours. Where did you get this?"

She turns toward him with eyes half-lowered. Like a spy. "What makes you think I didn't draw it myself?"

"What makes you think I'm an unrefined bonehead?" He studies the picture, eyes darting around the page. "I used to

111

do this for a living, remember? I didn't always live out here in the butthole of the West, ripped free of culture and civility."

Claire has checked the drawing so many times now (hourly, on occasion; though she won't share this with Max; what would be the point?) that she can practically match each flick of Max's eye with its corresponding component on the page. The debt-free hands, the weighted gaze, the line near the neck where flesh meets garment.

"This is marvelous," he says. "Who did this?"

Claire empties her face of emotion. "Sister Hilary. She gave it to me."

"A *nun*? A *nun* did this?" Max stretches out his arms, tilts his head. "She's trained. I'd bet money on it. Does she paint?"

"That's a study. For a painting." Claire hikes her bag off her shoulders and plunks it at her feet. In between her notebook and her American Film textbook, that's where the drawing will go, when she gets it back. "I haven't seen any, though. She does them at home. Not at the Center."

"It's odd," Max has the picture on a stack of boxes now, crouching over it with arms linked behind his torso, "it's technically fluent and yet emotionally raw in a way that's—I don't know. Not naïve, but," he loops a finger around his ear, stops at his chin, "awake. Or something. Fascinating."

"Yeah," Claire says. She shoves her foot into the bottom of her pack and senses the structure that is her interior life—or, more precisely, the sizeable portion claimed by one habit-less Sister—rise inside her as if on hydraulics. She could pinch off even a tiny bit, pluck it from the rubble, and hand it over to Max, relieve herself of some of the pressure, the drift and heft that taxes and aerates her inner shores. But she won't. It's hers.

"It's okay," she says, scooping her backpack off her feet and into her arms. "For a nun."

Pamela's Last Stand

They're picking three things when Claire arrives. It's Lupe's turn, apparently, and she gets ice cream, worms, and a sailboat. Claire, her own rudder fixed and intractable, glides past all the activity—Hilary, still Hilary; a barrage of paints and boxes and a bucketload of kids, including Enrique—and into the sanctuary of her sheet-enclosed editing room. The television, she sees, has been turned off but everything else, including her tape recorder and all the equipment, remains untouched or, at the very least, unmolested.

She'd like to stick around longer, play director a week or two more, but she's done enough. Her little movie is finished. Any additions, she's convinced herself, would be excess. Besides, a director can't work where a director doesn't belong. Everyone knows that.

It's an easy pick-up—inescapably easy, considering the energy employed in its creation. Equipment is polished, tucked in boxes, stashed away to the beat of Lupe's light and rambling tale. (The worms are building a sailboat. Ice cream has yet to make an entrance. Or maybe it was already mentioned. Claire's not sure.)

The final gesture of her deconstruction project (in the confines of her conscience, she's dubbed it Operation Run Away) is the removal of the sheet, an act Claire performs with as much conviction and as little ceremony as she can muster. It seems to work, in that she finds herself not being noticed but, rather, noticing.

Sister Hilary and her crew are embroiled in something bright and messy. The worm story appears to be over—Lupe is no longer talking and simmers in an aura of satisfaction—and the nun is instructing the kids in the finer points of icon-assembly.

"No one really knows," she's saying. "There are many different representations of what Christ may have looked like. You get to paint Him however you like—whatever the face of love looks like to you. That's Christ."

"Can I give Him a mohawk?" Enrique, who may be the only one aware that Claire is watching, dips his paintbrush into an orange the shade of radioactive warning signs.

"Is that what your face of love would wear? A mohawk?"

"Definitely," Enrique says. His smile is stretched and lazy, like a snake in the sun.

"Then by all means," Sister Hilary pries her attention from her own project to check in with Enrique and in that moment sees Claire, "a mohawk it is. Hello, Claire."

"Oh yeah," Claire says. "Hi. Didn't see you there."

Lupe harvests a cardboard box from a pile next to the table—it's huge, almost as tall as she is—and waddles over to Sister Hilary. Her three-sizes-too-big T-shirt, wine-red with blue stripes on the sleeves, is stuffed haphazardly into her shorts. "I'm going to use the whole box," she says. "I'm going to paint inside and out. La Virgen María on the inside."

Lupe, as usual, has said more than what she's said. Sister Hilary studies her as if picking through bones, at once appalled and reverent. "That's a great idea, Lupe. Painting inside the box and outside too. I'll have to try that."

"What did she say?" Lupe leans against her box, which leans against Sister Hilary. "Tell me again."

"What did who say?"

"La Virgen María."

"You mean the words from the Bible?"

Lupe nods.

Sister Hilary closes her eyes. She speaks slowly, her voice thick and resonant. "My soul doth magnify the Lord, and my spirit hath rejoiced in God, my Savoir. For He hath regarded the loneliness of His handmaiden, and behold, from henceforth all generations shall call me blessed. For He that is mighty hath done to me great things and holy is His name." She stays with eyes closed, sinking into an expression that is, somehow, the mirror image of her minute-ago reaction to Lupe.

Claire grips the video in her hand. This is all she can take with her, all she's allowed. She makes it to the hallway in about two seconds, waving only at Enrique, who scowls in return. Her feet initiate the process of final departure—one, two, three, headed for the outer hallway—when the door behind her opens.

"Claire. You seem in a rush. You have big plans for today?"

"No." Claire won't bother to lie. How can she lie to a woman religious with the aftertaste of the Virgin on her tongue?

"I thought maybe you were gone. It's been over a week. Are you—your movie, is it almost finished?"

"It is." Claire starts to slip the video behind her back, then changes course and leaves it at her side, tapping at denim. "Pretty much."

"Look," Sister Hilary takes a step toward Claire as if this is simply what people do when they're conversing, they get close enough so you can see the flecks of green in their mostly-brown eyes and the fluid connection between mouth and voice, "I wanted to have you over for dinner. At the house. As a thank you for your time here. For all you've done."

"I would stay and help, of course," Claire says, not answering, "but I need to start making some bucks. I've been too long on the wrong side of the bread-dough equation."

"And bring Pamela, if you'd like."

Claire blanches. *Pamela?* How would Sister Hilary know about her? Claire had a blackout the first time they were together, then almost had the experience replicated in a considerably

115

more violent manner when Pamela's boyfriend heard news of their affair. Luckily, he was a drinker as well and they settled their differences over a case of Budweiser and a few dozen shots of tequila.

But that's not who Sister Hilary means. Of course not. Sister Hilary knows nothing about Pamela. Claire would never tell her such a thing. It must be an accident, an unfortunate coincidence—unwitting penance from the unwitting nun.

"You must mean Shelly," Claire says. "My friend Shelly."

Sister Hilary, still near, still oblivious to the implications of standing close enough to smell each other's skin and inspect each other's eyes, says, "Yes, of course. Shelly. That's what I meant." She blooms into a smile. "Bring your friend."

Horror Show

Claire flaps her arm over her face, burying her lips inside the soft, indignant flesh of her inner elbow. Her mouth has been busy today.

It started at a morning meeting, offering a brief share of gratitude for the year that has passed, how far she's come. Next was Shelly, all about Shelly—her body, mostly. (The rest—Claire and Shelly, what that means, what the hell Claire is doing—is better left unexamined.) The subsequent program call was a surprise (Claire doesn't get many of these, other than Max), but Claire took it anyway, her lips and tongue forming the words and phrases necessary to erect a small shack of shelter for the person—a young mother, newly sober—on the other side of the call. That this call was an interruption—Claire and Shelly were in between rounds, but still both naked, still both swimming in sex—turned out to be an affront to Shelly, who immediately slapped on a shirt and pants and an expression of a gate slammed shut, a pocket emptied.

And so it is only now, after a day of selfless servitude and unquestioning loyalty, that Claire's mouth is finally bucking against the task at hand. She was all set to go, ready to ask her buddy Shel for one teeny little favor—about tonight, how Claire needs a bodyguard—when Shelly hopped in with an agenda of her own. Stymied by the mutiny, Claire and her mouth have been reduced to swallowed sighs and a covert exploration of her elbow.

"You have to say *something*, Claire. You can't just lie there with your arm strapped over your face."

"Whhufph uuh whoo maa whu uur aah?"

"Fine," Shelly flicks a finger into the top of a stack of papers on Claire's table, harassing them out of place, "I'll tell my counselor you weren't willing to discuss it. That I tried, but you went all Helen Keller on me. Can you *be* any more immature?"

Claire frees her face from the fort of her arm. "Hey. I just sorted those."

"Sort *this*, Claire." Shelly pounds her palms onto the table, causing further organizational upset. "We've been having sex for almost two weeks now. I just thought we should talk about it. About where this is headed."

"Where this is—Shel ..." Claire tucks her feet under the tattered blanket at the bottom of her bed. There's order, of a sort, right here. "Why you gotta get all directional on me all of a sudden? You've never talked like this before."

"You're right. I didn't. Neither did you. But maybe we should be more grown-up this time. Like, actually deal with it. My counselor says being in a mature relationship means talking about goals and priorities and shit like that. And since Kenny is history—I mean, it's *so* over with him—I just thought—"

"You're still married to stupid Kenny." Claire's voice is low, slithering under the blanket. She grinds it into the sheet with her heels. "Let's not forget about that."

"Yeah? Well, you went and turned your bed into a welcome mat for skanks and sleazebags. Let's not forget about that, either."

"*After* you left me for Kenny."

"There were *years* of 'after,' Claire. You can't blame all that on me."

"Sure I can."

"My counselor was right. This is a mistake. I should just say 'never mind' to this whole thing."

"Shel. Wait a sec—"

"Really. I mean, the sex is good. The sex is *great.*" Shelly's eyes widen, splashing the anger onto her face. "It's fine to just come and come and come. But we can't just have sex all the time. We can't just be *only* friends and then be *only* lovers, because that's what always happens, that's what we always do, and then—"

"Shel." Claire scrambles in place. She's still naked, but there's no time to do anything about that now. "Shel Shel Shel. Look. You're right. We should talk about it. Why don't we … why don't we go to this dinner and then talk about it after that. When there's more time. And we're not both so worked up." She swallows. *And I can get the nerve. Maybe then I'll have the nerve.*

"I told you I didn't want to go. You said it was fine if I didn't."

"That's true. I did." Claire hoists her naked body out of bed. The floorboards between her and Shelly are comfortless—stiff and cool and unrelenting. "But now I think it's better if you go. So you can—so we can …" She eyes the floor. What is she supposed to say? That she needs protection from a nun?

Shelly peels the sleeves of her sweatshirt, which is enormous on her, over her hands. "The only reason I'd go is that you look so goddamned pathetic. Naked and begging and all."

Claire shifts in place, floorboards firm under her feet. "It'll be fun. You'll see."

Claire is pacing. There's a lot about this dinner she wasn't aware of. That Sister Hilary, Sister Frances, and Sister Maria all live together in a modest 1940s bungalow-type house off Bearley's meager downtown strip: this she did not know. That all three women would be there for dinner and expecting a private after-dinner screening of Claire's little film: this she did not know. That Sister Frances would still be snotty and

Sister Maria kind and Sister Hilary alluring, this she certainly did know but finds, now that these previously established facts have intersected with the newly discovered items of cohabitation and expectation, that she is swamped in half-gulps of chaos and self-containment. She wonders how she'll get through.

"Where was this taken?" Shelly picks up a silver-framed photo on the coffee table next to the couch she shares with Sister Maria. Sisters Frances and Hilary are in the kitchen, and Claire is maintaining her nonstop patrol of the perimeter of the room.

Sister Maria peeks around Shelly's elbow. "In El Salvador. Just outside of San Salvador. Sister Hilary and I were there during the war."

"You were?" Claire makes a pass by couch and photo—a group scene with Sisters Maria and Hilary and a cadre of bare-footed children. "Sister Hilary never mentioned that. We talked about El Salvador once, but she acted weird about it. Changed the subject real quick. She never said she *lived* there." Claire tries to control her agitation. "Or anything about a *war*."

A bunch of things happen next. Shelly takes the temperature of Claire's response and finds it entirely unacceptable. Claire notes this reaction to her reaction and feels guilty and exposed: her unacknowledged feelings blasted into open air for everyone to see. Sister Maria observes it all—the layering of wounded glances on top of hastily constructed judgments—and pretends, gracious entity that she is, to notice nothing.

"It was a difficult time," Sister Maria says. "It's not exactly one of Sister Hilary's favorite subjects. We were only there a little over a year. We had to leave when the violence started to hit too close to home. We were in Oakland after that, working with the refugees. The strength of those people. It was unbelievable."

"I'll bet you speak Spanish. Right?" Claire enunciates the obvious. Then the unnecessary. "Sister Hilary does too."

Shelly bangs the photo back on the table. Her mouth is a tight line, with hooks on each end.

"My father was Mexican," Sister Maria says. "I learned from him when I was a child. Sister Hilary learned down there."

"I thought you were—" Claire stops herself. So many messes. She's already made so many messes tonight.

Sister Maria nods. "You thought I was black. Most people do. I'm a mutt, actually. Black mom and Mexican dad. Though the Latina in me was invisible until I went down there. Folks only see what they've been trained to see."

"Enough of that now. It's time for dinner." Sister Hilary is standing in the doorway to the living room and Claire can tell, by the lack of motion in or around her—the absence of elevated breath, the settlement of limbs—that she has been there a while.

Shelly and Sister Maria rise and Claire, already risen, already ambulatory, joins them in following Sister Hilary into the dining room. But not before Claire has the opportunity, like Sister Maria before her, to witness a glance of censure and remorse, this time between the two Sisters. Claire, like her predecessor, feigns inattention but stores the look, thick with right and wrong and the endless sky between them, into memory.

"So, how did you two meet?" Sister Frances' head is cocked and her mouth is full of string beans. She looks, Claire thinks, like a rabid parrot.

"In school, a long time ago." Shelly's fork clinks against her almost empty plate and she guzzles the remains of glass-of-wine-number-three. "I can't get rid of her."

Everyone laughs except Claire, who knows it's not a joke.

"Nice to stay friends so long." Sister Frances smiles and

Claire is reminded of her nephew Walt in his early days, when what passed for a smile was really just gas.

"Shelly's working at the new Wells Fargo in town, did you hear?" Claire attempts a change of scenery. One of the more unfortunate realizations of this already unfortunate gathering is that Sister Frances, who knows Claire through meetings, surely recognizes that Claire is gay (she doesn't hide it, in her "shares"). It's a tidbit Frances has probably divulged to Hilary who has, much to Claire's current consternation, never been informed of this fact by Claire herself. The lack of communication on this topic is certainly not news; Claire has made a habit of skirting the issue with a particular woman religious in the same way that she has steered clear of after-class conversations that might include phrases such as "sex" or "sticky" or "entangled." Phrases she can no longer avoid.

Shelly is peppy with stories about the bank and the Sisters are following along like there's a prize for best listener.

"Mid January, that's the latest," Shelly is saying. "By then, there'll be an opening in loans and acquisitions in either the Bearley or Point Firth branch. I'm keeping my fingers crossed."

"How marvelous." Sister Hilary, neck and neck with Shelly in number of glasses of wine consumed, dispenses the beginnings of glass number four. ("I don't usually drink this much," she says at the end of each glass.)

Claire squares her placemat against the edge of the table for the fiftieth time tonight. "Tell them about the band, Shel. How you might be singing with your branch manager's band at that party they're having."

"Actually," Shelly won't look at Claire, as that would violate the rules of Hating Her, "I wanted to ask you guys about the Pope's tour. With the Popemobile and all. What did you think of that?"

Sister Maria chuckles. "You mean the vehicle or the man himself?" She reaches for the salt and Sister Hilary slaps her hand away. They are, it seems, engaged in a long-running battle over the matter of Sister Maria's health. "Oh, come on," she says. "Just a little."

"Just a little more high blood pressure is not what you need, my friend."

Sister Maria groans. "I'm sorry, Shelly. You asked about the Pope. What do you want to know?"

"Nothing in particular. I was just wondering about some of the stuff he says. Like about how women can't be priests and stuff like that."

Sister Frances lops Shelly with an esteem-shrinking glare. "I don't know that this is really the appropriate—"

"So if the Pope is, like, your leader," Claire pops in, "do you really have to obey everything he says? Is that how it works?"

Sister Frances fixes her gaze on Claire. "You're not Catholic, are you?"

"No. Well, kinda. My mom was, and I—"

"Because if you were Catholic you would understand the relationship between Rome and the people of the Church. It's not simply a matter of leader and masses, it's more complicated than that. And it's not possible to explain or justify that relationship to someone outside the structures of the Church."

"Yeah? But the Pope does say things that are supposed to apply to all Catholics, right? I know that much."

"As I said, it's not that simple. But I wouldn't expect you to comprehend any of this. It's beyond the scope of your awareness to—"

"Beyond the scope of my—"

"Claire," Sister Hilary addresses her like they have an understanding, a shared history upon which to draw this aside of intimacy and, although they do, it is more than a little odd to have it aired in this setting, "there's a spirit in the Church that's bigger than personalities or politics. The

Church is its people. And the spirit of God within those people. That's what we serve."

"And serving God's children includes contemplative reconciliation to the apparent restrictions of the hierarchy." Sister Frances, seemingly disjointed by the subtle but marked connection between Claire and Sister Hilary, raises her voice to a level that obliterates opposition. "Which, I trust, concludes our discussion on this topic."

"Except for the women priest thing." Shelly, who thus far has been acting like the kid who's delighted to have tipped the starter domino, chimes in again. "I was asking, see, because I used to want to be a priest. Really." She nods. "Before I knew I couldn't. I'd sit in Mass and watch the Father and think, 'Hey, maybe I can do that.' Until my mom told me it wasn't allowed."

"Really?" Claire jabs her placemat out of alignment. "You never told me that."

"Hey, it's better than being a nun. Oops," Shelly pounds at her chest, "that's not what I meant."

"Good one, Shel."

"No. I'm sorry. That came out wrong. What I meant—"

"It's all right, Shelly." Sister Hilary's eyes are twin candles, patient flames excluding nothing. "Most young women feel like you do. That's why we have so few vocations these days. I'm almost forty," the flames flick at Claire, "and I'm one of the young ones. People both understand and don't understand this life, what it means. What it entails." This last word lands on no one in particular, but Claire suspects, and cringes at the notion, that this "entails," and its accompanying non-look, are directed at her.

"So don't worry about it," Sister Hilary says. "You were just being honest. I think," she stands and fetches her plate off its mat, "that we should see about dessert and a certain video. Shelly, why don't you help me clear the rest of the plates and set up the TV trays in the living room?"

"Sure." Shelly peels herself off her chair and, in a sweep of stunning dexterity, not only relieves the table of a majority of its plates and glasses and silverware but, with the removal of each item, fires furtive, nuclear-reactor-type glances at Claire to let her know how badly she, Claire, who said *nothing* about nuns and how worthless their lives are, has Fucked Everything Up. It's as she seizes the final item, the bowlful of cheesy string beans eaten only by Sister Frances, that Shelly adds volume to her already articulate display.

"Claire, why don't you tell them about your other movie, the one you did with that professor of yours. What was the name of it again?" She fake-thinks for the title as she makes her exit. "*Doctor Damned*, wasn't it?"

"It's not what you think." Claire raises her palms at her remaining tablemates.

"Enlighten us. Please." This from Sister Frances.

"It was a farce. Part horror flick, part commentary on the limitations of higher education in this country. There was this guy, see," Claire starts talking faster to compensate for probable lack of interest, "and he's a teacher at this college. Or, well, he's *posing* as a teacher, but what he really is, is an insane genius swamp-dweller who lives in the sewers under the library. And he survives by eating the brains of the students who get lost on the lower levels of the library when they're working on their research projects. And after he eats their brains he injects them with this golden goo that makes them way smarter than they were before they got lost in the library and had their brains chewed out in the first place. So then they all start running the college, these goo-filled protégées of the evil swamp-dwelling professor, who makes them call him Doctor Damned, and they decide to take over the whole town.

"But *then*—and here's the big surprise—Doctor Damned says 'No, I don't want to take over the whole town. What I really want to do, what I've always wanted to do, is write and star in television infomercials about those human-head-shaped ceramic planters that, when seeded and cultivated with alfalfa sprouts, appear to be growing hair.' So that's what he does. And that's the end of the movie."

The Sisters look completely flabbergasted.

"It did really well," Claire says. "It won a prize."

Sister Maria grins. "It's clear," she says, "how much these films mean to you, Claire. You light up like you're made of electricity. It's always wonderful to see someone who's found her calling. Wouldn't you say so, Sister Frances?"

Sister Frances is saying nothing of the sort. She's studying Claire with the same brew of ownership and malevolence as Doctor Damned himself, just prior to striking one of his unsuspecting victims: a desire to consume and destroy, leaving nothing but a thumbprint.

"I'm going to check on the coffee," she says, and exhales herself out of the room.

"If your other movie's as good as this was, I might have to see that too. I always did like horror flicks." Sister Maria laughs and her chin, her bosom, and the slice of lemon meringue pie in her lap jiggle with competing rhythms.

"I didn't know that." Sister Hilary stirs in the corner of the couch. Shelly sits beside her, fitful and frowning. Claire is on the floor in a neutral zone, equidistant from all parties.

"Sister Frances is out of the room," Sister Maria says. "I can say such things."

Sister Frances is not only out of the room, she was nowhere to be found for the entire screening of Claire's movie. Just as well, Claire thinks; she probably would have hated it anyway. The others, Sisters Maria and Hilary at least, seem to have loved it. Shelly has yet to voice her opinion on the matter.

"Are you going to tell her now?" Sister Maria takes another

bite of pie. She is, Claire realizes, possibly the happiest person Claire has ever met.

Sister Hilary wobbles forward. "Now? I thought you and I were going to talk first. Though," she scoops her hair out of her eyes and Claire notes this as a favorite gesture in a series of gestures that she shouldn't be noticing in the first place, let alone categorizing and enjoying, "we have already talked, in a way. And we've seen the film. Claire," Sister Hilary nods as if this alone should communicate her message, though it only confounds it, "we have good news."

Claire shifts her position from legs tucked under and sideways to legs straight out and flush against the floor. They're not kidding about the "hardwood" part of this arrangement, she thinks. Though none of the soft spots in the room are all that appealing, either.

"We applied for a grant," Sister Hilary is saying, "a calendar-year grant instead of a fiscal-year grant. But that doesn't matter. Anyway," she scoops again and Claire's gaze skittles away, then back, "we got it. We just found out we got the money. It's a three-year funding cycle and it'll give us funds to expand our domestic violence program and increase services to the homeless and ..."

She waits. Shelly coughs. Sister Maria smiles. Claire's impatience bashes against her patience.

"... and there's money in the budget for promotional materials. Media and the like. You see what I'm getting at?"

Claire does. She sees. But what would we be talking about here? Three hundred dollars? Three hundred and fifty? Claire needs a job, a real one. She has loitered far too long in the House of Hilary. It's time to pack her proverbial bags and hit the proverbial street.

"Ummm," she says. Does this suffice? Does this convey her skepticism? Or just the full range of her suckerdom?

"What with all the scandals lately, donations are down. A

video showcasing the Centers—our services, our successes—could be just what we need. You'd have complete control of the equipment—we know you'll treat it well. And we could pay you. Two thousand dollars for your time and expertise. If you'd agree to do it at that price."

The couch clatters as Shelly's pie plate slips off her knees and onto the floor. A chalky yellow smear glistens off her calf and the somehow-intact sheath of graham cracker crust lies belly-up at her feet. "Whoops," she says.

"Oh my," says Sister Maria. "Let me help you with that."

As they rescue the remains of Shelly's pie, Claire contemplates her own piece, asleep in her lap. She had only a tiny bit and the brown-rimmed tips of meringue shimmer up at her like frozen sea foam. She feels like God, gazing at a sliver of creation, pleased with the intricacy of its dip and flow. Except she's not. She's merely Claire, staring at the dessert in her lap, attempting to gather a response to Sister Hilary and finding herself unable to do so.

The sky is burnt black and the street they're stepping on is darker than that. Claire is trying to make as little noise as possible in the hopes that this, somehow, will postpone the heat-seeking darts certain to emerge from Shelly's mouth any second. Thus far, Shelly is implementing only silence—and quite effectively, Claire might add—as the medium with which to convey her dismay and disapproval of the folly that was this evening.

"Nice dinner," she says finally.

"Yeah," says Claire.

"Have you ever wondered what's up with Kitty and Donna?" Shelly says this like *of course* this is what they're going to discuss, here in the post-apocalyptic niche that is their walk home. "How they're always hanging out all the time? I never really noticed before I was staying with you, but they're, like, always together. I think they're dipping into more than just the brewskies, if you know what I mean."

"Shelly. That's ridiculous. Kitty's *way* into guys. What about Tex? And she and Donna are both totally femmy. There's nothing going on there. Believe me."

"You just can't see it because it's your own mom. I'm pretty sure they're a couple. And Tex is barely ever around, in case you haven't noticed."

Claire, no longer holding back on the sound effects, kicks away a stray beer can. It pops and rolls into the gutter. "A second ago you were just wondering and now you're pretty sure they're a couple? What is this, Shel? Is this about dinner? This is about dinner, right? That's not—"

"Did I say *anything* about dinner?" Shelly's voice rips apart the seamlessness of street and steps and air. "I was talking about Kitty and Donna. Why can't you ever just listen, Claire? Why do you always have to make everything about you? You and your movies. You and the nuns. You and your stupid ..."

"I didn't—"

"Whatever."

They sling back to silence. Claire searches for something else to kick—a rock, a bottle, a blow-up photo of her own face that says "kick here"—but there's nothing. Just pavement and pissed off and the persistent vision of Kitty and Donna traipsing blithely behind them, hand in hand, high on the morphine of imaginary love.

Paradise

The secretary's desk is flat empty and the mailboxes are full, stuffed with late nights and bleary, caffeine-induced displays of intellectual prowess. Claire considers depositing her own small treasure somewhere inside this scenario, but understands that this would not take into account the bigger reason she is here.

The door is sandwiched between the Xerox machine and a bulletin board fat with flyers. Claire pretends to examine the board for about half a second and then, as a kind of trick, sneaks a fist around the corner of herself and pounds on the door.

"Come on in," it says.

She steps across the threshold and stands in the shadow of the sun barreling in through the window. Jack glances up from his desk, packed with videotapes and piles of papers, and takes a look. Then returns to his task with a low moan.

"I was going to leave this out there," she says, "but your box was full and Mrs. Wong wasn't at her desk."

Jack's pen on his papers makes a scritching noise. It makes Claire think of a buried-alive person trying to escape: the futile effort, the hoped-for release.

"I finished my documentary. It's all done." Claire pauses for the "good job" that definitely won't get said. "And I got a gig making a video for a social service agency. Real money and everything. Yeah."

Jack continues to scritch his way out of the coffin, eyes fixed down.

He's behind, Claire thinks. This always happens. All the other professors are finishing up their grading in order to be done in time for Christmas break, and Jack, he's just barely getting started. She can practically smell the ethers from last night's party vaporizing off his brow. Not that it matters. All the old judgments—the things about him she found wanting and incomplete, the shoddy ammunition used to fuel the rickety rationale of betrayal—mean nothing now. She feels them clot inside her, then fall. What's left is a moment, a crucial one.

It was the Los Altos Film Festival, right after the screening of *Doctor Damned*. The audience response had been incredible; Claire and Jack's egos were in flames. Jack addressed the crowd, introduced Claire as his Assistant Director, and they sauntered off the stage arm in arm, draped in blankets of success and admiration. But it wasn't the applause or the laughter during the screening (at all the right moments, as if etched into the soundtrack) that held her up, injected her step with sense and purpose. It was the exact weight of Jack's arm on her own, the ounces of joy and integrity and collaboration. That's what she's lost.

"I've been trying to figure out who you are, and it's finally occurred to me," he says, eyes dark. "You must be the pure and noble twin of Claire McMinn. You certainly can't be your evil counterpart, who promised never to contact me again."

"Yes. I promised. I know I promised. Maybe that was stupid—that I promised." Claire bounces inside her anxiety. The backs of her knees are damp, like mini-terrariums. "I'm so sorry about everything, Jack. Really sorry. I'll never be able to forgive myself, for what I did. It was partly the booze, what made me act that way, but it wasn't just that. It was mostly me being stupid, wanting attention, wherever I could get it. I'm in this program now, see, and it's helping me get stuff sorted out. I'm still pretty much an idiot, I know that," her terrariums switch to ponds, "but I'm trying to be better now,

131

to do things better. And I know you'll never forgive me because you shouldn't, there's no reason to forgive such an awful thing, but I am sorry. More than I can ever say in words, because they don't even begin to say anything, really. It's just …" Claire clutches her tape. "I fucked up so bad."

"Ah." Jack straightens his papers just so, a gesture Claire finds strangely reassuring. "The noble twin speaks the truth."

"Or tries to." Claire stands in place, her brain hollow and inept. She can't do it. The idea that she would ask Jack for anything, that she ever thought she could, now seems unendurably absurd.

"But surely that's not why you've come," he says. "To apologize. Surely you have another, more self-centered aim for this little visit."

"No." Her head won't shake, though. Won't even budge.

"Please. Claire. You took me for a fool once already. Twice would just be …" he flicks his pen onto the stack of papers in front of him, "*unforgivable*, wouldn't you say?"

"Yes."

"So?"

Claire swallows. "Look, Jack. I wasn't going to say it, I was just going to go. I still can." She steps toward the door.

"And rob me of the opportunity to see you grovel? I don't think so."

"But—"

"You can do it, Claire." Jack settles back in his chair. He is fostering the beginnings of a smile. "I know you can."

Claire nods. She presses the videotape into her palms, its edges sharp against her skin. Sell the unsellable, that's all she has to do. "The reason I'm here …" She takes a breath, a big one, though not big enough to hold what comes next. "I never would have come except you're the only one I can ask. My application says I need a recommendation from a teacher who knows my work. And that's you. It's just for UCLA. SFSU doesn't need one and I'm only applying those two places. I was going to request it in writing, or just send it to you, but asking face to face seemed more ..."

"Manly?"

"Uh. Yeah." Claire gulps. "And I know it's insane, but I was going to ask if you could maybe just write a little something, nothing even really all that nice or anything, it could be real neutral, but just so I have a little recommendation from the film guy at my college. So there's at least something. Even something, you know, not that great. I mean, not that it wouldn't be great because of you, but because of me. My stuff." She brakes, starts again. "So, yeah. That's what I was going to ask. Or ... not ask. That's it."

"That's it?"

"Yeah."

"I see. I figured it was something of the sort." Jack folds his hands on top of his desk. They are hairy on the edges—always have been, still are—and this strikes Claire as one of the eminently likable things about him: he has hands and they are hairy.

"It doesn't surprise me at all," he says. "That you're here. I suspect it's the same amphibian portion of your brain that encouraged you to take liberties with my trust that shuttled you here today. So to hear your words, your request ... These things are emblematic of a core of entitlement that, frankly, amuses me." He shrugs. "And yet, though it pains me to say this, you do have a point. I do owe you a recommendation, in a way. You contributed a lot—to my movie, to my classes. And I am, as you say, the only 'film guy' on campus."

Claire's fingers, the ones fidgeting with the tape guard at the front of the video, cease their activity. Anything other than stillness will upset the balance, the undeserved parcel unfolding before her.

"And so I will not only give you a recommendation," he says. "I will give it to you now." His hands unlatch. "Get out. Get out of my office right now and do not come back. If

133

you can manage this much, then I will look at your tape and possibly pass you. If you are unable to accomplish even this simplest of tasks, then I shall be forced to rebuke you in a manner considerably more medieval. How's that for a recommendation? It's the best you'll get from me."

He swoops up his pen as if it were part of the attack, Robin to his Batman, and calmly resumes the grading of his papers.

Claire could be stunned but she's not. She's mostly sorry she ever attempted such a pathetic stunt to begin with. Though she also knows that it's good she did. That this is, as Max would say, a perfect rendering of krama: a vicious blend of karma mixed with drama. Unlike the usual "actions come back to you" jive (Max's gleeful voice throngs Claire's head), krama is invoked when the aforementioned actions return with an unusual dose of vengeance and flair—of a sort that knocks you on your ass and eats you for dinner. Claire stands duly munched.

The door to Jack's office reopens with the same lack of protest with which he greeted her arrival: as if it, too, is through with her. She trudges across the reception room— crunched, defeated—and realizes halfway through that she has failed in the only part of her mission she had an even semi-serious chance of completing. She turns to leave the tape with Jack when she is snared by an interruption. The empty secretary's desk beckons, a cool beach in an uninhabitable paradise. Claire is merely a tourist here—visa expunged, baggage irrevocably lost. She sets her tape on the bare wide surface, her illegible mark in the sand, and erases herself from the premises.

Venice

Claire is attempting a drive-by on her own house. Though technically it isn't, as she has no car to supply the "drive" for her "by." The only thing she has going for herself, really, is speed. She'll need it too; Shelly, Claire can see from the battered hunk of a car in the driveway, is home.

"It's about time. I thought we were doing something tonight." Shelly is flopped across the unmade bed, decorating her fingernails road-flare red.

Claire glides through the room as though this is not a difficult maneuver. "I was over at the Center, prepping for my movie. I'm lining up interviews, that sorta stuff."

"So?" Shelly attacks her thumb with the teeny red brush. "What about tonight?"

The eleven days and nights (not that Claire is counting) since the dinner of doom have seen a truce, of sorts, between the two friends. There's been tension, sure, but it's been a tension of topics and territory. These, once evaded, clear a space for another, more pressing alternative to pour its carnal tidings all over the two young women until—panting, grateful—they find themselves swimming in Switzerland. It's not, as it were, a lasting solution, but it's the only one they've managed to come up with so far.

"Not tonight. I can't tonight," says Claire. She hikes two bottles of sparkling cider from the fridge and stuffs them into her backpack. "I'm having dinner with Max."

"And ..."

135

Claire cinches the strap of her bag. This, instead of looking at Shelly. "What do you mean 'And …'? I'm having dinner with Max."

What is it with her? It must be Shelly's past and potentially future proximity to Claire's mouth and other orifices that creates in her a built-in alarm system for the false and fractious as they seek their escape from said portals.

"I mean, there's an 'And' there," Shelly says. "You didn't finish your sentence. I can tell."

Claire plunks her pack on the counter. Rigorous honesty, that's been Max's theme of late. It cuts at her now like a buzz saw, effortlessly shredding her attempts at deceit. "Sister Hilary will be joining us. Max wants to talk with her about art. He's been bugging me for weeks to introduce him."

"Oh, gosh," Shelly parks the open bottle of nail polish on the bed where, they both know, it could easily tip over and spread its viscous red all over the sheets, "I wonder why you didn't want to tell me *that*."

"Maybe I didn't want you making something of nothing. Maybe I knew you'd blow it up bigger than it is."

"You got it backwards, babe." Shelly wiggles on the bed, taunting the polish. "I saw the way she looked at you the other night."

"The way she … What are you talking about? Sister Hilary didn't look at me in any way at all. Just the regular way. The way nuns look at everyone. Like they can help them or protect them or whatever. You know that stuff better than me."

"Maybe I don't. Maybe I've been missing a whole lotta crap."

"Shel …" Claire plucks a stray nectarine off the counter and squeezes it inside her fist. She starts to assemble a story inside her head, a string of connecting lies to chase Shelly off her tail, but it's no use. The nectarine prickles against her palm, singed with defeat. She sets it back down on the counter.

"I was hoping you wouldn't notice," she says. "Because it doesn't matter anyhow. Nothing happened."

"Doesn't *matter?*" Shelly rolls into a sitting position, legs kicking the sheets. "What are you saying 'it doesn't matter'? Do you have any idea how seriously you'd go to hell for something like that? Corrupting a nun isn't like stealing a bicycle, Claire. It's like stealing God. You are seriously fucking with some fucked up shit here."

"I know. I know I am. And I've been trying not to. I have. I just suck at it. It's so hard to get this stuff out of my head. The only thing that's worked so far is ..." Claire stops. *Whoops.*

"What would *that* be?"

"What would what be?"

Shelly's gaze is steady, belying injury. "Whatever it is that's helped you out so much. It wouldn't have anything to do with me, would it?"

Claire swallows. If she could smash herself to pieces, all the parts that ache for the wrong things and damage everyone around her, she would. She'd do it right now. "I was gonna—"

"That's okay." Shelly retrieves her nail polish from the edge of the bed and starts in on one of her toenails. "I only slept with you to get over Kenny, so I guess we're even. Except that you're an idiot." She laughs, a hearty fake laugh. "At least I'm not going to be eternally damned and shit. At least I've got sense enough to—"

"Shelly. I told you. Nothing happened."

"See? What did I just say? You're an idiot."

Sister Hilary is driving. She promised this ahead of time, and when Claire arrived at the old downtown house, Sister Hilary was waiting on the porch, keys in her lap.

She is, it turns out, a horrible driver.

"Whoa. Watch out for that stoplight there." Claire tightens her grip on the passenger seat of the boat-sized Oldsmobile that is, according to Sister Hilary, "easy to drive." The car, like the house they live in, is shared among the Sisters.

"It's yellow," Sister Hilary says, gunning the accelerator. "Yellow means go faster. It's green that drives me crazy. So open-ended. At least with yellow, you know where you stand." Her hands cup the wheel, careening back and forth in response to the perfectly-missable-yet-not-at-all-avoided potholes littering the frontage road to Max's. She vetoed the interstate route for (and this was said without a trace of irony) "religious reasons."

"I just go straight here?" she asks.

"Yes." Claire sidesteps the obvious. "It's a few more miles down this road."

"I don't know what he wants, exactly." Sister Hilary's jaw snaps back into her head as the Olds encounters yet another pothole. "I'm not a professional."

"Just amazing."

"What?"

"Just an amazing artist. That's all you are. He wants to see that."

"Hmmm."

It's dark already and the beams of oncoming cars and passing street lamps flicker across Sister Hilary's features like warring strobe lights. Claire feels the draw, the current of invisible levers and pulleys that gets activated when you're attracted to someone, that forces you to imagine the smell of their cheek and the taste of their skin. Like oranges becoming marmalade, refusing to resist the transition.

"We'll be there soon," she says.

"It's like someone removed a part of my body. And I know I'll get it back eventually, but until I do, nothing's right."

Sister Hilary is explaining to Max and Claire what it's like to miss a day of painting. "So I try to focus on my day, I try

138

to stay centered, but that sense of something missing, it doesn't leave me until I'm painting again. I've been trying to get up earlier, to get some time in before I leave for work, but sometimes I'm so worn out from the day before, trying to paint and work and run the Center, that it just doesn't happen. And then I have the displaced feeling all day. I'm not used to this." Sister Hilary stops, dazed. She glances down at her just-released confession, scampering loose in her lap. "I'm not used to having this much of a deficit in light of the lack of something. Except for God, and that's different."

"But is it?" Max says, leaning into her confusion. "I don't know that it is."

"Well, yes." Sister Hilary smiles. "There is the way they're the same. Same source, same intention. But that's just the art, not all the other things we were talking about. You know?"

"Yes." Max's shoulders bump against his chair as he unhitches himself from Sister Hilary's gaze. "That's true."

Claire places her napkin over her plate of picked-apart food—a surrender, of sorts. They're been talking this way all evening. Who would've thought that Max and Sister Hilary would have such an affinity, that they would cleave to each other like twin sisters separated at birth? Their conjoint love for and knowledge of art are vast and, as far as Claire can tell, unending. The Things They Have In Common are similarly inexhaustible, first on the list being a mutual left-handedness that had the two of them espousing the virtues and wonders of this freak-of-nature affliction until Claire was tempted to take the back of her hand, her virile and dominant right hand, and slap them both silly.

Then there's the Secrets Shared, a category that has Claire feeling more and more like gondolier to Max and Hilary's love-soaked couple. Turns out Max was married—to a woman—before he got sober and came out of the closet. (Who knew? Not Claire. Though Max is sure he told her.)

And Sister Hilary was an orphan, raised by her grandparents and, after they died, a series of welcoming yet distant foster families, the best of whom, an old maid named Miss Kerry, taught little Hilary the "pick three things" game.

"But Max, you never told me," Sister Hilary flings her napkin on her plate in a manner similar to Claire-of-a-minute-ago and Claire clings to the inconsequential connection, "why you left the art world, what brought you here."

Max sweeps a runaway shank of hair off his forehead. He's wearing an oxford shirt the color of limes and for some reason it makes Claire think of how he must have looked in high school—new, hopeful, sullen.

"It was about three years ago," he says. "After Bert died. He was sick for so long, it was almost a relief when he finally passed. But then of course, not at all, as I was left without him and had to deal with his family who, the minute he died, turned on me like they had just put two and two together and realized it was all my fault. Though it *so* wasn't—I'm negative, for God's sake. But that didn't stop them from taking the house and the gallery."

"That's ..." Sister Hilary sighs. "They could do that?"

"Bert's father found a loophole in the will, said Bert was not in his right mind when he made the changes, even though those were made *years* before Bert started to get sick."

"Did you fight it?"

"I could have. I could have hired a lawyer, but Bert's family was a formidable foe—old money San Francisco. And I didn't have it in me to fight. I had already buried so many friends. I had to get out. When my mom broke her hip, it was more than enough reason to move back here, to stash myself into this little corner of nowhere. It was a blessing, really—that nowhere existed."

"I'm so sorry," Sister Hilary says. And she is, Claire can feel it. Sorry pulses through her limbs and shoes and outsized eyes like it was never even an entity till now. Like it just now got born on this hope-benighted planet. Sorry.

Max nods around tears brimming off his eyelashes. "Thanks. Talking with you brings so much of it back. I don't know if it's dreadful or luscious." He swipes his eyes with a lime-edged wrist. "I guess I should thank you?"

"Thank Claire," Sister Hilary says. "At least for the dreadful part. She's the one who brought us together."

They laugh, all three of them, and Claire's resentment at being excluded from the love fest, which was reaching nearly intolerable proportions, flakes off like dirt in a bath.

"I tossed too much in the garbage, though," Max says. "Bert's parents made it all too easy. But then I saw your drawing, and I realized there was something I wanted back. That I had sacrificed a huge piece of myself in exchange for freedom from Bert—or from his death, at least. As if you can ever find peace by chopping yourself apart."

"It doesn't work, does it?" Sister Hilary shakes her head. Her eyes grow dim and she slides once again into an energetic understanding of Max's pain—side by side, comrades in grief. Except, Claire sees as she shifts back and forth between the two faces—Max's worn and familiar and right next to her, Sister Hilary's pinched and distant and fending off vague swells of sorrow—that it's not Bert Sister Hilary is holding. It's someone else. Someone Claire doesn't know.

"Here's what I've been wondering," Max says. Max drives up out of the trenches and Claire knows precisely what he's going to ask. "How did you go from art major to nun? Not that your falling away was anything like mine, but how did it happen for you? If it's all right to ask."

"Of course it's all right to ask. It was completely different than yours, you're right. I wasn't ... That is, I ..." Sister Hilary's lips twist into a smile. Her harbored person, whoever it was, fades into a glint in the pocket of her eye. "It's been a long time," she says, "since I've told this story."

141

She strains into a view of Max and begins again. "I grew up believing. Or rather, I was raised Catholic and never questioned my faith. I loved church when I was little, unlike most kids my age. This was all pre-Vatican II; the Church still had that aura of mystery. It was wonderful back then—the ritual part, at least."

"And everything in Latin, right?" Max says. "That must have been powerful."

"Yes," Sister Hilary says. "It was. But it didn't last. The Church transitioned into the twentieth century and I lost my grandparents. They died within two months of each other. After that, I just stopped believing."

"It happens," Max says.

"It does," Sister Hilary says. She laughs. "You should have seen me—I was such an angry adolescent. Full of Sartre and de Beauvoir. The rise of reason and logic over faith. Art was the one thing that still mattered—the one thing that still made any sense. I wanted to go to art school out of state, but there weren't enough funds for that. The only affordable option was a Catholic college outside of Des Moines. My foster family put my name in for a scholarship. I was so mad." She laughs again, tones deep and heavy in her throat.

"But you went," Max says.

"I did," Sister Hilary says. "And right away I met this woman. Sister Frances. Claire knows her."

Claire nods. She wants to look at Max to catch the reflection of Sister Frances' lofty brow and miserly expression in his full and unguarded eyes, but she can't summon the nerve or stupidity for such a trick.

"She was unlike anyone I had ever met. She was a doctoral candidate, a rare feat for a woman religious in those days, though I didn't realize it at the time. She was so alive, so aware. She scared me, initially. I tried to stay away from her, but I couldn't. She was a teaching assistant in one of my classes that first semester. Then two in the next. I started to

142

follow her around, asking her about her beliefs, her commitment to her faith. I argued with her, tried to prove her wrong. I'd be damned if I was going to get caught in anything as saccharine as a life dedicated to Christ." Sister Hilary takes a sip out of the water glass she has left untouched the entire meal, sets it back in place. "And yet He wouldn't leave me alone. Like one of the kids at the Center when they want something from you. Like Enrique is with you, Claire."

Claire grabs onto a view of the painting behind Sister Hilary's head. She will share her reaction only with this—a conglomeration of reds and yellows and thick black lines that Max and Hilary had earlier declared "divine."

"It finally caught up with me one night when I was walking home from the library. I was almost to my dorm room and was watching a car rush past me, taillights in the dark underneath a sky that was about to rain. And for some reason I thought of Christ and the crucifixion—that sense of endings, maybe. And that's when it happened."

She turns to Claire. Why she's choosing this particular moment to glue the specifics of her tale onto someone other than Max, Claire's not sure. She squirms under the attention.

"My thoughts got bigger," Sister Hilary says. "And the crucifixion—except it wasn't just the crucifixion, it was the resurrection too—they planted themselves in the center of my mind. Though it wasn't just my mind. They were everywhere. I *felt* them, in a way I can only barely remember." She stops. She looks suddenly small, embarrassed. She searches Claire's face, then her own hands, then the other side of the room, pulling these fragments into her voice, which is now thin and low.

"There was this presence," she says. She appears to be continuing out of obligation, or force—a gun to her head, her life shoved against her. "It's difficult to describe. Love is the only word that comes close, though it was worlds beyond what I'd ever thought of as love. It was palpable. And full of clarity. It was like, for a flash of a second, I understood everything Christ was trying to say. Or as much as I could contain, in that moment."

Sister Hilary blinks. She is no longer entirely in the room, Claire can see this. "And included in that was my vocation," she says. "That I was supposed to become a woman religious. That I *am* a woman religious. I tried to push it away, even after that experience, but it was too late. I knew who I was after that."

"Mmm," Max says.

"Mmm." Claire tries it too. Unlike Max, though, who is involved and interested, but from the safety of his own person, Claire is spinning in a whorl of resonance. Is it her turn? Is she supposed to tell her own, similar story now? Though what would be the point? A cosmic face-off, a matching of bliss and obligation and embarrassment? Claire tightens her mouth, traps her words inside. She has nothing to say.

"I'm sorry," Sister Hilary says. "I'm not ... Anyway. That's what happened."

Max nods. He unbuttons a shirtsleeve and folds his shirt once, twice, three times up his arm. "And the art?" His tone is gentle, precise. "What happened to the art?"

Sister Hilary shrugs, her shoulders clumping down. Her gaze returns to her plate. "I tried to make it work, but my art professors weren't really supportive of my calling. You'd think they would be, in a Catholic college, but no one was joining the Order anymore—it was already seen as an anachronism by then. And after I joined the Sisters of Divine Mercy, Sister Frances' order out here in Oakland, there was no time for painting. The president of the community back then wasn't, shall we say, encouraging of my endeavors in that direction. So I let it go."

"That's too bad," Max says.

"Yeah. Too bad." Claire tests her voice, attempts to reset her upheaval. Though it hardly makes a difference.

"Perhaps," Sister Hilary says. "But now it's found me again. Life has a way of catching up with you, if you let it." She picks up her fork and uses it to reconfigure the leftovers underneath the napkin over her plate. "I haven't told many people about my art work yet, other than Sisters Frances and Maria. I'll have to talk to our president at some point, to get some sort of official permission. I should have done it already, really." Sister Hilary's cheeks flush deep red and Claire realizes she's never seen her blush before; that she assumed, hoped, she would be the catalyst for such an event.

"We need to get together, you and I." Max tips toward Claire but his eyes are on Sister Hilary. His breath is spiked with coffee and lasagna. "I'd like to see more of your work. Would that be possible?"

Sister Hilary's focus on her food-shuffling project increases, like she's reached the crucial stage where one wrong move could wreck the whole thing. "That would be all right," she says.

Everyone is quiet for a minute or so, a roomful of inhales and exhales and things to say that don't get said. Claire uses the time to reinvent herself, to snap back into a version of Claire who is absolutely unaffected by anything Sister Hilary has shared tonight. Though the only way to do this is through a kind of makeshift lobotomy, extracting memory and emotion and fabric of thought until all that's left is anger and feelings of worthlessness. It's a crappy strategy, she knows this, but she's too pissed and apathetic to do anything else.

"And you." Max ends the silence by firing his attention on Claire. "You mentioned when you first came in that you had news. Something from the Shelly front, perhaps?"

"No." Claire digs her heels into the cluelessness of Max's question. Though how would he know she's still stashed in the closet as far as Sister Hilary is concerned? Or maybe he does know and is prying the door open on her behalf. Either way, Claire can ignore him.

"I got a letter from Jack," she says, voice full of rough. "He changed his mind about the recommendation. He saw my little movie on the Center and decided to give me a break. I lucked out. Totally."

"It's more than that," Max says. "What's that story in the Old Testament—the Prodigal Son?" He confers with Sister Hilary, who shakes her head, confused. "It's Biblical, is what it is. You've had a moment of grace, babycakes. Best to savor it. You never know when something that good will fly down the pike again."

He grins at Sister Hilary who, as though she knows exactly what he's talking about, as though she's in on every nuance of the whole Jack debacle, grins back and the two of them beam at Claire like they're the sunny, punch-drunk couple she's been gondoliering all evening. Except, Claire thinks, a gondolier implies a measure of control she cannot even pretend to possess. She's more like a hole in the bottom of the boat.

The car is technically parked in Sister Hilary's driveway, though given her limited capacities in this arena, most of the car is shoved over to the side of the house against a shaggy row of bushes. Claire offered to walk home from here, but the nun, intentionally or not, has restricted her exiting options to bushwhacking through the bushes or crawling over the lap of the driver. Claire refuses to be snared by either strategy. Instead she's sitting tight, stewing through a slough of potential responses to Sister Hilary's just-asked question about her future. The one about how she didn't realize Claire was possibly going *away* to school next year, and how she wonders when Claire will know more about her plans.

"I'm not sure yet," Claire says. "Depends where I get in. And what I can afford."

Sister Hilary tilts her eyes to avoid the glare of the bald bulb blaring off the corner of the garage. "You and Max seem close. That's great you have him as a friend."

"Yeah," Claire says. Visions of dinner spill back into her brain, sway inside her like just-watered flowers.

"I was sorry to hear about his partner. It's clear he misses him a lot."

Claire squints into the light. "So it doesn't bother you, then? That he's gay?"

"Oh, no." Sister Hilary's head bobbles from side to side like her neck is made of water. "The Church has been sorely remiss in its response to the AIDS crisis. It's another area where the official doctrine of the Church has yet to catch up with the realities in the field. When Sister Maria and I were working in Oakland, we saw—"

"Because I am too, you know. I never told you directly, and I thought maybe you already knew, but I am too. Gay. Or lesbian. It gets called both things." Claire taps her own knee, keeping time to a frenetic, inaudible song.

"No," Sister Hilary says.

"No what?"

"No, I didn't know." Sister Hilary sits quietly. Claire's plip-plip on her kneecap bounces against the car's interior.

"But it's not a problem, is it? I mean, if you're cool with Max, then I figured—"

"Of course it's not a problem. No." Sister Hilary seems to be shrinking. It's as if an inner switch has been activated and her skin and her clothing and her speechlessness are rolling out of sight.

Claire has seen this before. Many times. The old friends, former teachers, and down-the-street neighbors who hear from someone else or from Claire herself and pretend to be okay with it, even though they're not. They turn away, like Sister Hilary is doing now, retreating into the folds of their ordered lives, and when they turn back, if they do at all, it's

147

with a look of vacancy: a clean removal of all the jokes and stories and gossip they might have shared, if only. If only.

Sister Hilary sinks deeper into the driver's seat, her retraction undeniable. She tries to move, or maybe talk—her lips split apart and come back together—but she manages only a strange, squeaking sound.

"I'm glad it's not an issue." Claire says this mostly to herself, waving her hand at the Cosmic Forces who have slammed her with yet another lost connection. "Because it often is. People freak out and stuff. So I'm glad you're not doing that."

There's a vibration emanating from the base of the Oldsmobile, the source of which Claire initially thinks is a seismic tremor, then a passing car, then Sister Hilary's foot. It's with this final (and accurate) identification of the shaking's source that Claire realizes she has been wrong. Sister Hilary is many things, but horrified is not one of them. She is—like Claire, like Claire has been from the beginning—attracted. Smitten. Claire can feel this in the vibration under her feet, can taste it in the scent—spicy, petrified—filling the interior of the car, can sense it in the tremulous emotion lapping the air like freedom. It's all she can do to stay on her side of the seat.

"So late," Sister Hilary says. "It's so late, isn't it?" She smiles at Claire, an overwhelmed smile that confirms everything, unlocks her door *(it was locked? why was it locked?)*, and pours herself out of the car. As she does so, the cross around her neck, the one Claire perpetually tries to ignore, smashes into the light off the garage and crashes into Claire's consciousness in a manner so corny and overwrought that, if it hadn't happened, Claire would be sure she made it up.

Sister Hilary marches up to the porch and inside the house and Claire stays put, struggling to comprehend what just happened. Off to her left, the driver's door hangs open like a broken jaw.

148

◆◆◆

Dueling nips of flame from the porch next door greet her return home.

"What time is it?" Claire barks at the two shadowy figures, presumably Donna and Kitty, lingering under the porch's awning.

A cough. Probably Kitty. "Dunno."

The cougher takes another drag off her cigarette and a noise like whooshing slides off the porch.

"Why don't you come set with us for a bit?" This one is Donna, Claire can tell. The way she says "set."

Claire's entire life thus far has been an assembly of reminders that "comfort" and "Kitty" are mutually exclusive terms. That they are instead at war, clashing and clanging with a force that invariably leaves the two intact and Claire in pieces. And yet, as she does from time to time, crumbling under the weight of accumulated need, Claire, amnesic moth, hurls herself into the distance between herself and her mother.

"Kitty was just telling the story of AJ's last days. You ever heard this one?" Donna is dressed in a blue-and-black checkered shirt that makes her look like an off-duty lumberjack. Claire had never noticed, till just now, how much Kenny looks like his mother.

"No, I never did." Claire plops onto the deck chair at the far edge of the porch. Kitty and Donna are sharing the fashion-impaired couch that made it out of Donna's living room but never any farther than that.

Kitty cackles and nestles her head against the couch. "He said he had to go to the office late to check on the books. Books my ass. I gave him fifteen minutes, then hiked it over there. He was with that woman, that whore. What was her name?"

"Mini. Mini Calhoun." Smoke courses from Donna's throat like steam, blending into the damp dark. "What a bitch."

149

"Tell me about it. I never figured AJ used those plumbing tools on anything but plumbing, but there they were, working that plunger like it was *born* for the chore. I'd always suspected AJ liked to play in the back yard more than he'd admit, but the way that woman was going at him, you'd think she was trying to retrieve a thousand dollar bill out of that man's ass."

"Kitty." Claire attempts to pry her ex-stepfather's sodomized image out of her brain. "Why you gotta tell me stuff like that? You think I want to hear that? As if I wasn't damaged enough, growing up in this family."

"Whatever," Kitty says, going teenage. "I'm surprised you even care. You always hated AJ anyhow. Now you've got more—uh—hard-pressed evidence against him. I'd think you'd be jumping for joy and shit."

"And shit." Claire takes a whiff of beer and stale air. Why is she here?

"Besides, I don't know why you're prowling around at this hour in the first place. They don't make them alkie meetings this late, do they?"

"No, Kitty. You know they don't."

Kitty pats the pile of clothes in the corner of the couch, which, it turns out, is not a pile of clothes at all but Sinatra, curled up in a ball of warmth and simple motives. "Must be a boy, then," she says. "What would keep you out so late."

"Why say 'boy'? You know it's not a boy." Claire's legs flex down and her chair screeches against the porch. "I know a lot scrams by you, but you can't tell me you've missed this one. That you can't see what's right in—"

"Don't talk to me about what I see and don't see. You don't know shit about that." Kitty remains still but her rage flares forward like a pistol. Donna, on the other hand, is staging a retreat in inverse proportions to Kitty's lashing out. It's as if the two of them are on an energetic teeter-totter, each woman launched in opposite directions in reaction to Claire's stab at revelation. And yet, as Kitty rides the higher octaves

150

of retort (against Claire's selfishness, her ingratitude, her inability to grant Kitty even *one solitary speck* of the respect she so rightly deserves) and Donna disappears into the dark checks of her jacket, Claire realizes that the agent of this complementary activity is not her, but something else entirely. Something like the inside of a tent—damp, sweaty, a recycling of breath and bodies and buried inclinations. Shelly was right. There's more going on here than Claire could allow.

"This has been just swell," she says, interrupting the tail end of Kitty's speech. "Really. But it's time for bed." Claire blanches, lurching off her last word.

She turns her back on the two of them and everything this implies, pushing her body across Donna's lawn and over to the gate. The window to her little house is soaring with light, and Claire is struck by the relief this brings her. It's funny, the combination of solace and pain-in-ass one person can provide.

"I know it was a shitty way to leave," Claire stutters as she's opening the door, but there's no one to say it to. Her floor is splattered with a layer of papers—the former contents of her table desk, to be exact. The now-refuse is punctuated with jabs of color that appear to be (Claire toddles over to check) the shredded remains of hundreds of candy wrappers. Over by the bookshelves, Claire's video collection has not only been emancipated from the tyranny of alphabetical order, but most of the tapes have been stripped of their jackets as well, splayed across the room in a manner that clearly articulates both the "Fuck" and "You" of Shelly's parting sentiments.

Holy

They've started over. Claire began the interview with Sister Hilary in a long shot and saved the zoom until the end, then got discombobulated by the corner of Sister Hilary's mouth, the way it seemed to be signaling to her in code, and was forced to back up off her shot after having already started to zoom, which, of course, ruined the whole thing.

This time, she began with the close-up, ignoring the mouth, and zoomed out early on, capturing the Christ on the cross above Sister Hilary's head. In the late afternoon light drumming through the window of the office, it looks as though He is nodding in agreement with everything Sister Hilary is saying.

"When the roof caved in at our first site, Sister Maria and I thought it was all over," she says. "We didn't know how we'd get the funds to rebuild, or if that was even possible. Then we got the grant from the Brill foundation, and everything started to fall in place. So to speak." Her forehead fans open and the cross above her glimmers. "The next step was to build the GED program, which we began in the basement of the church in Point Firth. One of our first clients was a young man who insisted on bringing his dog in with him. Said that his dog, whose name was Heidi, had all the answers inside her head and if he could just have her nearby, he'd be able to pass his GED in no time. And of course our first volunteer teacher was terrified of dogs, and we had to strike a compromise by having Heidi sit over in the corner. The young man passed, though. Did remarkably well, in fact.

"And then there was the incident with the rats and the exterminator." Sister Hilary smiles, her teeth tidy and smooth inside her mouth, "I'd forgotten about that. It started with a strange noise coming from the fridge in the back of the room ..."

Claire smashes her face closer to the viewfinder and tries to pay attention. Sister Hilary is full of stories—she has acres of them, it seems—and if Claire can keep her eyes and ears on the story itself, perhaps she won't have to be so overwhelmed by its source. Since she came out to Sister Hilary over a week ago, the two of them have successfully managed to avoid any further discussion on the topic, let alone acknowledge the now-unearthed, now-undeniable spark between them. For her part, Sister Hilary has maintained a friendly, unflappable front—the essence of openness and understanding. At least, most of the time. The remainder of her interactions with Claire have the quality of a backtracking river: a steady, established flow that decides to abandon the ocean destination and return to the mountains from whence it came. Back to that single, solitary, instigating drop.

Claire reminds herself frequently that none of this matters. That, as Shelly would say (Shelly who refuses all calls, who has moved back in with her evil sister Viv, who has left the scent of Sweet Tarts and solitude in Claire's small house), chasing a nun is like catching the express train to Hell. No stops, no side streets, just a straight shot to perpetual heat and lousy neighbors. And yet, Claire says to the Shelly inside her head, isn't Hell where Claire is bound anyhow, given a life on the margins of acceptability and common sense? And if so, if any of it's even true to begin with, why not follow that tender voice within that might, in its innocence and clarity, be the closest thing to divine Claire has ever known? Why not, indeed? Shelly-in-her-head always agrees with her at this point, though at this point Shelly-in-her-head has taken up with a nun of her own and is championing the cause of nun-civilian relations.

Sister Hilary tells more stories about the GED lab and the job training facility, then the domestic violence shelter and the after-school program and all the grants and plans and dreams and inspirations stuffed under the tent of charity and good works that are the Bearley and Point Firth Community Centers. Claire wrangles it all inside her camera, down to the last drop, and shuts off the video with the awareness that, aside from a few more interviews, she has almost all the footage she needs to make one bang-up promotional film.

"You did great," she says, ejecting the tape to make sure it recorded. "You're actually quite chatty when the camera starts rolling. Most people start out all flustered and self-conscious, but not you. You were like a sportscaster—all oomph and snappy delivery. We'll splice your voice into the action shots. You'll see. We'll keep it all real peppy." Claire closes her mouth. Only with Sister Hilary would she use a phrase like "peppy."

"Thanks." Sister Hilary inspects her knees.

"There was another thing I was going to ask you about," Claire says, grasping at a conversational track that will leave her faculties of speech intact, "but then I thought maybe it was too off base. Sister Maria mentioned that you two were in El Salvador and I thought it might be cool to talk about that too, but with all the other stories and stuff, I forgot to ask you about it."

Sister Hilary's gaze lifts off her knees. Her face is the color of dusk. "I see."

"That was a while ago, though. That you were there?"

"It was 1979. We left in 1980. It was a short stay."

"What did you do, when you were over there?"

"Not enough."

Claire tucks the tape into its case. "So did you—"

"How do I get this off me?" Sister Hilary wags a finger at the clip-on microphone pegged to her blouse. "Can I just—"

"Here." Claire barrels forward. "It's pretty easy to ..." She grabs at the blouse. Her fingers, which have amassed the thickness of sausages, struggle with the microphone. "At least, it's usually just a matter—" She tugs at the mic, useless.

"Perhaps it would be easier if I try." Sister Hilary slips her hand under Claire's. Only she doesn't try to remove the microphone. Just keeps her hand there. "I made a mistake," she says. "The other night. After our dinner with Max. Do you remember that?"

Claire stops with the microphone. Sister Hilary's skin underneath her own is thin and calm. "Umm. We sat in your car. I told you stuff about myself."

"You did." Sister Hilary studies her hands. The veins on her eyelids look like tiny rivers on a map. "I shouldn't have left so abruptly. I was scared. When you told me you're gay."

"I'm gay?" Claire grins.

The eyelids snap back up. "See, that's just it. I know what you're doing."

Claire blinks. "You do?"

"Of course. You try to fool me, pretending you don't care about anything, that everything is just a joke, but I know that's not true." Sister Hilary takes a breath. The fabric on her blouse lifts, falls. "I'm the same way."

"You are?"

The blouse stops moving. "It's not easy to walk around the planet with a gap between you and everyone else, is it?"

Claire swallows. Her pulse is thumping at a pace that would murder a less-fit individual. "No. It's not."

"But how long am I supposed to live like that?" Sister Hilary shakes her head, exasperated.

"Well ..."

"Am I supposed to keep the padding for my sake? For other people's sake? What's the point of any of it?"

Claire steadies her voice, her nerve. She presses her hand into Hilary's. "You were protecting yourself. There's nothing wrong with that."

"Maybe. Or maybe it's the same as death." Sister Hilary shifts her weight over her feet. Her torso sways out, then back toward Claire. "The other night, in the car, when you told me you were gay, it disappeared. All that space. It was just you and me and no more *stuff*. That's why I left. I couldn't take it. I always wondered how it would feel to be with another person without any barriers and there it was and I couldn't stand it."

"You're doing okay right now."

Sister Hilary sighs, stares at Claire. "And how about you? How are you doing?"

"Oh." Claire flicks her thumb off the microphone and rests it on the button of Sister Hilary's blouse. "I feel like I'm about twelve."

"Yeah, me too."

"Really?"

"Yeah."

Claire gears up for a speech. About the rightness or wrongness of all the things that could happen. About all the thoughts she's had but kept to herself. About the breath-removing wonder of standing face to face with the person who's lived inside of you for so long that it's like you've been turned inside out and are now gazing at your own imagination. These ideas and a million others crowd Claire's mind, but they disintegrate before they make it past her throat. In the absence of words, she tries something else. The only thing. She kisses her.

It's exactly like she imagined it. That's the strangest part. Claire is gentle, extremely gentle, letting their lips touch, nerve on nerve, then pulling back, waiting, before trying again. The only thing that's different, the only detail that didn't make it into Claire's frequent previews, is the power with which Sister Hilary kisses her back. What in fantasies was an initial terseness, a slow unraveling of desire, is in real life an exact matching. Skin and pulse and lips. Claire lifting her hand from Hilary's and sliding it behind her shoulders, easing Hilary's

156

weightless torso into her own. Groans and murmurs that seem to emanate from neither one of them, or both.

When the interruption happens—a rap on the door, cautious at first, then louder—Claire can't pull herself away. Sister Hilary can't either, not at first. When she does, with a snap, palms against Claire's stomach to push herself back, she looks as though she has just received either marvelous or horrible news. A birth or a death, either one irreparable.

"Is anything wrong?"

"No," Claire says, realizing only after the word has left her that Sister Hilary was addressing the still-closed door.

"The contractor's here." The voice through the door is deep and muffled. "He said you had an appointment."

"I forgot." Sister Hilary's face is pink, blushed. Claire can see herself there, can see the part Hilary took with her when she pulled away.

The door speaks again. "Should I tell him to come back later?"

"No." Sister Hilary sneaks a hand back over to Claire, traces the skin on Claire's arm from elbow to wrist. "Tell him I'm coming. Tell him I didn't forget." She opens her mouth as if to say something else, but she doesn't. She plucks the microphone off her blouse and steps back, then away. Then out the door, closing it behind her.

Claire finds herself unable to move. Finally, after a few thwarted attempts, she picks up her feet and allows them to guide her to the chair under the cross by the window. Once there, she crumbles onto the seat and gazes upward.

She needs to be alone with Jesus.

True Story

She was supposed to meet Max for coffee before the meeting but begged off, citing fatigue and video-production woes. Better than incapacitation due to post-kiss-with-Sister-Hilary aftershocks. Claire has a feeling Max wouldn't take too kindly to that particular excuse.

The hallway outside the Point Firth Library annex is clogged with the usual pre-meeting smoke and she wanders through it, greeting puffing bodies along the way.

"Yo, Bob. Are those some extra pounds I'm looking at, or did you just get back from playing Santa at the Mall?"

"Wait till you're my age, Claire. You'll see."

"Jerry. Rode by you at the golf course the other day. Looked like you were doing some damage."

"Only to my pride, girl. Only to my pride."

"What's the word, Hank? Is your wife feeling better?"

"Much. Thanks for asking."

Max is already inside, a self-imposed quarantine from the nicotine appreciation society. He is resplendent in an earth-toned version of himself, loam-hued pants topped with a browny beige shirt. He's sitting alone and Claire can tell, by the twitching activity in his ankles and fingers, that he's jonesing for a smoke.

She plops onto the folding chair beside him. "You could just give in, you know. I'd still love you."

"Sure you would. You could soak in superiority next to your addiction-riddled sponsor."

"Come on now." She jabs a leg of loam. "You know my superiority's already been established. Why prolong the agony?"

"Speaking of which, I got you tickets to my play. Opening night is in two weeks."

Yet another of the seemingly endless number of things Claire didn't know about Max is his history on the stage. A double major in college, it turns out, along with a current and chunky part in a local production, bequeathed to him when the previous inhabitant of the role (a friend of his mother's) died unexpectedly of a cerebral hemorrhage.

"You said tickets. You know there's nothing plural about me these days." Claire closes her mouth, sealing in the lie. Hilary's taste, a glaze of cinnamon and secrecy, balances on the back of her tongue.

"The other ticket is for Sister Hilary. She said she wants to go."

"She told you that?"

"No. She told the Pope, and he told me. Of course she told me that."

"Oh." Claire sits inside the intersection of curiosity and censorship. "Then it must be true."

"Please," Max says, "don't put me through another minute of this. Can't we just stop pretending that I don't know you're madly in love with her?"

"With who?"

"Stop it."

Claire melts into her chair. She can't tell him. Can she? His disapproval would ruin it. Maybe the kiss was wrong, it was probably wrong, but doesn't she deserve to enjoy the wrongness a little longer?

"We're friends," she says. "That's all."

"Claire, really. Isn't it time you trust me just a wee bit? I know you've got your reasons for protecting that vault of secrets you've got locked away there, but this Hilary thing isn't something to hide. Besides, I already know."

159

Claire gulps. "You do?"

Max laughs. "I'm your fairy godmother, remember? I know everything."

Claire leans away, limiting his view. "Well," she says. "Maybe you're right. I do like her. But it's crazy. And I already know what you'll say."

Max clasps his hands over his knees. He looks like a child at an amusement park, all glee and anticipation. "Which is ..."

"Which is that I couldn't have picked a less likely object of romantic interest. Unless I had homed in on, say, your mother."

Max chuckles. "Your grasp of the absurd is formidable, my friend."

"And that I'm just setting myself up for a huge disappointment." Claire lowers her voice into the Max range, striving to simulate his tonal flair. "I'd be better off trying to make a life with Shelly—or even, yes even, trying to go straight—than to make a play for a woman so firmly ensconced in the Way of the Catholic. Though what I really need to do is get my head screwed on straight enough, as it were, to see *myself* more clearly. Then, and only then, will I start to make choices more in line with my true, God-given nature."

"Why am I here?" Max looks around. "Is there a reason?"

"But wait," she tugs on the sleeve of his cream-colored shirt to prevent his arms from flailing about, "wait. There's more to it than that." She stops. Can she do this? Can she tell him just enough to get it sorted out in her own mind? She wraps her resolve inside her like a knot, a fortress. Of course she can.

"At first I thought it was just my sidelined libido," she says. "Raring to get back in the game. You know, projecting all my crap and madness onto whoever happened to stand in front of me. But it's not just me, Max." Claire realizes she's still holding onto his shirt. She lets go. "It's her too. It's both of us. She *gets* it. Everything. I've never known someone who has so many pockets I can go into—not just the attraction, but all the other stuff too—and she's there. Every time." The knot inside her yawns, widens. "She's so amazing. So smart and funny and sensitive about all the stuff that really matters. And she likes me. You know, like, *likes* me. She ... I ..."

"Oh, Lord. Don't tell me."

"What?"

"Buttercup. It's worse than I thought, isn't it? You didn't. Did you?"

The words flee from Claire's lips. "It was just a kiss. At least, I think that's all it was. It wasn't ... I mean, it's never really been like this before. So intense like this. I think maybe—"

"I take it back. You do need me. Desperately." Max fixes his posture into that of a school marm—tall, rigid, ready for battle. "We'll continue this conversation after the meeting."

"What do you mean, after—" she stops, interrupted by the warmth and weight of the bodies behind and in front of her. "Whoah. I didn't even notice them come in."

"You'd notice a lot more if you could keep your head out of your pants." The school marm sighs, slaps a withering glance at his wayward charge. "But hush up already. It's starting."

It's the day before Christmas, another fact that had escaped Claire's notice. For a special Christmas Eve treat, Red from Concord, a boisterous fellow semi-famous on the meeting circuit for his tales of transformation from gutter-dwelling drunk to man steeped in salvation, is the speaker for tonight. Claire has never heard him speak—has only heard Max's reverent recaps and was always a bit skeptical anyone could be *that* good—but she soon discovers that everything Max ever said about him is true. Her amorous adventures fade from sight as Red shares his story: of a life so wasted and broken it redefines "bottom"; of an intervening grace so pressing and alive that its presence in the room, as he talks, is almost edible. Even after he has finished and others have started to share, Claire is still chewing, then swallowing, his words.

161

A bap on her shin brings her back.

"Hunh?" She flinches.

Max points and Claire follows the trail of his finger to its natural end. The forehead. The facetiousness. The fine-tuned condescension. Sister Frances speaks.

"It's been a little over four months since my last drink," she says, hands folding and refolding on her wool-lined lap. "My sponsor tells me I need to start sharing more in meetings, and I tell her I will. Though being perpetually in the future, 'will' cuts me some slack, you see."

The room laughs. Sister Frances smiles. Claire commits to a double cross—arms and legs both—in an effort to protect herself.

"But it's not funny, in the end. Why I'm here. I've been able to restrain myself so far, but today I find I'm compelled to speak." Sister Frances' hands settle in her lap. "Most of you in the room don't know this, but I'm a nun. People outside these walls might not understand, but I suspect everyone in here knows that this disease can find you no matter where you hide. In my case, it was under the cloth, deep in academia. I thought no one would find me there. But someone did." She gulps, her chin listing in reaction to the pressure on her neck.

"I'd been drinking for years by then. Ever so slowly escalating to the point where everything in my life was completely organized around my next drink. Even God got pushed farther and farther away until any notions of faith or blessing were only so many cracks in the floor. I thought maybe He'd given up. I knew I had."

Sister Frances' head tips forward. She seems to be corralling a giant force, elusive and undefined. "It was a fellow faculty member who noticed first, my co-chair in the Religious Studies department. William. He was ten years my junior, a brilliant scholar and a truly remarkable human being. He knew something was wrong. He was the first person to drill even a dent of reason into my addict's brain. Unfortunately, that wasn't the only trespass. I let in his words because I had let *him* in.

"Alcohol, you see, had compromised my boundaries to the point where I had begun to think of him as more than a colleague. He was married, I was a Sister—where's the sense in that?" Her eyes flip from face to face as if taking a poll. "He told me he was in love with me, he wanted to leave his wife, he couldn't see a life without me. It wasn't exactly a surprise—I felt the same way—but somehow, seeing how reckless I'd become, it helped me. I took a leave from the university and came back up here, to our motherhouse in Oakland. I told our president I was in trouble and she put me in a treatment facility. You'd be amazed how many Catholics I encountered there. It was hell. So to speak."

Another laugh from the crowd. Sister Frances blushes in its wake.

"I've been doing a meeting a day ever since," she says. "But quietly. Waiting. For what, I can't tell you. Or maybe I can. Maybe I was waiting to realize that, even though I've tried, I can't compare out. I need to be here just as much as every one of you. No better, no worse, no holier, no less wretched. Just here." She pats the seat of her chair, a metallic plap. "And I am very very very," she smiles, "very glad to be here. Thank you for listening."

The meeting moves on, packed with more stories, more lives wrecked, then rearranged. Claire can't hear any of it. She's too busy making nice with Sister Frances in her head, apologizing—or is she the object of apology?—for the intractable structure through which they had been attempting to communicate when really, all along, it was only a measly fence, traversing a field of so much common ground.

The end of the meeting finds the group standing, holding hands—Claire and Max included, Sister Frances across the room—reciting the serenity prayer and reminding each

163

other to "Keep coming back, it works if you work it." It is somewhere inside the envelope of this send-off that Claire fires her first signal over to Sister Frances, a flash of "Thank you" meshed with "Is there more to say?" The answer, when it comes—through a pair of blinking, dead-end pupils—is *No.* Is *Not on your life.*

Give It Away

Claire is in pursuit of treasure—an old gift about to become new. A thorough, soda-propelled inspection of her hovel, however, delivered nothing and now, having strained mightily against the ever-expanding parameters of her search area, she has collapsed into their borders (what else could she do? she had no choice) and given in—her feet skimming damp land, racing across the back yard—to the always-unctuous notion of an expedition to the Big House.

It's still early; this is to her advantage. No one will be up yet. Only Tex who, as she sneaks into the kitchen through the back door (unlocked, as always), heralds her arrival with a sloppy grin and the lift of a spatula full of scrambled eggs. Around the corner, in the living room, Claire spies a pair of bare feet dangling off the end of the sofa. Kitty. Someone else—Donna most likely, Claire won't ask—is bundled on the floor next to her under the Cinderella blanket that Kitty gave Claire for her eighth birthday. Sinatra lies between them, snoring soundly. The whole house smells like burnt toast.

"Happy New Year. We missed you last night," Tex says, motioning for her to join him in the kitchen. His favorite T-shirt ("Property of the Oakland Raiders") hangs off his hunched and lumpy shoulders and a pair of lowriding jeans shows off his absolute lack of ass. "Did you do anything fun?"

Claire thinks it over. Let's see—does bringing herself off to the thought of Sister Hilary wearing nothing but black leather boots and a nun cap count as "fun"?

"No," she says.

Tex laughs. "I guess you missed the fire trucks."

"Fire trucks?" Claire checks the kitchen for signs of foul play, but aside from the handle of what looks *way* too much like a sawed-off shotgun poking out from among the stacks of yellow newspapers and boxes of empties and plates and bowls and cups and saucers full of half-eaten, almost-eaten, forgot-to-be-eaten food, the kitchen looks exactly the same as last time she was here.

Tex, who had been patiently waiting for Claire to finish her perusal, points back toward the living room. "In there. Kitty and Donna were cracking up about something, we didn't know what. Then me and Kenny and Angela—we was all in here, playing cards—we look in there, and that candle doohickey your mom got Donna for Christmas, it had caught on fire. Not just that, but it was lickin' the table too. Those two broads thought it was the funniest thing they'd ever seen. Like it was a goddamned bonfire. Me and Angie put it out pretty good, till it caught on the rug and started up one of them chairs. Walt was watching the whole thing and he went and called the fire department. Says they taught him how, in kindergarten."

"Hmm," Claire says. She peers deeper into the living room. The charred remains of the TV table, along with a scorched rug and blackened chair, have been stashed off into the corner next to the old La-Z-Boy recliner. The recliner, also abandoned, was rendered thus the day Bunny and Walt decided to use the chair as a diving board for the plastic kiddie pool they lugged in from the garage and filled with pitchers of water from the kitchen sink.

"Kitty never was too good with fire," Claire says.

"She misses you. She was talking about it last night. How y'all used to hang out a few years back. Watch TV, shoot the shit." Tex pries a clod of eggs out of the saucepan and slaps them onto a neon-pink plate the size of a serving platter. He is,

166

Claire realizes, still a little stoned. Not too much, just skating down the last shards of a fat, wasted evening.

"Want some?" he says. Egg steam curls off the plate and into his pale, patchy beard.

"No thanks."

"She was saying how you'd yak all night about nothing, how she'd tell you stories from when she was a kid." Tex props his plate on top of the saucepan, chops his eggs into bite-size pieces with his fork. "And you told her all kinds of shit she never heard before, about all the wild stuff you did when you was little."

"We were tanked, Tex."

He nods, cheeks puffed with eggs. "I know."

"There wasn't a day went by back then that I wasn't shit-faced. It's the only time in my whole life me and Kitty ever got along and we were barely there, either of us. How messed up is that?"

"Yeah, maybe." He squints. "You can't say it didn't happen, though."

"No, I can't." Claire looks for a place to sit down. The kitchen table is her only option, but it's piled high with clothes and newspapers and too far away from Tex who, in spite of his hazy nudging, is undeniably comforting right now. "I'm not saying it wasn't fun," she says. "It was. It was a blast. But it's not like that anymore. You know that. I'm not going to start drinking again so I can bond with my mother."

"You don't have to be shit-faced," he says, "to bond with your mother."

"Right. And she didn't need a match to start that fire." Claire turns from Tex and his egg fest. "Have you seen the Russian doll? The one grandma gave me for Christmas a few years ago?"

"I thought you hated that thing."

"Not hate. It wasn't hate, exactly. More like I didn't under-stand it. I think I understand it now."

167

"What do you mean?" Tex picks up his platter and transfers another heap of eggs onto its shiny pink crust. "Like it's got some sorta special mojo? Tap it three times, and you can fly? Like that?"

"Yeah," Claire says. "Something like that."

"Where's my mom?" Walt, sleepy and disorganized in a pair of Power Rangers pajamas, plods into the kitchen. He approaches Claire automatically, like there are magnets involved, and butts his head against her stomach. "Do you know where she is?"

"Umm." Claire thinks to circle her arms around her nephew's back, perpetuating his impulse, but she can't. Her body feels clumsy and unused, a vapid charm.

"She's still sleeping." Tex ruffles Walt with his paw, completing what Claire can't. "You don't want to bug her right now. Come have some breakfast. You want cereal?"

Walt peers up at Claire. "Do we have Power Rangers cereal?"

Tex pads over to the cupboard, rummages inside. "I don't think they *make* Power Rangers cereal, bucko."

"Do too." Walt springs off Claire and rushes over to the counter. He pulls the sawed-off shotgun—a toy, after all—out from under a pile of potato chips and commences to whap it against the sink.

"Cheerios," Claire says, eyeing the box in Tex's hand. "Cheerios is the official Power Ranger's cereal. I saw it on TV."

"On TV?" Walt turns toward Claire. He studies her with equal parts suspicion and blind trust.

"Sure," she says. "You saw that too, didn't you Tex?"

"Oh yeah," Tex says, pouring the blond oats into a just-rinsed bowl. "A bunch of times."

Claire fingers the face of Christ. Or maybe it's not Christ—maybe it's someone else. It's a saint of some sort, she knows that much, and inside him is another saint, and inside him another. When she first received this gift from Kitty's mother a few years ago, she chalked it up to an excess of religious fervor: the old woman's Catholicism bleeding onto her then-unbelieving granddaughter. Wooden, pear-shaped Christians sheltering each other in a series of ever-smaller believers. Who on earth needed those? Certainly not Claire. Certainly not, she thought, anyone.

But here she stands, positioning the doll on Sister Hilary's desk as if she is performing major surgery. As if she has snipped the veins and arteries from her most central organ and is returning it, humble and unadorned, to the only place it can survive.

She hasn't seen Sister Hilary all week, locked as they are inside the dead frame between Christmas and New Year's. The Center had a big shindig for Christmas—presents for the kids, food for the homeless—but since then the place has been thrumming at a low idle and Sister Hilary has slipped inside its quiet drone, nowhere to be found.

This will bring her back, Claire thinks. For sure. She rubs the doll's belly for luck (though that's Buddha not Christ, but they're like cousins, those two) and says a quick prayer.

"Thank you," she says.

Limelight

"Max is worried he'll forget all his lines." Claire folds her program in half. "He called me right before we left. He said he's remembering everyone else's, but not his own. He thinks he's going to deteriorate into a heavily made-up echo with fake hair and bushy eyebrows."

"What did you say?" Sister Hilary is running her palms up and down the lap portion of her black cotton skirt. She's been milking this gesture for the past five minutes.

"I told him to make stuff up if he starts forgetting. He's good at that. The whole thing is pretty corny anyway, according to him. It would probably just make it better."

Sister Hilary laughs, though it sounds more like liquid nerves than a laugh. She checks her watch, trading her thigh-polishing maneuver for a watch-winding, watch-checking, watch-twirling one. "They're late. It should have started fifteen minutes ago."

"It's Max, I bet. Freaking out backstage. We could be here a while." Claire folds her program in half for the sixth or seventh time, fortifying the fat little rectangle in her hand.

Everything about this evening so far has been awkward. It started with the drive over, side by side in silence so thick they were choking on it. Their arrival at the theater wasn't much better; Sister Hilary caught Claire staring at her four times in the ticket line alone. Given that this is the first time they've spent together since It happened, Claire was sure there would be at least some mention, some acknowledgement of the fact that their lips and arms and interests were—for a moment, anyway—one. But honesty appears to have been removed from the menu tonight. Denial is knocking everything else off the plate.

Sister Hilary yawns and her jaw makes a faint popping sound. "What else did Max tell you about the play?"

"Nothing. Just that it's corny. Did you look at your program?"

"They're running out, remember? We're sharing." Sister Hilary gazes at Claire's lap, at the scrap of paper stuffed inside her fist. "Worried it might escape?"

"Oh, no." Claire relaxes her grip and the program buds open. "Not much chance of that, is there? Here." She tosses the wad into Sister Hilary's lap, then changes her mind and snatches it back, saying "Sorry," saying "That was stupid," unfolding the paper until there's nothing left to unfold, until it's just a program with letters stamped in black ink, letters that clearly elucidate what Claire had thus far failed to notice.

Her jaw tumbles open and, unlike Sister Hilary's, makes no popping sound but merely hangs there like a sloth.

"What's the matter?" Sister Hilary says. "You look like you're about to be sick."

"Nothing," Claire says. "It's just—I know the person who wrote this. She's a—she's the wife of one of my professors. We … She … There's a—" She stops, nipping the warm pool of her lower lip. "I know her."

"I can see that." Sister Hilary leans back, but it's like she's only inches away, breath parting the hairs on the skin enveloping Claire's cheeks. "Are you sure you're all right? You don't look all right."

"I'm—" Claire flips the program pages in search of something to make it all go away. There's an ad for a local cleaners, maybe that will do it. *Here's an affair*, she'll say. *Here's a past catastrophe clashing with my future. Can you fix this?*

The house lights dim (Claire makes sure of this by raising her head and shaking it several times to confirm that this is an outside phenomenon and not the prelude to a faint), and she hunkers down, eyes awake. Sister Hilary's presence beside her is a distraction at first, but this swiftly fades inside the voltage of the activity on stage.

The play is a hoot. Max neglected to mention this. He was right about the corniness, but it's corny in an elemental way: a farce with its feelings attached. Claire, knowing Rita, understands that not a word is uttered, not a gesture or grimace exposed, without its opposite, complementary word and gesture and grimace buried beneath it like a crime.

The plot, involving a sinister professor (inhabited by Max with an unrestrained glee that has Claire reconsidering the wisdom of being left alone with him), wriggles around and through itself with such dexterity she can hardly keep her head upright. The evil genius, it seems, has a penchant for students of the female persuasion and uses his stature and sleaziness to boink them every chance he gets. That is, until his wife finds out and conspires a revenge so brutal and meticulous that no one is left standing. So to speak. It's not until the show is almost over (in one act, Rita's specialty) that Claire starts to realize the plot is not so much twisting as twisted, that the wind squeezed out of her with each new line of dialogue has more to do with the cool truth of recognition than the play's inherent wisdom. She begins to harbor the horrible notion, a kernel at first, then sprouting inside her like weeds, that this whole thing—Max's "accidental" casting, Claire's attendance here tonight—is one big screeching setup. Though the paranoia upon which this thought is based, Claire notes, is outstripped only by the self-centeredness that brought it to bear in the first place. Hers and Rita's both.

"So in that final scene," the lights are up at last and Sister Hilary is stretching her elbows over her arm rests, "were we supposed to think those extraterrestrials were real or just a figment of Professor Feeley's imagination?"

Claire gnaws on the edge of the program. "They were real."

"Ah." Sister Hilary stands. Her jittery rhythm seems to have disappeared. She is solid, all of a piece. "We should go find Max. Before he takes his makeup off. I want to see that awful wig up close."

"I don't know if we're allowed back there. We're probably not. I think it's just an actors-only thing." Claire bites down. The program tastes like smoke and fingers.

"Don't be ridiculous. Of course we're allowed back there. Max asked us to come find him." Sister Hilary's foot lurches forward, crashing into Claire's. (By mistake? On purpose? Both?) "We're going. Come on."

Sister Hilary's blouse is tucked into her tighter-than-usual skirt in such a way that, when she walks, the intersection of blouse and skirt wafts in and out like an apology. Claire keeps her focus on this interchange of fabric—no lower, no higher—and wonders, as she trots behind Sister Hilary in quest of disaster, how their just-completed verbal exchange might translate into the bedroom. Then pinches herself for indulging such a thought.

"Darlings. You came." Max is mingling backstage with a small clump of cast members that does not include Rita. While his costume on stage made him appear evil and debonair, up close he looks more like an over-the-hill clown. "You have to tell me what you thought. And I'll know if you're lying, so don't even try."

"You were wonderful." Sister Hilary clasps Max's arm and permits him to smear her cheek with whatever it is he's got on his lips. "The play itself was a bit strange, but you held it all together. Down to that last scene with the space ship and the massacre, even then. See?" She raises a finger. "I told the truth."

Max grabs Sister Hilary's other arm, shaping the two of them into a human square. "I would expect nothing less from you, Sister Hilary. Nothing less."

"It's me he'd expect the fibbing from. Right, Max?" Claire's words bust apart the square. She gives Max a hug. "I loved it, though. You *and* the play. You didn't tell me—"

"Max, you have groupies. I told you this would happen. We'll have to start screening who we allow backstage."

The newcomer is attired exclusively in gold, the wardrobe choice of the Gods. Her hair, straight and black and unbearably glossy, descends from her scalp and drives past her shoulders with searing satisfaction. Her face—hot, cold, full of itself—appears to be unsure which countenance to display and, as a result, is shifting back and forth between amused condescension and thinly veiled alarm with such speed that an entirely new expression is being birthed between them.

"Rita, meet Claire and Sister Hilary. They loved it."

Sister Hilary shakes a gold-fingernailed hand. Claire does nothing. Her kneecaps are like bombsites, barren and splattered with once-noble intentions. She's still standing, just without the aid of her knees.

"Claire said she knows you," Sister Hilary says.

The Gold One grins. "She did, did she?"

"She does?" Max perks up, as though this is good news.

"From before," Claire says. Her tongue is chapped and swollen. "It was a long time ago. We're not really ... It was a long time ago."

"Sister Hilary." Rita's grin slides into a leer. "You must be Claire's latest."

"Rita—"

"Latest what?"

"Leave her alone, Rita," Claire sputters in place. "She has nothing to do with this."

"Nothing to do with what?" Rita's arms arc in feigned ignorance. "I'm sure I don't—"

"Oh dear," Max says, "there's Esther. Claire," he tugs at her arm, "come meet my mother."

"No." Claire yanks back, hard enough to reset the infrastructure of her knees. "I mean—Sister Hilary should come

174

too. She needs to meet your mother just as much as I do."

"I've already met his mother," Sister Hilary says, her voice both bruised and innocent. "I'll catch up in a minute."

"But—"

"Hurry up." Max clutches Claire again. "Before she starts cataloguing my charms to the first potentially gay man she meets. Come on. It'll just take a second."

"Mmmph," Claire manages, then submits to being shuttled across the room and dropped at the awning of one Mrs. Esther Kamminsky for a jovial exchange of handshakes and greetings.

"Well I'll be damned," Esther inspects Claire with an inspired display of clucking and head-waving, "if you don't look almost exactly like Bert. You could be his daughter. Or his little brother." She reaches forward and plies Claire's face with a gentle tweak.

"I guess." Claire fights the blush blooming from the portion of just-pinched cheek.

"You're obviously a woman, of course. Though you do look an awful lot like a boy. But I suspect," the clucking and head-waving commence again in earnest, "that this is what you're going for. Am I right?"

Esther Kamminsky is so far removed from Max's description of her that she might as well be someone else's mother. She is a good deal taller than the old-lady-short popular in most comparable models. Indeed, she seems to wear her body like an afterthought, a remnant casually acquired in order to make this appearance here tonight, but one that could be disposed of later without an ounce of compunction. She is a revelation, this woman—a person who, it seems to Claire, has material-ized this very moment to sand bumps into cinder, to mitigate the sting of—

"Max. I'm sorry, I don't mean to be rude, but do you understand who that is over there? Rita? *My* Rita?"

Max adjusts his wig. "But that one was older. And married. This one is—"

"Over fifty. And married to my ex-professor.

"But she doesn't look—"

"She is."

"And she never mentioned—"

"She wouldn't. She's an independent contractor, Rita. She probably kept Jack away so she'd have a better chance of scoring some fresh catch. Sorry," Claire bows her head into the warmth and beam of Max's mother, "it really is excellent to meet you. I just need to get back over there before something terrible happens."

"Say hello to Sister Hilary for me, won't you? We had a marvelous dinner the other night. Such a fascinating woman. She paints, you know."

"Mmmph." Claire is assessing the damage. Rita is laughing with a vigor most folks are unable to attain without the aid of snorted or otherwise ingested substances. Though Rita, Claire knows, needs nothing of the sort. Just the tussle and lift of hearts seized and smashed to the shape of her fierce and exacting will. Not a problem, really, if you don't mind the stench of revenge. Not that Claire doesn't deserve it. But still.

She takes a few steps toward the unholy alliance and immediately affects the outcome. Rita spies the oncoming interruption and flits off to embrace a particularly young, particularly male member of the cast. Sister Hilary stands alone in her wake like a corpse.

"Sister Hilary," Claire says, the words immediately evaporating off her tongue. She usually calls her nothing at all, rather than this.

Sister Hilary blinks. "We need to leave. Now."

Her driving, remarkably, improves with the strain. Sister Hilary takes her turns like a pro, bypassing potholes with the verve and acumen of a city maintenance worker. Yet it's not until they are parked (in front of Claire's house, at a rakish angle) that she attempts to add speech to her newly elevated skills.

"So that woman tonight. You and she were—"

"Yes." Claire stares out the passenger-side window. Unlike the other night, when she was confined by greenery, tonight she is unencumbered. Free to go.

"And you and Shelly, what about that? Were you with her as well?"

"Yes. But that was a long time ago. Well, mostly a long time ago. We tried something recently, but it didn't work out. You can probably guess why."

"No I can't, Claire. No, I can't." Sister Hilary is pecking at the car keys hanging off the ignition. The sound splinters the air around it.

"Sure you can." Claire swallows. "It's not like I take this lightly, you know. I used to, that's true. Like with Shelly, and Rita. But how it is with you, it's nothing like that. It's serious. Everything. Sometimes I'm scared I'm not paying enough attention—to you, to how it is when we're together—that I'm losing parts of it already. Because it's too good. Or something. Max told me it would be different when I was sober, but I didn't expect this. I didn't think anyone like you would ever—"

"What are you doing?" Sister Hilary stops with the keys. Her face is blunt, contracted. "I can't do this, Claire. I can't sit here with you and talk like this. Do you know how absurd that is? How ridiculous it is that I let things unravel to this extent? I don't think you understand. I think you're missing some basic—"

Sister Hilary grinds her keys into the ignition and the Oldsmobile howls in response. She continues to speak but is no longer audible above the churn of the engine, the blare and blend of fuel and initiative spurred on by a foot that pounds the gas again and again. Every so often, a phrase pokes through, words like "wrong" and "sense" and "respectability," but mostly the vowels and their supporting structures melt into the heat of the surrounding clatter, disappearing inside its justified roar.

Free

"Have you seen—"

"I told you already, I haven't seen her today. I don't think she's coming in."

Claire hooks her fingers behind her back. Is "Fuck you" a proper rejoinder to the secretary of a Catholic social service agency? She doesn't think it is. "Thanks," she says.

She slips out of the office and into the hallway. Steel-rimmed windows line the path to the Rec Room and Claire pauses to contemplate their message. The windowpanes are puckered and obscure so no one can see out. The light through the glass, the way it shoots through the windows and into the hallway like a yelp, causes Claire to stumble, then drop onto the bench behind her. She pinches her eyes closed and instead of opening them afterward, like she should, leaves them blanketed under fatigue-thin lids.

She should have slept. She should have forced herself to lie flat and allowed her subconscious to undertake the impossible task of processing the annihilation of last night, but she couldn't. Staying awake all night seemed like the best approach, the strategy most likely—from her crazed, sleep-starved stand-point—to bring Sister Hilary back.

It didn't work. Indeed, all it brought was fizzled nerves and hallucinations of nuns and priests prancing across her ceiling. Finally, somewhere past morning and heading toward noon, Claire realized that the only way to bring Sister Hilary back was to go to her. And so she did. Or tried to do. No matter that

178

all she has so far is absence; surrendering to Sister Hilary's categorical cut-off is simply not an option.

Claire rises from the bench, ignoring the freaky windows, and strolls down the hall toward the Rec Room. She'll wait there. A solid plan, this. It's almost three-thirty, and in half an hour the after-school program will start. Sister Hilary will have to arrive for that; she'll have to walk through the door and say "hello" to Claire and let the mess and jive of last night float off into the distance. They can both be there, to wave it bye-bye.

The Rec Room is empty and Claire makes a bogus check of her equipment. She's not editing yet, still has a couple more interviews to snare and some footage at the homeless shelter to garner, but she makes a pass anyway, affirming the existence of machines that, when last activated, were powered into motion by her own hands—her will, her motivation. The upcoming editing process will be useful, Claire thinks; it will plant her to a spot where good can grow. Where she, by her daily presence, can effect changes in the formerly obdurate others with whom she will surely come into contact.

The door blows open and a brittle swish accompanies the creak of hinges.

"Sister Frances. How nice to see you." Claire hits Record on the VCR. There's no tape inside, so nothing happens. "I was trying to find Sister Hilary. Do you know where she might be?"

"Yes." Sister Frances drags a cardboard box out from under the largest of the tables and begins picking catechisms out of its innards. "Of course I know where she is."

"Is it somewhere you can tell me?" Claire jabs Stop. "She's not secretly working for the Mafia, is she? Because if she is, I'm gonna have to seriously rethink my presence here."

"Sister Hilary has gone to our motherhouse in Oakland for a few days. Not that it's any of your business." An exceptionally eager catechism escapes from Sister Frances' clutches and

179

lands on the table with a *bapph*. She nudges it forward, closer to the others. "As for your presence here, you're on the right track. Sister Hilary has requested you finish the remainder of your movie away from the Center. That is to say, nowhere near the Center."

Claire nods. Her heart wilts inside her chest.

"She said you were almost finished anyway. So it shouldn't be a problem."

"Not a problem," Claire says.

"She said to take any equipment you might need. As long as you're not working here." Sister Frances' face curdles into an expression of sympathy. "I think you'll realize you couldn't have done your best work at the Center anyway. Not with all the noise, the distractions."

"Right." Claire rams her thumb into the opening of the VCR. She scrapes it against the tape plate, which should hurt, but doesn't. "Like you would know anything about editing videos. You who've spent your whole life locked up in a cage are going to tell me, who's always been free, how to live my life. Sure. That makes a lot of sense." She pulls her thumb out of the machine. Now it hurts. Now it feels like a burn, impudent fire like the words out of her mouth.

Sister Frances finishes with her catechisms and whisks aside the empty cardboard box. She props her arms against the table, leaning into them like they're the only support she'll ever need. "From one cage to another, dear, you don't look all that free to me."

Feud

The phone rings, brisk and insistent. Claire can tell right away who it is—the way the tones kick against the high end of the register like tiny divas, vying for attention and a quick pick-up time.

She lets the machine handle it.

"Claire, it's me. Will you *por favor* pick up the goddamned phone? I know you're there. I can smell your breath. You're eating pickles again, aren't you? I can tell. It's the odor of—wait, I want to make sure I get this right ... bitterness. Y-e-e-e-s, that's it. Bitterness and stewing. The kind that sits in your fridge for too long and you just have to throw it away. Because, quite frankly, who needs it? Rancid cucumbers in science-experiment-worthy broth, floating around like Martians, waiting to beam—"

"Pickles last forever, you know that."

"Apparently." Max huffs. "Apparently they last longer than sponsors, who are, as it turns out, completely and totally expendable."

"Max. Don't even start."

"What am I starting? You've been avoiding me for over a week now. I tried to talk to you after last night's meeting, but you scurried off like the revolution was calling."

Claire pulls the receiver off her ear and examines it, as if Max's obliviousness could be viewed inside its batch of holes. Then returns it to her ear. "What do you want me to say? That you were right? That I'm an idiot? That I had no business fooling around with her highness, the God-pledged virgin? Though I probably don't have to tell you a damned thing, Mr. 'I had Sister Hilary over for dinner and forgot—*forgot!*—to mention it to someone who might have been extremely interested in that particular piece of information.'"

"There's a reason for that."

"Not that it matters now anyway. She's refusing to speak to me. She basically kicked me out of the Center. Though I'm still supposed to finish her precious little movie. Like a servant." Claire tightens her grip on the receiver. It would be so easy to cry. If she could.

"Sister Hilary kicked you out? When did she do that? She never mentioned this to me."

"Ah, yes. Well, that was a huge mistake on her part. God forbid she doesn't share every last tidbit of her romantic escapades with her new best friend. You two should start swapping clothes or something. I can just see you in one of those denim skirts. Though they'd probably make your hips look fat."

"She asked me not to tell you."

"About the skirts?"

"Sweetheart. About the dinner. We were talking about her art. Her plan to take it to the president of the order and get permission to start devoting more of her time to her painting. She said she didn't want you to know because she didn't want *anyone* to know. She said she wanted to be quiet about everything until the sanction was there, though I ..."

"Though you what?" Claire scrapes her hand against the top of her scalp. She shaved her head again recently (the day after her run-in with Sister Frances, though the timing, she tells herself, is random and not at all causal), and the prick and burr of chopped hair against her palm is at once soothing and energy-inciting. "You feel bad about getting all confidential with the nun? Like maybe that wasn't such a spiffy idea?"

"Not exactly." Max waits. When he starts again, he sounds

formal and denuded, as though his vocal chords have been starched. "I was concerned about the way she was handling it. That she specifically asked me not to tell you, which I was fine about honoring, but it seemed peculiar, considering the other things you told me about her. About the ... connection between you."

"Yeah, well, thanks to Rita, the connection is shot. Two minutes alone with Hilary, that's all she needed. She's a viper, that woman. I still think the whole thing was rigged—that she pulled you in, pulled me in, so she could slice and dice me after the show. Even the plot, even that was part of the setup—like she was frying me in code. All those lines ... and having *you* say them—I mean, how corroded is that? What kind of person—"

"How many program calls have you been making?" Max makes a sound like a sigh.

"What?"

"I mean, besides going to meetings and ignoring me, what else have you been doing for your sobriety?"

"Max." Claire flips open the Yellow Pages on the table next to the bed. Moving Companies, that's what the page says. The urge to cry, or not cry, returns. She shoves it away. "I haven't been drinking, if that's what you're implying."

"Maybe not, but you're in it. It's just the aftertaste that's different, that's all."

"Nice."

"You know, when they say 'turn it over,' they're not talking pancakes. You don't get to keep it. 'Turn it over' means give it *up*. Give it to God. Where's God in all this, Claire?"

She flips the page again. Musical Instruments—Rentals and Sales. Just what she needs. In the top left corner, there's a man with a tuba, wound inside its brass. "God's all over this, Max. Hadn't you noticed? And speaking of Gods, when did nicotine make it back into the pantheon?"

"Pantheon? What kind of term is that to throw into a

conversation? You've been chewing on the dictionary again, haven't you?"

"Interesting. So you can call me on my crap and sidestep yours. That's fair." The tuba man puffs his cheeks, Claire swears she sees this.

"Okay," Max exhales, fully this time, "you got me. It was the stress of that damned play, my nerves were in a twist. Well, that and ..."

The two of them sit in the silence evoked by Max's lame attempt at withholding.

"You are such a lousy liar," Claire says. "What is it this time? You're thinking of converting, right? From now on, you'll be known as Sister Max."

"It does have a ring to it, doesn't it? But, no. It's business— a little business opportunity that's come my way. A potential art-space-type-thing. In Point Firth, of all places. One of the guys in the play is an artist, and he and a group of his friends are starting their own gallery. Very do-it-yourself. A far cry from the high money '80s, that's for sure. I'm helping them get set up. I do know my galleries." He chuckles. "And you probably don't want to hear this, but it's that ex-friend of yours who got me going again. I'm trying to talk her into showing some of her work, once the gallery's up and going. She's got a few pieces that are just spectacular. Did you ever see any of her paintings?"

The tears start falling before she can stop them. Fat tears, useless tears, dropping down her face. "Nnnn," she says.

"Completely original. And yet steeped in tradition. It's hard to describe. She's playing around with this dual panel, diptych motif: Joseph Cornell meets Stations of the Cross. Or something. There's a facility there with light and rhythm that's outstanding. And she's experimenting with structure and scale in a way that's—it's breathtaking, actually. I've never seen anything quite like it."

Claire is bawling now, eyes squeezed shut in an attempt to

fend off the flow of sorrow heaving through her chest. Though it's no use. It won't stop.

"Claire?"

She tries to talk, but can't. Can only eke out a wet gulp.

"Oh, hon. I'm sorry. I got carried away. I shouldn't have … Are you all right?"

Claire nods. Then shakes her head. Then starts to cry harder, audibly this time.

"That's okay," Max says. "I'm here. I'm right here."

"I'm such a moron." She spits the words through her sobs. "Such a stupid moron."

"Let's not—"

"No, it's true. I am." Claire's crying streams through her throat, her arms, her sense of shame. "That I ever thought— that I ever tried to …"

"Don't hurt yourself, darling. It'll just make it worse."

"But I'm so good at it." She forces a smile, lips dripping with tears. "It's like my specialty."

"Well. Maybe it's time to pick a different area of expertise. Like horseback riding. Or golf. I hear that's very big with your sort."

Claire would laugh but she's too busy crying. It's like a store of upsets—this hidden wound, that subterranean slight—have decided to suddenly make themselves known and trounce all over her body. Where have they been, all these years? So much sadness, so much caved-in grief. It's about Sister Hilary, but not just her.

A field of minutes go by—sobbing, stopping, sobbing again—and Claire lets it run, lets herself expand into a vast background against which Big Tears can have their way, thrashing and roaming against the limits of her skin. Until they're done.

Claire feels like vapor, when this happens. Like all she's good for is crying and now she's not even good for that. She blows her nose with a wad of tissue she finds stashed next to

185

the Yellow Pages and turns her attention back to the receiver pressed against her ear. She feels lightheaded, spent, and vaguely embarrassed.

"I'm sorry," she says.

"For what?"

"For being such an asshole. None of this is your fault. I shouldn't have taken it out on you."

"I'm hard to offend, you know that. Though the line about my hips was pretty harsh. I'll get over it, though."

"I won't." Claire pushes a hand across her face. "I'm sick of being such a jerk. A jerk and a whiner. And a cry baby too, apparently."

"Nothing wrong with that. You can't always be the man, Claire. All that pent-up emotion. Gotta let them babies fly free."

"You make it sound so easy."

"I do." Max shuts up for a minute, presumably an unfiltered one. "I shouldn't have mentioned her art work."

"Max. It's really not your fault. Not at all." She jabs her hip into the corner of the phone table. "I should probably get going."

"Going where?"

"Nowhere. Just here. I have to work on my movie."

"Ah yes," he says. "The movie. How's that going? Banishment notwithstanding."

"It's going all right." This is accurate only in a technical, things-already-accomplished sense. Claire and her productivity have been separated by the exile, buffered from each other by its series of endless, nunless days. "I'm hoping to be done with it in the next few weeks." This is true—the hope part, at least.

"I wish I was there," Max says.

"Why?"

"No reason."

Claire traces the rim of the Yellow Pages with her finger, then slams the book shut. The back cover is home to Gil

Andrews, Bail Bondsman. He's wearing a shirt composed of dark and light blue stripes that make him look, presumably unintentionally, like a prisoner. "So," she says.

"Will you be at the meeting tomorrow morning?"

"Yeah."

"Have coffee with me after?"

"Of course." She waits. "You're the best, Max. Really. I'd be screwed without you."

"I'm not going to touch that." He chuckles. "Keep it simple, sugar pie."

Claire's version of keeping it simple, for now, is to hang up the phone. Then pick up the Yellow Pages, like there's a product or service hidden inside that needs ferreting out, and carry them with her over to the couch, where she collapses under their weight and folds herself onto the corner cushion like an abandoned puppet.

It's all such a wreck. Her body, her past, the search for cohesion and belonging among erratic offers of affection. Will it always be this random? A conveyer belt of options that either fail to satisfy or fail to stay? And what's Claire's responsibility in all this? What is she supposed to do?

She sighs, sinking deeper into the couch. She could chuck it all, that's one option. Float off to film school in the big city—San Francisco or LA, either one—and never look back. The geographical fix. Though she knows it's not that easy. And that there are probably people worth keeping. That there *are* people worth keeping.

But who? Who can she trust with her still-beating heart? Not just romance-wise, but anyway-wise. People-wise. Who's in her life? And what are they doing there? A review, says her mind. Let's review.

1. Max. The man, the legend. Like bones in blood, his essential presence and integrity.

2. Sister Hilary. Woman religious and scaredy-cat. Burdened with baggage. Baggage with crosses.

3. Jack and Rita. The perilous pair. Fated to replay themselves in a ceaseless cycle of Chump and His Mistress. A production in which Claire needs no part.

4. Kitty. The anti-mother. What is she but air? An element that sustains one, in its way, but is essentially ungraspable, ineligible for touch or tangibility.

5. Tex. Stoned and steady. A model not of sobriety but of love. At least of love.

Claire rubs the pads of her fingers along the telephone book's spine, curved inward with age and questing. So it's Max, so far. And Tex. Only them. That's something. But what about the other candidate for the Hall of Heroes? The other person who has managed never to make leaving a permanent condition. The other individual who has always injected a sense of loyalty and faith into Claire's free-floating affectional spectrum. What about her?

Claire sets the phone book on the floor, then kicks it out of reach. She needs to do something about Shelly.

Interest

Two weeks later, she does.

The lag time between inception and manifestation is mostly a matter of approach. Given how they left things, Claire wants to make sure that her first conversation with Shelly post Move Out is peppered with just enough but not too much sentiment and a few well-thought-out and perfectly placed apologies. Only she can't think of any. Everything she comes up with just sounds weak and pathetic—second-string versions of Olympian apologies.

Finally, after being unable to summon either the definitive statement or appropriate emotional stance, Claire submits to the only thing she can think of: an unannounced visit at Shelly's place of employment.

She spots her immediately, sitting at a desk by the window with the view of downtown Bearley. (A few stores, cars driving through.)

"I guess you got that promotion, hunh?" Claire decides to ease into it. She takes a seat in one of the two chairs perched in front of Shelly's desk. Classy numbers, these, with thick maroon padding and business-ready arms. "What's your title now?"

"Assistant Credit Manager." Shelly scrunches her shoulders inside a body that has realigned itself to a new dimension. She's wearing a blouse—not a shirt, but a blouse—with a pointy collar and buttons that are round and to be taken seriously. There's a bracelet around her wrist Claire has never seen before—silver, with a geometric pattern that's probably ancient or from the pyramids or something. Her hair is drawn back in a bun (Claire can't see behind her head to confirm this, but it's probably a bun), and her eyes, without the hair to shield or distract them, seem cleaner than Claire remembers—as if they've been polished, perhaps, or replaced altogether.

"I shouldn't have taken so long to come find you," Claire says. She's wearing her usual T-shirt and jeans and feels like a workman at a rich lady's house. "I should have come sooner."

"A month-and-a-half is a while," Shelly says. "I figured you had taken your vows by now."

"No, not at all. Nothing like that." The muscles in Claire's thighs pinch together, like fright. "That's totally over. I'm really sorry, Shel. Really, really sorry. Like, really. I never should have pulled you into all that. I wasn't even thinking about you, about how I might be hurting you. Or I was, but not enough. Not enough to stop me from screwing everything up. And I did. I screwed up everything with you and everything with Sister Hilary. You were totally right. I shouldn't have messed with any of that."

Shelly adjusts the nameplate in front of her desk (Shelly Flanagan, New Accounts). "I told you."

"You did. You did tell me. And I didn't listen. I should listen more. I should do a lot of things better. I'm trying. I'm trying to not be such a retard."

"Claire."

"See? Like that." Claire fidgets with the chiseled-crystal candy jar next to Shelly's nameplate. "I'm not supposed to say that, am I?"

"No." Shelly tamps down a smile.

"But I wanted to come see you. To tell you I blew it and to say that we've been friends for a long time, and if we're ever *not* friends, I don't want it to be me that makes it happen. I want to stay friends. And not mess it up with sex and all that. Because that never works. And I love you, Shel." Claire lands inside the renovated eyes. "You're a totally excellent person. And I think I should be around to remind you that."

Shelly twirls her bracelet to its other side, where it looks exactly the same. "I'm sorry about trashing your house. It was sorta—I don't know. I was pissed, I guess."

"That's okay." Claire sits up, hands clutching the edge of the desk. "I deserved it. And it was inspired, actually. All my videos, co-mingling with your candy wrappers—like a piece of modern art or something." She stops, skidding into the poorly conceived analogy.

Shelly seems not to notice. "I have a two o'clock," she says.

"A what?"

"An appointment. In three minutes." Shelly nods but it's a strict nod, an Assistant Credit Manager nod. "Maybe we can continue this discussion later."

"Oh. Sure." Claire, the workman, is being dismissed. She feels the rejection like a pile of bricks in her lap: dense, coarse, useless without a structure in which to insert them. "Sure," she says.

"No." Shelly springs from her chair and bursts onto Claire's side of the desk, grabbing her hands and pulling her up so they're both standing there, hands attached, in the middle of the bank. "I'm not blowing you off. I promise. I was going to tell you—you should come by the Pearl on Friday night." She takes a thumb, one of the flat-like-a-saucer ones, and insinuates it into Claire's palm. "Our band has a regular gig there. Fat Earl and the Bedwetters. I sing lead in about half the numbers and background in the rest. We're seriously not bad."

"The Bedwetters, eh?" Claire grins. "That's awesome. I'll have to stop by. I will. I'll bet you're amazing, Shel."

It's funny, Claire thinks. She lets go of the sex stuff with Shelly and then here they are, holding hands in a public arena, looking totally like dykes. But that's probably why it doesn't matter. Because it's not about that.

"So you'll come?"

191

"Sure." Claire nods. At Shelly, but also at the young couple, blond and khaki with blunt haircuts and matching checkered shirts, stationed just inside the radius of the New Accounts airspace.

Shelly sees them too, but instead of acting like she's embarrassed or shy or bolted down at the edges, she holds onto Claire's hands a good five seconds longer than she has to before releasing them, finally, with a slew of words.

"Congratulations on your new mortgage, Ms. McMinn. Me and the staff here at Wells Fargo look forward to fully satisfying any and all of your future household needs."

No one's in the parking lot except a young mom and her kid getting out of one of those high-rise trucks with wheels as tall as a person.

"There you are," the woman says. "I was looking for you."

"Angela?" Claire eases toward the truck. "You look—so. Different."

Claire's sister is drenched in darkness: tight black jeans, a black Led Zeppelin T-shirt, freshly dyed black hair curling in and over on itself, eyes rimmed black like they're leaking dirt. Claire suspects that both the truck and Angela's new look are borrowed from her latest paramour, a drummer in a Bay Area band who, according to Tex, likes to eat live hamsters on stage.

"Claire! Look what I got!"

Bunny, decked out in pink, the vibrant underbelly to her mother's gothic gloom, charges toward Claire like she hasn't seen her in weeks. Which she hasn't.

"It tells time." Bunny lifts her wrist to display a pink plastic Little Mermaid watch. "It came outta the bubblegum machine. It looks like she's under water, see? You wanna give me a piggyback?" She slips her hand, light and airless, into Claire's.

192

"Not right now." Claire swings her arm and, with it, Bunny's tiny hand. "Maybe later, okay?"

Angela pinches her daughter's shoulder, drawing her away from Claire. "Honey, go play in the truck. Mommy needs to talk to Auntie Claire."

Bunny scampers from her mother's grip, runs a figure eight around the two adults. "Don't wanna!"

Angela rolls her eyes, blue inside black. "Damn kids. Look, Claire. You have to talk to mom. You're the only one she'll listen to."

"*Listen* to? That's not how it works with me and Kitty. We're not—"

"Yeah, I know how it is." Angela glances at her daughter, now attempting a handstand with the aid of someone else's Buick. "But here's the thing. She ave-gay alt-Way some eer-bay. And it wasn't just a little. He was, like …"

"He was like what? Unk-dray? Like that?"

"Kinda."

Claire slumps. "Jesus," she says.

"She promised she wouldn't do it again. But you know how she is. And she's the only one I got to help me watch them. Maybe you could tell her about that program thing. Get her interested or something."

"You've got to be kidding. She won't listen to me. She thinks program is a cult—thinks we're all a bunch of freaks and whiners. You should call the cops, Angie, or those child endangerment people. They'll set her straight."

"I'm not calling the cops on my own mother. Jeez." Angela rolls her eyes again, harder this time. "I just asked for a little help, is all. And you gotta start talking cops and welfare people."

Bunny has abandoned her handstand project in favor of whirling herself around and around until she is so dizzy she can no longer remain upright. "Whoa," she says.

"It's not like she hasn't done this before," Claire says.

193

"Kitty's not going to change just because you tell her she's doing something wrong. Remember? With us? How she used to do it with us?"

"She used to do it to you, Claire. To *you*. You were the rowdy one."

Claire has nothing to say to this. She'd forgotten that part.

Bunny, in a puddle beneath them, twists her face around an emerging thought. "Gramma gave Walt beer—that's what you said. Gramma gave Walt beer! Gramma gave Walt beer!" She lifts out of her collapsed state and into a full run, loops inside loops on the gray and wide pavement.

Souvenir

Sister Maria is wearing a sweater the color of wolf's fur. Not that Claire knows what wolf's fur looks like, exactly, but if it were tufted off and made into outerwear, she's pretty sure it would look like what Sister Maria's got on.

They've spent the last two hours in a basement office of the Catholic church in Point Firth. Not the most inspiring of locales, but one that has served its purpose as the launching pad from which Claire has flung herself back into her movie. Seeing Shelly yesterday was enough to jump-start her into action mode; as far as her relationship with the Bearley and Point Firth Community Centers, it needs to be over. This just-completed interview with Sister Maria should give her all the footage she needs to polish off her film in no time.

"Do you know the Calzados?" Sister Maria is leaning back on an old wooden chair that's not a rocking chair but seems to accommodate this motion. "Are there still people by that name around here?"

Claire peers up from her packing job—tapes, camera, microphone, wires. "The Calzados? How do you know them?"

"I grew up here. Didn't I mention that? My mother worked for them—in their kitchen. My father worked in the fields. That's how they met."

"There was a kid in our high school. Chris Calzado." Claire slides a pack of batteries into an exact-sized pouch on the outside of the camera bag. "He went to some fancy private

195

school in Pleasant Hill but got kicked out for drugs or something and had to come slumming in Bearley. Junior year. Do you know him? Chris?"

Sister Maria tips her chair sideways, toward the lusterless filing cabinet next to the wall. She starts to tug on the lower drawer, then changes her mind and sits back up in her chair. "Chris. That's their grandson. Sally's boy. Sally was a few years older than me."

"Were you friends?"

"Oh no. Not friends. My parents were the help. You don't make friends with the children of the help."

"Because Chris was kind of a jerk. Well no, not kind of. He got booted out of our school too. For selling crack or pills or something. I don't know what happened to him after that."

"Hmmm." Sister Maria seems to be finished with this line of discussion. She bends down, all the way this time, and scoops a large brown bag out of the bottom drawer. Oil stains the size of oranges dot its exterior. "How about a chip?"

"Umm," Claire says.

"Don't look at me that way. You're acting like Sister Hilary. You gonna to have one or not?"

Hilary. Claire attempts to remain immune. It's just a name, after all. "Oh, yeah." She swipes her palms across her pants. "Definitely. I was gonna say yes the whole time, really."

Sister Maria holds out the sack with both hands. "I can see that."

Claire takes one to start, wraps her mouth around it. She is flooded with corn and oil and salt, all in exactly the right proportions. "These are fantastic." She snatches a handful, stands munching. "Wow."

Sister Maria pours a hefty pile onto a paper plate and sets the bag between them. "My mother made these."

"Your mother? She's still here?"

"She's had a hard time, since my father passed. I've got

a couple of brothers, but they don't live around here. I've traveled enough for a lifetime. It's nice to be back here, at least for now. Keep an eye on her."

There are two options. Claire can see them both clearly. One involves a few more pleasantries, a few more chips, and a hearty good bye. The other consists of a foot-first jump into a pile of mud that Claire knows well enough to leave alone. Way alone. But she can't. It's the only way to keep Sister Hilary in the room.

"Can I ask you something?" she says.

Sister Maria plucks a runaway chip off the bosom-slope of her sweater. "Depends what it is."

"It's about El Salvador. About how you and Sister Hilary were there. I tried to ask her about it, a bunch of times. But she wouldn't really talk about it."

"Well, no. She wouldn't."

"Why not?"

"Because it was horrible, that's why not." Sister Maria sheds a few shades. "And it's impossible to explain unless you were down there."

"Explain what?"

Sister Maria tries to smile, but it doesn't quite happen. "Do you know anything about what went on down there? About the war?"

"No." Claire swallows. "You should tell me, though. You should."

Sister Maria angles back on her chair. It creaks and pops like ammunition. "You're a persistent child, aren't you?"

"Uh." Claire thinks. "I guess."

"You don't know what you're asking." Sister Maria's head slants forward. Is she praying? Claire's not sure. After a while, her face lifts back into the pocket of space between them.

"Sister Hilary and I went down in '79 to help out," she says. "I'd been doing missionary work in Chile for about seven years before that, so I thought I knew what to expect. But it

197

was worse than Chile. At least, as far as what we were able to do."

"What do you mean?"

"I mean there were no rules."

"Rules?"

Sister Maria's chin pulls in, tightens. "You don't understand. Like I said."

"I'm sorry." Claire sags backward, attempting to appear innocuous. "So it was bad? Like, chaotic or something?"

"Yes." Sister Maria waits. "Chaotic doesn't even begin to describe it. The U.S. had already gotten involved at that point, supporting the government of El Salvador. But they were on the wrong side. The crazy side. There were these men—death squads, they called them. The Salvadorian military claimed they had nothing to do with them, but they did. These squads, along with the army, they were killing everyone—not just the rebels fighting against them, but anyone suspected of being sympathetic to the rebels' cause. And the U.S. government was supporting this. That's what I mean by no rules. Teachers, labor leaders, church workers. They were all being killed. It was unimaginable. Sister Hilary and I had no idea what we were getting ourselves into. No idea."

Sister Maria stops. Her voice kicks against itself. "Are you sure you want to hear this?"

Claire tries to shake her head, but it comes out a nod.

Sister Maria sighs, pushes her breath back into the room. "We were doing band-aid work, mostly. Trying to keep the civilians out of harm's way. Bringing them to the Sanctuary in San Salvador, where they would be safe. Or safer. The army, the squads, they would take people from the shelters too. Shoot them in the street. I'll never forget the first time I saw something like that. There was a puddle in the road outside the church. They had taken the body away and all that was left was a pool of blood in the dirt. Full of flies, I remember that." She shudders. "You can't know."

Claire is still holding a bundle of chips in her hand. She searches for somewhere to put them, but there isn't anywhere. Just back in the bag and she can't do that. Sister Maria was right; Claire can barely take this in. She hears the words—blood and dirt and government-sponsored death squads—but they slog in her mind like stones in soup; they won't be allowed to stay.

"The president of our order encouraged Sister Hilary and me to leave the country, but we couldn't. There was just so much to do, so many people who needed our help. And even in the middle of all that death, I could still feel God. He wanted me there, I knew that." Sister Maria's feet clap against the floor—stomp and step, an insider's dance. "But then. Well, then the Maryknoll Sisters were murdered. And Idalia right before them. We had no choice after that. Our president ordered us to come home."

"Idalia?" It was a rough string of syllables, coming from Sister Maria. Eee-*da*-lee-ah. Claire offers them back to her.

"Idalia was a college student there, a friend of Sister Hilary's. She was a friend of mine too, but she and Sister Hilary were especially close. They would talk and talk—about the war, the role of religion in the struggles of the people. Idalia was involved in the Church, the whole movement there—helping with the refugees, speaking out against the government. She was probably a target for longer than we realized, but when she and Sister Hilary became close, it was too much of a threat, I guess. The death squads started posting notices on Idalia's door, said they'd kill her if she didn't shut up. Idalia would laugh at that. She'd say it was just another rumor. Though I know it scared her. How could that not scare you?" Sister Maria's eyes rise up, glints of light.

"They shot her one night, in the courtyard of the village where we were staying. Just like that. It was so easy, then. To die." Sister Maria is perspiring—her face, her neck. She dabs her brow with the sleeve of her sweater and a piece remains behind, pale gray thread against a forehead the color of a new field.

"Sister Hilary had a real hard time after that. It was like every corpse we saw was Idalia's. Every arm or leg or piece of skin. We were burying bodies by then, you see. There were just so many of them, and no one would touch them for fear of being killed. So we, the church folks, we'd take them and we'd bury them. The Maryknolls—Ida, Maura, Dorothy, Jean—they were doing the same. And they killed them too."

Sister Maria's hand is in a fist. Her other one surrounds it loosely like an oversized coat, trying to soothe or protect or whatever it's doing, but being entirely unable. "I bet you're sorry," she says, "you ever asked me about this."

"No," Claire lies. "It's okay."

Sister Maria's hands come to a rest. She regards them wistfully. "It took the both of us a long time to recover when we got back. Though it was a lot harder on Sister Hilary than on me. She didn't smile for two years. Not once. She was only a few years in the order at that point, too young to be faced with such destruction, to have her faith tried to such a degree. She thought of leaving us, you know. She never told me that, but I know she thought about it." She groans, a muffled rumble.

"A couple years after we got back, we started working with the refugees in Oakland. Somehow that shifted it all around. Didn't take away the parts that were still wrong, but it helped Sister Hilary—and me, too—find our way back to what was right. What *is* right. It's like the only solution to such horror is to let God in. Not push Him away and wail against the world. Though sometimes you have to do that too, I suppose. You know?"

Claire nods. She supposes she does.

Sister Maria folds the brown paper sack into a tight lump and shoves it back inside the filing cabinet. She sits with her palms relaxed and facing downward and her spine straight and mighty against her chair. Claire peeks over at her every now and then, but mostly she zips and unzips the side flap of her camera bag and tries to either forget or remember everything she's just heard.

After five minutes have gone by, maybe twenty, Sister Maria clears her throat.

"You and Sister Hilary had a falling out a few weeks ago. I don't know the details, but I understand you're no longer speaking."

"Yeah." Claire plucks a videotape out of the bag, stashes it back inside. Just for something to do.

"I'm sorry about that. Though I suspect it couldn't be helped." Sister Maria sits unmoving, a sphinx on sand. "It's funny," she says, "but Sister Hilary has always understood me, better than most. Not in El Salvador, but here in the U.S.— being brown in an order of white women. She always *got* that, more than she should have. Being outnumbered. Different. I never knew why that was. But now I think I do." Her eyelashes wave like tiny hands. "Not that it changes anything."

Claire plugs the zipper's end into the depression at the bottom of the bag. So it's a package deal, is it? And instead of Hawaii, she's being treated to the terrors of war: the bombs and blows and shrieks of damage in a place she doesn't know; the wounded psyches of two women who witnessed it. Is it possible, Claire wonders, that Sister Maria has invented these horrors? Constructed the madness to prove a point? No. Probably not. It's probably more like a puzzle Claire was never expected to solve. The trauma, the tendencies, the absolute impossibility of her having a part in any of it. Of course. She sees this now. Sister Maria is offering her a gift—a ruined gift, but a gift nonetheless. One that Claire, adjacent and wild, can stuff in her pocket and run with. She'll take it as far as it goes.

The camera bag is unnaturally light against her shoulder— a burdenless burden, free of taint or consequence. The tripod in one hand is the same, as is the tape case in the other.

"No," she says. "It doesn't change a thing."

Creep

Early February in Bearley is a showcase for spring. It's the same thing every year. The calendar flips over to that second page, and suddenly the rain and the cold and the hard edge of damp simply forget to show up for a few days. Sometimes even a week.

The first Saturday in February, the day Claire breaks the ban, is one of these days. There are clouds in the sky, sure, but they're of the light and frothy variety: divinely arranged props that elucidate the blue of the sky in the same way a favorite shirt calls forth a stripe of red in the cheek, or marbled-green in the eye. Birds *(were they gone? now they're back!)* dominate the skies like victory, mouths full of chirps and oxygen. Magnolia trees, those harborers of buoyant blooms as yet in bud form, stand as patient observers to the gaiety, busting ranks only every so often to reveal their mirth in solitary splashes of color and creation.

Claire notices none of this. Or rather she does, but in a peripheral way, the way a child on a scooter notices the rotation of wheels under her feet. She was told at the Bearley Community Center that Sister Hilary was in Point Firth, told in Point Firth that Sister Hilary was at home. And now, not five paces from the front porch of the old bungalow house on Flagg Street, Claire gets the distinct sensation that no one is here.

The doorbell appears to be out of order—repeated ramming of the thing brings only a dent in her thumb—and a series of knocks on the front door brings a similar response. Nothing.

Claire plunks down on an old wicker chair on the front porch. What to do? In the old days, she would have broken into the house, taken the vacancy as an opportunity to peruse the lives and possessions of the not-at-home. But she's evolved since then. She's no longer the girl with the untethered impulses. Her impulses now are aimed toward the good, even if they don't always land there. If only her current impulse—to see Sister Hilary—wasn't so strong. Then she could pick herself out of this chair and sail away with the assurance of a search complete. But her body has other plans. It's not going anywhere.

Claire sighs. She's been having a rough week. Sister Maria's Tour of Hell, her crash course in Central American atrocities has unleashed in Claire a tour of her own. It starts at night, when she shuts her eyes. There, her dreams are populated by hatchets and flies, rivers of feces and piles of rotting Bibles. She's looking for Sister Hilary but never manages to find her, finds only men in search of missing limbs, children in search of missing fathers. When she tires of this, or it tires of her, Claire ends her quest the way she always does—at least for the last week's worth of alwayses. She slips into a bar—in Bearley, in El Salvador, she's never sure which—and drinks herself drunk. It's an unmitigated departure from her previous nocturnal benders, the breeze and benevolence of those. These are raw and ragged, reeking of the damage from which she has escaped—or maybe caused. And still no Sister Hilary; still no guarantee that a corpse with her face is not among the vats of dead and abused littering the towns and streets outside the bar.

Claire has discussed this with Max (after a period of not discussing it with him): the dreams, their source, her interview with Sister Maria. And while this helps a little, softens the sting of lugging such horror alone, it has yet to persuade her that Sister Hilary has made it through this horrendous past—now Claire's present—alive. Max insists that he's seen her, shared a few tête-à-têtes about art, but these claims are about as soothing as Claire's dreams: specters in a wasteland.

She stands. Given that the house is off-limits, maybe a peek in the backyard will alleviate her anxiety. She remembers Sister Hilary mentioning a garden-like area behind the house. Maybe she's there now, sunning herself. It is, after all, the beginning of spring. Who wouldn't want to revel in its majesty?

The driveway is mostly gravel and broken asphalt, a combination that makes Claire's legs feel even more tentative than they already are. The surface segues into concrete at the lip of the garage, spitting her into the tiny backyard next to it. A yard that looks nothing like Sister Hilary's description. Where's the beauty? Where's the inspired landscape promised by Claire's favorite woman religious? Other than a crop of emaciated bamboo at the back of a small stretch of land with more dandelions than grass, this yard offers nothing. Nothing decent, nothing worthwhile.

Claire wanders into the center of the dandelion patch and yanks one of the weeds from its stem. Then tosses it back on the ground. Instead of making her angry at Sister Hilary, the ratty yard only makes Claire miss her more. Only Sister Hilary would describe this yard as beautiful. Only Sister Hilary would gaze upon the shabby and incomplete and proclaim them cherished. Like she did Claire.

The ground is still wet from months of rain and Claire's feet, as she lifts them in a stroll back toward the driveway, make obscene sucking noises. It's in spite of these noises—or through them, somehow—that she hears the other thing. The voice. The back of the house has a screened-in porch whose door has been left or has been blown open (open!) and it seems to come from there. *Claire.* Is that what it said? Or was it *here. Over here.* Claire steers her feet toward the porch. (Though this is crazy! What is she thinking? She's thinking that a porch is not a house. That exploring some-one's porch, especially one that has called your name, is nothing like breaking into someone's home and rifling through their photo albums and medicine cabinets. That stepping onto a porch is the same thing she did five minutes ago, on the other side of the house.)

The back steps acknowledge her arrival with the requisite creaks and bounces. Proof, perhaps, that she has made the right choice by treading upon them. The screened-in porch, as she eases inside it, is bigger than it looks from the outside. There's a table and set of chairs at one end and at the other, the back door to the house. A door that just happens to be ever so slightly open.

Inside the house, a radio is playing, a sound that must have morphed into the signal that entered Claire's ears as a beacon. So someone is home. Someone who couldn't hear the knock on the front door over the blare of the radio and someone who has yet to welcome Claire inside.

"Hello?"

The door opens onto a hallway, dark and shady and offering nothing but inscrutability.

"Hello? Anyone home?"

Claire stands at the entryway, neither inside nor not. It was so easy, as a kid. Walk inside, slink around, sneak out before you got caught. It's different now—Claire's feet and blood frozen in the thick spill of good intentions—but the compulsion is the same. Like an itch. Or a scab that begs to be picked.

"Sister Hilary?" Claire takes a step into the hallway. Just one. "Is that you?"

What if Claire had left a piece of equipment in Sister Maria's possession after their interview? One that she had to have back. That would be reason to stop by, reason to enter the seemingly occupied house.

"Hellooooo?" Claire permits herself two more steps, long

205

generous ones that leave her standing across from another partially opened door, this one to a bedroom. Her breath catches in her throat, hangs there like a small bird. This is bad. For whatever reason, she knows exactly whose room this is. Perhaps her intrinsic psychic powers have finally kicked in; perhaps little Lupe's gifts have been instantaneously transmitted from afar. Either way, the only sane option is to scram, bolt off the premises quickly enough to save everyone from harm. So what if she loses this opportunity before her? This possibly ordained, probably meant-to-be chance that has been tossed in her path.

She tells herself this: she could just take a peek. Seeing what is almost certainly Sister Hilary's room would, Claire's pretty sure, achieve what seven days of talking and not drinking have failed to provide. They would convince her of the safety and vibrancy of a person who, once this safety and vibrancy is assured, would (Claire is pretty sure of this as well) float to the back of her consciousness like an extra piece of plankton in a vast and ever-expanding sea. So simple, this.

Claire nods. Her skin shrinks around her bones, pinches closer to the black impulse within. It's horrible, it's lame, it's unforgivable. But she'll do it. The voices telling her not to have simply lost their strength.

"Hello?" She tries it again as she enters the bedroom. The answer returns in the form of absence. No sound, no refusal, nothing to stop her.

It's a large room, though its size is immediately over-shadowed by its condition, which is an unabashed disaster. Claire didn't realize it was possible for a grown person's room to be such a mess. The bed is not only unmade, it's mostly mattress. What little sheet remains is crimped up next to the wall like it's blocking a draft. Clothes are everywhere—on the floor, under the bed, draped over what might be a desk, streaming out of what seems to be a closet. The two windows opposite the door—the old-fashioned kind, with ropes to make them go up and down—are open, and their sills, thick and heavy and full of purpose, are jammed with the cups and plates and bowls of previous feasts. It's like the pickup window at a diner, only backward.

Claire, pulse flying but still functional, steps around a hefty pile of towels and heads toward another almost-all-the-way-closed door on the left side of the room, next to the bed. It's not a closet, she can tell: there's light and importance peering out of this place and she knows that any sign, any confirmation of Sister Hilary's aliveness will most likely be found here.

Swiftly, as though the speed of her actions will save her from detection, Claire nudges the door forward. It opens with a jolt, revealing what would technically be called a bathroom, though it appears not to be used for this purpose. The room is crammed with papers and boxes and canvases and exudes an aura of both focus and frenzy. It's the last place on the planet Claire needs to be. She knows this. But it's too late for that. She steps inside.

The paintings are familiar—similar in style and subject to the drawing Claire keeps stored under the couch, pressed between the pages of *The World Atlas* and *The Joy of Lesbian Sex*—and they throng the room like old friends, though more dramatic and articulate than she remembers these friends to be. The boxes are new—a dozen or so wooden crates standing on end with paint beaming off their sides like something's for sale. The figures on the boxes—both inside the crates and out, on doorlike front panels—appear more earth-bound than the regular canvases. Indeed, some of them are people she knows: Enrique, Lupe, kids from the Center. There are other folks too, ones she doesn't recognize, with deep brown skin and not nearly as happy—people from Oakland, maybe. Or somewhere else.

Forgetting to be cautious, forgetting everything but the steady pull of the room itself, Claire investigates another box, this one off in the corner next to a stash of paint supplies.

The door on this one is closed, with a character on the outside who looks like a priest. He's wearing eyeglasses, black and sturdy rims on top and clear glass on the bottom, and all the other components of his face—ears and nose and chin and forehead—are larger than one would expect them to be, as if they've been infused with extra molecules. Perhaps I will meet this man, Claire thinks, though it's a strange notion to have about a two-dimensional being rendered in oil, who may or may not be a real person. There's a hook on the door, unlike the others, and she picks it open.

It's death, inside. At first she can't tell what it is—just blotches of black and a red that's scabbed. But then she sees the pieces—the legs and elbows and parts of faces—jutting out of the mound of mess and darkness. She can almost hear the accompanying screams, the guns and the whoops and the smell like a stain. Evil, her mind says. It says it again, then again. Then again. Finally, she shuts the slender wooden door to make it stop.

The rest of the room is still in order, which seems wrong. Though now that the glasses-man and his sideways hook are back in place, Claire understands that all the other pictures are unharmed precisely because this one door is closed, that her humble act of confinement is responsible for a level of preservation she can only guess at.

The radio, which until this moment had lapsed to a murmur at the edges of Claire's ears, blasts back into her awareness. It's time to go; no one needs to tell her this. Except her shoes are like just-licked stamps, adhering to the floor and impeding her progress. *Stay*, they say. *Stay just a little while longer.*

She pauses at the bathtub, next to the door. There are paintings even here, under the tub. She jabs at the shallow pile with her toe and it seeps out onto the floor. A particularly feisty canvas, face down, its wooden frame and stapled edges almost sinister in their blocking capabilities, crashes out of its underground hideaway and into the next section of her getaway path.

There's a photograph tucked into one corner of the painting, wedged under the back of the frame. Claire picks up the painting and tries to pull it free, but it won't budge. It's a snapshot of a small woman with a large smile, standing in front of a mud-colored building. Her eyes are both bright and heavy and she knows things Claire doesn't—Claire can tell by her stance, the weight of her stare. She must be that woman, the one Sister Maria mentioned. The one who died. And the painting on the other side of Claire's grip must be her. Idalia.

Claire whispers the name to herself a few times before taking a look. She tries to prepare herself—will this be like the priest painting? or worse?—but finds that any courage, any specks of bravery have been siphoned off by the actions that brought her here. No matter. She has the sense that this painting is what she came here for, that seeing it will allow her to, somehow, let Sister Hilary go. She flips the canvas over and props it against the tub.

The features are so familiar that Claire doesn't get it, at first. That it's a picture of her. It would be a self-portrait, if she painted. But she doesn't. Claire's legs shift in such a way that all of her weight is suddenly beneath her ankles. She allows this to crumple her, dropping her on the floor in front of the painting.

It's not Idalia. It's Claire. But how did this happen? How did she come to find herself—twice—in a place she shouldn't be?

Claire brushes the surface of the portrait, the lumps and ruts of dried paint cool beneath her fingers. Her hair is longer, like it was a few weeks back before she clipped it free. She's sitting on something—a box or a ledge or a smoke-blue square with a thin cover pad that's orange and soft—and she's facing the camera. Or no, not a camera—this is a painting. She's facing the painter.

Did she pose for this? Claire wonders. It's like she did. The painting looks so much like her. Or rather, it looks like how she would want to be. If she were beautiful and unconcerned and had never done anything wrong in her entire life. She saw a movie once, about a guy and a painting that held all his bad stuff, soaked it into blips of design and depravity. Perhaps this is the opposite. Perhaps this picture is giving Claire free reign to be human, to toil and scrape and manufacture the thousands of useless injuries the girl in the painting would never dream of.

The front door of the house opens and shuts in quick succession. A bump and a bang. Then silence. Claire thinks to stand in response to the arrival but she can't; she's cemented to the floor. The only things that move are her eyes, which scurry off the painting and over to the door. She understands. A noose is around the house, fresh and corded and inching toward her neck. The grating sound she hears, like fingernails on raw meat, is probably just her heart, sharp and pounding, but could also be the cord, creeping closer.

It's only one person, Claire can tell by the lack of conversation and the uneven, unselfconscious rhythm of the steps as they dribble around rooms at the front of the house. She turns back to the painting, which, now that she takes a second look, is stuffed with flatness. There's no perspective in it at all; the shapes and angles are wedged against the front of the thing like they're glued to it. Like they're escaping a world behind them.

"So?" Claire whispers. "You got me into this. Now what?"

Flat Claire stretches, stifles a flat yawn. "You don't even know who it is. Maybe it's Sister Hilary. Maybe she'd love to see you. Look," she flicks a finger inside the painting, inside herself, "how much she loves to see you."

The meandering steps start meandering down the hall.

"Shit," Claire says.

Flat Claire smirks. "You shouldn't swear," she says.

"Yeah? Well you shouldn't represent yourself as such a

fucking angel. That's the whole problem here. You and your fucking—"

The steps are right outside the hallway now, then inside the bedroom.

"Sister Hilary?" A tired, gravely voice, the voice of Sister Frances, pokes around the muddle and hum of the outside bedroom. "Is that you?"

Claire and Flat Claire remain motionless, breathless, out of any ideas except concealment. It almost works, too; Sister Frances sounds like she's about to turn and go, when Claire, in a gesture of three-dimensional stupidity, is smacked with the impulse to clear her throat. And not just a polite tap, no, but an all-out straightening of the vocal chords and anything hindering their path to free expression. It's impressive, in its way.

The bathroom door opens and Sister Frances steps inside. "Claire? What are you … What's … What's going on here?"

"Uh. I had to, uh … I had to stop by?"

Claire's not sure who says this, her or the painting.

"I can see that." Sister Frances takes a step back, as if this will enhance her information-gathering abilities. "I stepped out for a minute, but I knew someone was here. You left your bike out front."

She's not her usual self, Sister Frances. Instead of wool, she's sheltered in casual clothes of the cotton variety. The items, a pair of "ladies" jeans with stitched-on front pockets and an impossibly pale yellow blouse, harbor a trace of— Claire sniffs twice to confirm this—lilac perfume.

"Does Sister Hilary know you're here?" Sister Frances scoots forward once again, closer to Claire and the bathtub and the flat dry portrait. "I'm assuming you wouldn't have entered the house without some sort of permission."

"No. I mean, yes. I stopped by because I left one of my microphones with Sister Maria after our interview. I had to …" Claire allows the lie to crawl out of her mouth and

211

onto the floor. But only one. "It was Sister Hilary. I was trying to find her. I've been having these dreams …" Her eyes sting with the thought. "They're stupid, though. You don't have to tell me. I know she doesn't want to have anything to do with me."

Sister Frances addresses the painting. "We both know that's not true."

"Do we?" Claire eyes her alter ego. "Then why did she say that? Why did she tell you to say that? For me to stay away."

Sister Frances sighs and shuffles in place, her new-but-used jeans swishing against themselves. "Do you really want to hear it out of my mouth? Wouldn't that just ruin it? Or was I supposed to pretend I didn't know?"

Claire curls her knuckles into the linoleum. "No."

"Because Sister Hilary and I have a history. Anything she's tried to hide from me, she can't. That's how it is with us. With all of us here. Not that you would understand. As I said before—"

"Try me."

"Claire. You don't—"

"No, really. You're right. I don't get any of this. Her. Me. None of it. So anything you have to say, I want to hear it. Like you said, you know her better than me."

Sister Frances plucks a box of brushes and paint-spotted rags off the toilet and sets it on the ground next to Claire. The radio, which up until now had been spouting off traffic and the weather, switches over to music. Classical.

"All right," she says. "But you aren't going to like it. I can tell you that already."

Claire laughs. "I don't like most things. And of the things I do like, Sister Hilary's way up there. Way up. So if it's about her, I'll like it. Even if it's bad."

"If you say so." Sister Frances' forehead gleams in the light snaking in from the outer bedroom. "But let me talk, will you? Don't interrupt. Can you do that?"

"Mmm." Claire maneuvers her neck in such a way that the outcome, while looking very much like a nod, evokes enough left-to-right-and-back-again action that she could, if she needed to, later claim it as a shake.

Sister Frances shoos away the paint box with her heel and settles down on the edge of the tub. "The first time I met Sister Hilary was at a seminar in ethics at Holy Names. She approached me afterwards to challenge my interpretation of the text we were studying. She told me I'd got it wrong. That my assumptions were based on faulty logic. As if it were ever about logic." She smiles.

"That was the beginning of her conversion. Though she didn't know it. Every time we talked after that, I could see her struggle. Trying to fight it, then giving in. Then fighting some more. And she was a little bit in love with me, I'll tell you that right now. Not that we ever talked about it, because we didn't, but I could tell. It was in her attention, her affection. Though it was ultimately God she was falling for. Not me. She realized that, after a while. We all do."

Sister Frances bends forward and lifts a fresh tube of paint from the box at her feet. She opens the cap and spreads a stripe of orange, fat and glossy like a slug, on the top of her finger.

"Celibacy is misunderstood as repression," she says. "It's not. To be celibate you have to embrace your sexual feelings. All of them. You need to bring them to Spirit, through prayer, and transform them in the service of Christ. The energy doesn't leave, it just gets rechanneled. Most people fail to understand that. Even those within the Church. Though failure's not an excuse to give up." She squishes her paint finger into the palm of her opposite hand, crushing the brash orange into her unbroken skin.

"Sister Hilary knows that. So do I. For you, it's different. Sexual attraction, to someone like you, means acting on it. Expressing it physically. But we've chosen something else.

213

Something that's difficult, but vital." Sister Frances grabs a rag, redistributes the paint from hand to cloth. "We can't give in to that. We can't give in to the intensity of a sexual bond with another human being. It drains energy away from our community. I've seen it happen. It doesn't work."

Claire's mouth opens without her consent. "But that doesn't make sense. If everything's in God, if God is in everything, then isn't God in sex? Isn't it all just part of—"

"What did I say?" Sister Frances' eyes are sharp, almost hurt.

"I'm sorry. I'm just trying to—"

"You're really not Catholic, are you? I told you this would be lost on you."

"But it's not. I mean, I—"

"Our strength as an organization comes from our bond with each other. Not in special relationships, but in a commitment to our community. And service to others through Christ and the Church. It's a choice, Claire. You can't argue with a choice." Sister Frances' face flattens, sets. "It would be pointless, you see. You can't change any of the outcomes here."

Claire stuns her gaze to look only at the painting, at Flat Claire, who has been listening to this entire speech along with her benefactor. The oscillating blues and pallid oranges of her canvas home are shining with a muted enthusiasm that belies their power. The colors are so pure, so sure of themselves. It's as if the light within has been tamped down only to hold back the shock that would undoubtedly arise if they were allowed to reveal themselves fully.

"It's just hard to let go," Claire says. She turns away from the portrait and back to Sister Frances. "I can't pretend that I haven't been affected, or that I haven't affected her. And it's making me ... I don't know. I can't—"

"But that's the problem. Your effect on her." Years of authority and chastisement surge through Sister Frances'

214

voice. "You've disturbed her. It's not healthy. And I think you know that."

Claire traps a stray paintbrush under her foot. "I told you. I don't know anything."

Sister Frances sighs. As she does so, her face seems to fall apart. What's left is raw and red, like a stain.

"Perhaps you've misunderstood me," she says. She stands. "I'm not sharing these things with you to amplify your misguided affair. Or so you can use them as bait for your little fishing excursion. Quite the opposite. I'm trying to get rid of you, Claire. To get rid of everything you stand for, everything you've dragged into our lives with your impudent, arrogant—"

"Whoah. Watch it. You don't want to piss off the Big Guy, do you?" Claire shoves off the linoleum and trucks out of the room, leaving her two-dimensional counterpart to fend for herself.

Before she gets in the door, even, Claire hears the answering machine blaring across the room.

"Claire, it's Sister Hilary. We need to talk."

A low thrill clips Claire's stomach. Two words remain. *Need. Talk.*

She doesn't stop, doesn't ponder, doesn't wait to package up her feelings with ribbons and a bow, one of the fancy kinds meant to convince the receiver that you have really gone out of your way to get them a nifty gift. She just goes. All the way off her property and across the six-and-a-half blocks between herself and one twisted-up woman religious.

Sister Hilary is in her office when Claire arrives, but they won't be talking there, she makes this clear. She shuttles the two of them outside, onto a bench next to the portables under a cool wide tree with pinecones the size of cats' heads.

"You broke into the house, apparently. Into my studio."

Sister Hilary crams a chunk of hair behind her ear. It's shorter than it was a month ago and seems, though Claire knows this is impossible, thicker. Her face is changed as well. Shades of gray float beneath skin that has clearly been deprived of rest. Or at least respite.

"I was wrong," Claire says. "Totally wrong. I wasn't thinking. I was just trying to find you. I wanted to know you were all right."

"As if that has *anything* to do with you. Or justifies invading my personal space. If I'd known how troubled you are, or how unstable, I wouldn't have ..." Sister Hilary presses a palm against her forehead, as though checking for fever. "I would have done a lot of things differently, let's just say that."

Claire tries to respond without shaking. "You wouldn't have painted such an incredible painting of such a crummy person. For example."

"We're not doing this, Claire. I'm not discussing this with you."

"But I saw it."

"That's not the point."

"Not the point." Claire is sitting on the front tip of a pinecone. She snatches it from underneath her thigh and flings it onto the grass. "What is the point, exactly? I've lost it."

Sister Hilary sighs. "The point is we never should have ..."

"What?" Claire chokes out the words. "You can say it, you know. It's not like saying it will make it happen again."

"And what about Rita? Will saying her name give you the same immunity?"

"Rita." Claire's vision scrambles out of place. "No."

"Not that you need it," Sister Hilary says. Her face is stiff and strangely calm. "Rita, Shelly. The fact that they're married isn't even pause for concern, is it? You just roll along, bedding them left and right. You probably couldn't wait to add me to your little collection. Though I suspect 'little' is probably the wrong word. I suspect I can probably count myself among scads of conquests."

"No. Not even close. You're—"

"That's what this is to you, isn't it? A game?" Small stars of pink dab Sister Hilary's cheeks. "One where you make all the rules? One where no one else even knows it's a game? In some circles, your lecherous antics are probably praised. Though Rita wasn't quite so generous." The pink stars flush red. "I guess it must be fun. For people like you. Bragging about the women, racking up the numbers."

"Oh yeah." Claire hangs her head in exasperation. "Like that's all this was. Like my scorecard wasn't complete without a nun."

"Woman rel—"

"I know what it's called. What did Rita say, anyway?"

Sister Hilary fiddles with her lower lip, grinding it in and out against the top one. "She said the two of you made a movie. If you could call it that. She told me *all* about it."

"Jeez." Claire winces. "Listen—"

"What? What do I need to listen to? You telling me that you were drunk? That you made a mistake? That you dressed up like a pirate and filmed yourself having sex with a married woman in the bed she shares with her husband because *you just weren't thinking*? How much of this do you think I really need to hear?"

"Oh God." Claire remembers the eye patch. She found it stashed in the bottom of her backpack and wondered where in the hell it had come from. "I am such a moron."

"See, now," Sister Hilary swings a black-panted leg into the air in front of them, "*that* I agree with."

It's still a sunny, show-offy day, the sky drenched with incoming spring. Loquacious birds and a distant mower shoot into the space made vacant by Sister Hilary's wrath and Claire's stupidity, by her unwillingness to defend the indefensible. She thinks about Max, how he'll crack up over the pirate. It's the only thing that keeps her from puking.

"Sister Maria probably told you," she says at last. "About our interview."

Sister Hilary nods. Her jawbone jabs against her skin.

"That's really the reason I came to find you. I know I wasn't supposed to, and I knew you were upset about what happened with us, but Sister Maria told me such awful stuff. It was like you got all wrapped around inside of it. You couldn't find your way out, at least not in my head you couldn't. I had to come find you, just to get you out of there."

"You shouldn't have."

"But I did. I did, see, and I found all that stuff. All those paintings. The ones about the war. The one with all the bodies. It was just like Sister Maria said it was. Like everything was gone and there was just screaming. I don't know how you did that. How you got through that."

Sister Hilary's chin has lost its stability. She wipes it off with her hand. "It's debatable," she says. "Whether I did or not."

Claire stays quiet. Her mind is back with the glasses-man and the horrible painting inside the box.

After a few more minutes have been absorbed between them, Sister Hilary pulls the fabric of her pants tight around her knee. Then tugs it back. "We lost a lot of people," she says.

"Oh?" Claire tries not to breathe.

"They're still inside me, so of course I still feel it." Sister Hilary addresses the pine tree on the other side of the yard. "I thought it would help to put it on canvas. I don't know if it did or not."

Claire imagines touching Sister Hilary's hand, or her face. It would be sad and intractable. Or afraid. But they would feel better, for her having done it. "I wish you didn't have to go through that. I wish none of that had happened."

"But why?" Sister Hilary seizes Claire's gaze for a moment before turning back to the tree. "It did happen. Wrestling over that inevitability is futile. And any residual pain I may have is nothing. At least I'm alive."

Claire's hand, still on her lap, curls like a useless thing. "Sister Maria told me. About your friend."

"Sister Maria told you far too much."

"I'm sorry." Claire waits. She flexes her fingers. The feel of stretched skin bolsters her. "Was that her? The photograph behind the painting?"

Sister Hilary shakes her head. "What is it, I wonder. That makes you so entitled. People. Information. You think it should all be yours, don't you?"

"No."

"Do you consider it? At all? How this grab for experience affects others? That they might be damaged by your intrusion into their lives?"

Claire shuts her eyes, keeps them closed. "I guess they are. Sometimes. I thought things were getting better, but maybe not. You deserve what's good, that's all I know. I wanted … I was thinking that was us." Her eyes slide open. "I still think it is."

"This is precisely it." Sister Hilary hurls her hands into the air. "This is precisely why I can't see you anymore."

"What is? You're the one who called me here."

"Please. Claire." Sister Hilary slopes forward, spine bowed, her feet revving the gravel. "I called you here because I wanted you—I wanted to make clear in your mind what apparently had not been made clear before. At least, judging by your actions earlier today." Her hair falls off her ear but she leaves it, eyes hidden in a plane of brown. "If you understand nothing else, understand that you are not to come to my house, or sneak into my bedroom, or drop by my office when no one is there and leave gifts on my desk. None of these are good ideas. I called you here to make it stop."

Claire lowers her voice, gentles it. "Getting rid of me won't make it stop, you know." She mimics Sister Hilary's tilting motion, but in the opposite direction. Her shoulder blades crunch against the bench's scratchy back. "But I bet you already knew that. I bet you're starting to figure it out."

Sister Hilary spikes her heel into the gravel. A cluster of stones flutter onto the grass. "I never should have let you make that damned movie."

Lover Boy

Viv is scowling through the screen. After four long rings of the buzzer and five blasts of viciously insistent knocking, Shelly's sister has finally come to the door.

"Shelly didn't say nothing about you stopping by."

"Yeah, well, if your phone wasn't disconnected, then maybe I could have called ahead of time and you could have gotten all gussied up in anticipation of my arrival." Claire sneaks a peek through tiny screen squares. Viv is wearing a wound-red bowling shirt belonging originally to someone named Flash. Her once-blond hair has been dyed pond-scum brown, though the roots, gold and naïve, are already attempting their escape through the crown of her skull. "That probably still wouldn't have given you enough time, though."

"Shelly's back with Kenny, you know. So you might as well stick your tail in your mouth and waddle on home. Ain't nothing for you here."

Claire tips toward the screen. The house reeks of matches and hot dogs. "What the hell are you saying? I just saw Shelly a few days ago. At the bank. We were talking about—"

"You were talking bullshit, is all. Like little kids on the playground making up shit about how everything's gonna be. You ought to leave Shelly out of your lame schemes, Claire. She's never been part of any of it. You're just too thick to see it."

"Shut up, Viv."

"You gonna make me?" Viv slams the door open, a flying

smack. Her teeth are gleaming and her pupils are jagged, like they've been lashed. "You gonna haul your sorry wannabe-boy ass on in here and make me?"

Claire is struck by how unchained Viv is. She's like Shelly, but without the societal constraints. She's like Shelly when she's coming. Or making Claire come.

"Let it out, Viv. Free the passion. You're just jealous because I picked Shelly over you. Gotta get all frothy and dangerous so I don't see how bad you want my wannabe-boy ass. Who do you think you're fooling? Sure as hell ain't fooling me."

Claire puffs up, T-shirt flapping at her back, heels digging into the slats of the porch. It's a tired stance, though. Threads of apology spool around her tongue.

"You don't know nothing." Viv clutches the edge of the screen door, as if only this will keep her from pummeling Claire with rage. She holds this pose for a few seconds, then unleashes an expression that completely confounds Claire's already confounded bravado. For there, underneath the ridges of fear masked as anger and insolence, lies a flare of unadulterated desire. Viv unmasked. She tries to bury it by coughing and wiping nonexistent sweat off her brow, but it's too late. They both know it's there.

"I'll go get Shelly," she says. "Don't come in the house."

"Sorry about that." Shelly barges through the door and joins Claire on the steps of the porch. "Viv can never just tell me you're here. She always has to make a production out of it."

Claire taps the ball of Shelly's bare knee as a hello, then the nape of her neck. "Remember that time she caught us in your bedroom?"

"Dude. That was so fucked up. She went on about it for months." Shelly stows her hands inside the pockets of a brand new zip-front sweatshirt. "She never did tell mom, though."

"Viv said you were back with Kenny. She's full of crap, right?"

Shelly's shoulders hunch inside her sweatshirt. "Sorta."

"What?" Claire lurches forward and her bike, which was sunning against the blistered-paint post of Viv's porch, speeds to the ground in a clatter of aluminum and shock. "How could you be back with Kenny? You weren't with him when I saw you last week, were you?"

"We were together at Christmas. You know, *together*. I sorta got lonely. And now I'm sorta ..."

"No."

"Yeah."

"Shelly. What the hell? You didn't use any protection?"

Shelly bops her knees together. "Nope. Freestyle."

"Does he know?"

"No. Not yet. I just found out yesterday."

Yesterday. Claire slaps the wheel of her bicycle tire, makes it spin. Yesterday was Sister Hilary and her pathetic reiteration of the Stay Away order. Yesterday was the fall and rise of Claire's longing for a woman who can only be touched by God. And then today. The weirdness with Viv and now this.

"Are you gonna tell him?"

"Probably, yeah. He's gonna be a daddy. He should know."

"So you're gonna—"

"Yeah. I'm almost twenty-six. It's about time."

"But, Shel ..." The tire is still rolling on air. Claire grabs it, rubber squeaking against her palm. "You know what'll happen if you get back together. You know what he'll do to you. How could you even think about it, after all that crap—I mean, seriously. It was *bad*. Don't you remember?"

"He stopped drinking, Claire." Shelly's eyes are reflecting light like she's crying, but she's not. "He's a lot nicer now. You don't know."

"He's on probation, Shel. Everyone's a lot nicer when

223

they're on probation. Look at your brothers. And besides, he's got a girlfriend, doesn't he? That Rhonda?"

"Yeah, well, I kinda have you, don't I?' Shelly cocks her head toward the sun, which is shining on her like that's its only job.

"No. Not really. Not like that. I thought we decided—"

"We did. I was just messing with you."

"Oh."

"Besides," Shelly bumps Claire's shoulder with her own, "once you go there, you can't take it back. That's kinda what I meant. Like, we'll always be different than regular friends, even if there's no more sweaty times."

"Yeah. That's true." Claire picks a scab of paint off the step underneath her feet. "Anyway. I guess I should just shut up about giving you shit. It's not like I'm any better. I'm still all gone over Sister Hilary. She thinks I'm trash, but I think she's the best. How lame is that?"

Shelly scratches her ear, puts her hand back in her pocket. "So that 'it's all over' crap you said to me last time was a lie?"

"Kinda. Except I really thought it was." Flat Claire flashes on the step beneath Claire's fingers. She winks.

"Cut it out," Claire says.

"I didn't do anything," Shelly says.

"I know." Claire stares into the sun for as long as she can, which is no time at all. "Do you think we'll ever get what we want? Either of us?"

"Don't get weird."

"I'm not." Claire stomps on the paint chip with her foot. It breaks into three pieces, a big one and two tiny ones. "But you should be with someone who thinks you're the bomb. And no offense, Shel, but that's not Kenny. Nothing can make that happen. There's nothing can make that person be him."

Shelly yawns, or pretends to yawn. Her eyes are blunter now, more absorbent. "I'm not saying it's for certain for sure I'm going to get back with him. And I'm not saying he didn't fuck up big time. But he also gave me this." She pats the front pocket of her sweatshirt. "And he is my husband still. That's the part I have to figure out. What to do about the husband part."

"The husband part." Claire coils around the phrase, tries to crack it open by the strength of her resistance around it, but finds herself slack, rubbery. She remembers Shelly and her weenie game, her ability to scan and rank men's egos in relation to their Shelly-imagined private parts. Maybe it's all for sport. Maybe there's nothing she can do about it. Though she knows, even as she thinks this, that it's just a thought, and thoughts can go in all directions. She tries for a different one, a better one.

"A baby," she says. "Wow. I guess we'll both have to stop swearing."

Vampire

"Lord." Max releases the stream of smoke he's been hoarding for ages. "And she might go back to him?"

"She says she doesn't know. She says she's undecided."

Claire and Max are lounging on folding chairs in the lobby of the Green Monkey Gallery, Max's new art space. Given that the grand opening is still weeks away, the only artful aspect of the place so far is the mound of tarps littering the floor with a promise of transforming the Monkey's sidewalk-gray interior into something more compatible with the "fabulous pieces" Max claims will soon grace its currently gutted walls.

"I'm not going to say 'I told you so,'" Max says, "because that would be cruel and malicious and well," his lips suck the life out of what's left of his cigarette, "it wouldn't really help matters, would it?"

"I'm so glad you've got that part of yourself under control. That obnoxious, shit-giving troll-of-a-self you're keeping hidden away there."

"I'm trying." He crushes his cigarette into the folding chair's seat. "I can't help it. I saw this coming. I warned you about Shelly just like I warned you about that person whose name you won't let me mention."

Claire winces. "You take pleasure in this, don't you? You get your jollies by watching my wreck of a life. I never should have told you about the painting. I never should have told you anything."

"Gumdrop," Max swoops Claire's hands into his own and

226

coddles them on his lap, "you *had* to tell me about the painting. The painting is *huge*. The painting is elemental. It's just that," his grip gets tighter, more fierce, "it also points to a larger issue here, one of—how do I say this?"

Claire swipes her hands back. "Oh boy. Here comes the speech."

Max pauses to feign offense, then starts primping in front of the imaginary mirror hanging between himself and Claire. "I'd like to thank the Academy," he says, voice quaking.

"I'll just go." Claire relieves her backpack from footrest duty and slings it across her shoulder. "I can see the door from here. Two seconds, tops. I'm gone."

"No, don't." Max lunges for the pack and shepherds it back to the floor. "I'll be good. I promise."

"No you won't."

"You're right. I won't. But I'll tell you the truth."

"The truth. What? You've been lying to me up till now?"

"Not exactly." Max crosses his legs knee-in-air style, his ankle snug against his thigh. He's barefoot and his toes, thin and interrupted, look like fingers. "Withholding is probably a better word."

Claire blinks. "You're scaring me, Max. What is it?"

"No need to be frightened." He wraps his fingers around his toes. "Though I suppose it couldn't hurt. Perhaps fear is the appropriate—"

"Max. Cough it up. I'm on the back of my seat here."

"Well." He sighs. "Remember when you and you-know-who came to dinner at my place?"

"Yeah." Claire leans in. Max looks embarrassed. She's never seen him so tentative, so tippy in his own skin. "We sat in chairs and ate food. What about it?"

"I noticed something that night I never told you." Max squints like he's assessing twigs in his path, potential hitches. "Chose not to tell you. Probably shouldn't be telling you now. It's why I didn't mention the other dinner, with my mother. So as not to perpetuate this whole *thing*."

"I know about the *thing*, Max. I know it's wrong. You don't have to say it again."

"But what you don't know is what I saw that night." He plucks a cigarette from his pack and parks it between his lips. He doesn't light it and won't—his trick, Claire knows, to keep him from smoking too many.

"I've seen you with Shelly,' he says. "Hell, I've even seen you with Rita. And I've seen how you get when you talk about the others—that pumped-up despair that spills into the sheets and gets confused with love. But when you and this woman showed up, this serious Catholic," he shakes his head one way and his cigarette wags the other, "and believe me, the irony of the situation was not lost on me, but when I saw you two together, it was like you were on the same ride. It reminded me of how it was with Bert—that sort of gliding along next to a companion, someone planted there just for you. You're separate beings in separate skins, but somehow there's another, larger skin that stretches around you, that moves you through it. I'm sorry," he says, "but it's true. I told you I wasn't going to say it."

Claire, who's never been a smoker, considers the consequences of snagging one of Max's cigarettes and toking up. Lifelong nicotine dependence? Chronic halitosis? A slow, ever-encroaching death courtesy of the very thing that makes life worth living?

"Wrrrmp," she says. "Mffrrmrrmp bbbmmtrmm." She waits. "And you're telling me now because ..."

"Because of what else I have to say."

"Oh dear."

"It's just that, Claire, tell me something." Max yanks his lighter out of his pants pocket, then thinks again and puts it away. "What do all the women you've slept with have in common?"

"Uh ... They all pee sitting down?"

"Okay, smarty. What else?"

Claire stares at the messiest, most chaotic paint tarp, as if the answer might be embedded in its flat depths. "Ummm. They were all ..." She scratches her head. "I don't know."

"Well, from what you've told me, and correct me if I'm wrong here, every single woman you've slept with has been a virgin to the Sapphic Seas. Am I right?"

Claire has to think for a moment. Not for long, though. "Whoah," she says. "That's weird. How come I never noticed that before?"

"Because you have me. That's my job, pumpkin. To shed light on these subterranean matters."

"But what does that mean? Is that bad?"

Max shrugs, though it's not a casual shrug. Claire saw him do this once before, when they were talking about Bert. "I'm not saying there's anything wrong with being first in line at the recruiting station, it's the consistency that concerns me. That is to say, perhaps lesbian vampirism isn't ultimately for you. At least, not as an enduring pattern. Perhaps it's indicative of something else, something eluding you, in its way."

"You're losing me, bud."

"Okay. Like, for instance—and this is just a thought ... homophobia. We all have it, you know. Even if we think we've cured it by having too much sex or outing ourselves to everyone we meet doesn't mean it's not there, screwing with us. As it were. And sometimes—again, this is just an idea—it keeps us stuck with the first-timers. It's not even about them, really. It's about not stepping into who we are—all of who we are." Max extends his arms, as if to demonstrate. "It's a tough assignment. But you're a tough broad." He draws a fist back to his chest, pounds it.

"But I'm not—"

"And I know what I just said about your saintly friend totally contradicts what I'm saying now—although not entirely, as I certainly wasn't suggesting that anything else *untoward* should happen between you two—but I've been keeping both of these observations to myself for far too long and the guidance I've been getting is to spill the beans. And so I have. All over my lovely friend Claire."

She shivers.

"Hey, come on. Where's the snappy comeback? I count on you for those." Max unearths his lighter and sparks up a smoke. "You could thank me, at least."

"Thank you, Max," she says.

She stares at his chin, the way the skin stretches around it when he takes a drag off his cigarette, then relaxes back in place when he exhales. It's like they've just been made, both of them: his skin and the fresh crop of hairs poking out from wherever they've been stored to mark the beginnings of a beard; her head and the flock of thoughts—more of these than he has hairs, even—that tumble inside with a velocity that mutes her. She knows he's onto something, but to fully absorb this, or even attempt to let it in, is beyond her current capacities. Twelve Step slogans swing through her mind with a rhythm that comforts and unnerves. *First Things First. Easy Does It. One Day at a Time. Progress, Not Perfection.*

Claire knocks her temple with the heel of her hand. "So what do I do now?" She punches the words through the slogans.

"You do whatever you want, honeybunch. I supply the ingredients, you bake the cake."

She groans, prelude to a covey of complaints about Max and his totally unhelpful advice, but her tirade is cut short by the entrance of someone new. A tall, friendly man carrying a ladder and a store-load of painting equipment.

"Max." The man waves.

Max waves back. "Gregory."

The man sighs, then drops his equipment in a pile by the door. He bends over, and with a poise that strikes Claire as studied—like he was a dancer or involved in an endeavor where every movement was dismantled, then reassembled to approximate effortlessness—he begins to break down the large heap into many smaller heaps.

"I'm sorry if I've confounded you." Max pats Claire on the knee and she understands, by his eyes-closed inhalation of cigarette and a volume of voice cranked down only a few notches, that they are to continue as if undisturbed.

This is challenging, for Claire. Gregory's presence is making it impossible to concentrate. It's not about him, of course, but that's beside the point. Max's news, or Claire's lack of processing thereof, has left a vacancy for a certain woman of God to worm her way back into Claire's brain. And it was just this morning, before breakfast, that Claire finally booted her out of there. Told her to pack up her beauty and her eyes and her chicken-shit ways and stay the hell away from Claire's hopes. It was a plan rooted in desperation and wishful thinking and, like all such plans, never had a prayer of survival.

The only solution for now is this man, this Gregory. He's standing upright again, arranging brushes and gallons of paint on the front window ledge, and Claire locks in, allowing him all of her attention. It's not difficult. He's wearing a yellow T-shirt the color of confidence and the shock of this hue against his dark skin—he is black, this Gregory—is a pronouncement of sorts, a tattoo on the moment, that no one else, save this handsome man, should ever again attempt to wear a shade this precious or complete. It occurs to Claire that Gregory and Max are probably lovers, that this would account for Max's deliberate indifference, his insistence that nothing has changed even though everything has.

"Maybe I should go," she says. "Leave you to it."

"What do you mean?" Max wrinkles in place and Claire sees that she is right.

"I mean my battered heart isn't getting any business. Maybe it's your turn."

Max blushes, a tone of red complementary to the yellow.

"It'll happen for you, babe," he says. "God's still warming up the engines as far as you're concerned. Just give it time."

"I wish I could give it something else," Claire says, eyeing Gregory's broad back. "Time hurts."

Scraps

It's getting late and the windows are leaking streetlight into Claire's eyes. She closes them and presses the button one more time.

"We're extremely hopeful," Sister Hilary says. "Things are really looking up."

Claire stabs Stop, rewinds, plays it again. "We're extremely hopeful," Sister Hilary says, stronger this time, more sure. "Things are really looking up."

"They certainly are," Claire says, head in hands. "In fact, they couldn't get any better."

The thing of it is, she's nearly finished. Dubbing Sister Hilary's voice-over narration into the final edit (a procedure akin to performing surgery on herself with a dirt-encrusted spear) is almost done, and other than a few odds and ends, including the odd end of re-listening to this tape fragment again and again, Claire is just about ready to deliver the excessively polished product to its funder. The only problem with this endeavor, other than avoiding Sister Hilary in the process, is the act itself. The enunciation of over.

Claire should be relieved. But she's not. For one thing, these weeks holed up in her house with her equipment have been an oasis of consciousness and control in an otherwise unruly environment. Audiotapes, videotapes, scripts, and dubbing machines—the instruments beneath her fingers have followed her commands with unerring accuracy and innate responsiveness. Drunk with solitude, she has watched her

233

little movie piece itself together virtually on its own, as if she is simply the agent of its overarching wisdom and capacity for coherent, thought-provoking filmmaking. She need do nothing but obey its wishes, punch its buttons, and the Universe will deliver its video.

And it's not just tape and metal that have supplied Claire these weeks of absorbing, albeit agitated, distraction. Her brain, soaking inside the shots of food bank recipients and GED students and the snips of Sister Hilary's voice, has proven to be an equally peppy companion. She never knew, for example, that a perpetual reiteration of Max's remark about her connection with Sister Hilary, in combination with the video and audio versions of said soul mate, could produce the sensation of an actual relationship with an actual person. And while Max's other, more cautionary statement shadows her fantasy like a hurricane warning in paradise, Claire has nevertheless allowed herself to indulge in the effervescent sweetness of a realm in which she and Sister Hilary, travelers together, are dipping their toes into the same brief, intelligent stream.

Until the stream revolts, the hurricane hits, and Claire is left with worry and water. What is she supposed to do, for instance, with the homophobia Max mentioned? She knows it's there, crouched inside her, tossing stink bombs at the target of her self-esteem. How to get rid of it is another matter, one about which Max has been surprisingly vague. And why—oh God, why?—did he preface a warning against "first-timers" with an ode to Claire and Sister Hilary? It's like one of those koans they talked about in her World Religions class, where you're supposed to overcome the contradictory nature of some statement by a period of focused meditation. Though the sound of one hand clapping, as far as Claire is concerned, was always *whoosh whoosh*. No long-winded contemplation there. In the same way, her connection with Sister Hilary, basic and complete, is—perhaps—an answer unto itself. Thick with potential, endless in its spiritual, emotional, intellectual, and—yes—sexual possibilities, Claire has never encountered such bulbous hope, such ripe and burgeoning fodder for a relationship of consequence. Not even (and this is a time for honest comparisons) with Shelly. And yet. And yet she plays the tape just one more time and is at once overjoyed and deflated, stuck inside her koan-ish self like a nut inside a squirrel. (Or is the squirrel inside the nut?)

Ever in need of a second opinion, and always up for another round of Zen-infested mental mastication, Claire consults the tape deck once again.

"What do you think about all this?" she asks. "Am I the biggest idiot on the planet or am I just following my heart?"

"We're extremely hopeful," Sister Hilary says, more optimistic than ever. "Things are really looking up."

One week and four hundred and seventy-five replays later, Claire skulks over to the Center. The tape is in the mail, sent certified and addressed to Sister Hilary in a spurt of panic and self-consciousness, but the rest of the equipment—video camera, sound mixer, tapes, and a camera bag stuffed with various cords and cables wrapped with such meticulous care that they needed to be checked repeatedly to make sure they were retaining their meticulous condition even with the bag shut—is a tougher unload.

Indeed, Claire was swimming in entropy for days until she realized (while chopping carrots, of all things, the corny orange chunks like sawed-off digits) that Sunday morning, during mass, would be the ideal time to drop her load. What better distraction than Christ Himself, especially during the late morning, Spanish-speaking service, when scores of folks pack the pews and spill over into the aisles, fans flailing, babies wailing, without so much as an extra eye or glance available for the boylike girl who could slink past the ruckus

235

and into the empty Rec Room like an extra drop in a pitch-perfect sea.

And she's right. It works.

Claire pats the trio of just-relinquished boxes, stashed hastily inside the portable closet in the back of the Rec Room, and shuts the door. She should have a tag-along orchestra, for moments like these. Or at least the violins—that quivering thing they do when something's sad. Instead, she gets a rumble of steps and faraway prattle that quickly morphs into right-outside-the-hall-way and then spewing-into-the-room people. Children, to be exact. Most of whom she doesn't recognize but a few, like Enrique and the calm-faced kid with the braid down his neck, she does.

"Enrique. My man." Claire gives a wave. She's feeling a bit nostalgic and, sans the violins, thinking that perhaps a chat with her old buddy might lift her out of the fog.

"What are you doing here? Didn't you, like, die or some-thing?" Enrique seems in no mood for fog-lifting. He's grown since Claire saw him last, his height and weight reapportioned so that one has gained at the expense of the other. His white collared shirt is tucked into a pair of pants that are not so much too big as too beautiful, giving him the air of vanquished royalty.

She inches toward him, ignoring his indignation. "How about you? What's this? Children's group?"

"Duh." His hands disappear inside the pockets of his pants. "They send us out after the first song."

"Who's the teacher?"

Enrique nods in the direction of a teenaged girl with stage-worthy mascara and a gap-toothed smile. "Her."

Claire salutes the girl, who merely blinks in reply. "She looks nice. Better than Sister Frances, eh?"

"Sister Frances left." Enrique scoots back toward the group.

"Left where? What do you mean 'left'?" Claire had noticed

236

the absence in the last few meetings, but had figured the older woman was probably avoiding her, Claire, around whom the world revolves. "You mean left the after-school group or left altogether? Where'd she go?"

He shrugs, but not like he doesn't know. More like he knows but won't tell her. "She just stopped showing up. How should I know where she's at?"

"Enrique, look. I'm sorry I didn't give you more of a chance. I should have let you help me more. I'm sorry I was such a grouch. That was dumb."

"Unh hunh." Enrique loses some of his height but none of his resolve. "She's about to start." He pokes a thumb toward Mascara Girl and subtracts himself from the conversation.

Claire stands, watching his reentry into the group (his smacking of another kid, the tug-fest that follows, the teacher's gentle prodding them out of it) and understands, like it is she who has lashed out and then been patiently admonished, that she is not forgiven. That sometimes, when you fuck up, the objects of your carelessness and misuse will simply get out of your way.

The hallway is unoccupied, save two small girls with matching haircuts and dress lengths ambling toward Claire with their arms linked together.

"There she is," says one, her stubby legs shifting to a skip and her companion following along. "She finally got here."

Claire stops. "Lupe," she says. "I didn't recognize you with your hair like that."

Lupe's once-hacked bangs have grown into a curtain of black stretching over her eyes. "They grew," she says.

"I can see that. You two must be headed to the kids' group."

"Maybe," Lupe says. She's staring at Claire in that strange way of hers. Like she's x-raying her soul.

"What's your name?" Claire turns to the other girl who, though sporting a bang-clearance almost as dramatic as her friend's, carries none of the same intensity.

"Lupe," she says.

"Your name is Lupe too?"

"Yup." Lupe the Second starts jerking her knees back and forth at a frantic pace. Claire's not sure where to place her eyes.

"Enrique told me Sister Frances left." She speaks to a spot between the two girls. "Did you two know that?"

"Enrique's cute!" Second Lupe swings her arms forward and down against her dress. Her knees are still knocking about in a super-charged frenzy.

"Do you have any idea where she went? Sister Frances?" Claire tries to pretend she's not excessively curious, that she's not interrogating kindergarteners for this scrap of information.

Second Lupe scrunches her forehead underneath her bangs. "Las Vegas? I think Las Vegas." She grins. "Mi abuela lives there."

"No," Original Lupe clucks. "She went to Los Angeles. She went back there. She had to go back. To that man."

"What?" Claire is evaporating. Either that or the girls are growing larger. She slams her shoe against the hallway floor to regroup.

"The man who lives there." Lupe shifts and her bangs sway gently. "She had to go back to be with him."

"Graham crackers!" Second Lupe screams, her feet scurrying forward. "Let's go get graham crackers!"

Original Lupe smirks at Claire, amused like an adult would be amused, and the two girls fly away, spinning down the hallway like a brand new song.

238

Verge

Claire is awake, but a second ago she wasn't. A second ago she was in El Salvador. On stilts. It was a battlefield, or maybe a regular field, but either way it was brimming with bodies, some of which were sticking to the bottoms of her stilts and thwarting her progress, if it could even be called that, as she made her way West (how did she know it was West?) in search of Sister Hilary.

The alternative, the glow of her bedside lamp splashing onto her knees and furnishing thin shadows against the sheets, is hardly any better. These caves of wakefulness, more and more frequent of late, accompany her nightmares like force-fed intermissions. They are, she knows, merely a holding pattern—a pale stretch of time in which the dreams can't touch her, but instead can only taunt. It's hard to say which is preferable: fear, or waiting for fear's return.

Claire unhooks from the clot of sheet at her feet, pulls on shorts and a T-shirt, and drags herself over to the fridge. It's on her way back to the couch, strawberry banana yogurt in one hand and spoon in the other, that she sees the face at the door.

She jumps, then stumbles. It's Sister Hilary.

Claire blinks. How can this be? She found her without the stilts, without the sleeping. Or maybe this is just an extension of her dream, one of those unbearably lifelike kinds. Claire's spoon clangs to the floor. She picks it up. The person at the door—who is undoubtedly Sister Hilary, a fact that in several ways is just now registering in Claire's muddled head—turns her face as if to leave. Claire charges toward the door, spoon first.

"I'm sorry to interrupt your snack time." Sister Hilary stands on the outside step, a dark blur against the wash of streetlight behind her. "This is unorthodox, I know. To show up without an invitation."

Claire nods. Her legs, hollow up till now, fill back in. "Consider yourself invited." She kicks the door closed with her foot, shuttling Sister Hilary into the room.

"Thank you." The visitor, though she's never been here before, makes herself right at home by trotting over to head-quarters and taking a seat next to a stack of unpaid bills. "It's such a strange night. I tried to sleep, but it didn't happen. I was driving back from the store, and I noticed your light. We need to talk about your movie."

"My movie." Claire and her yogurt settle into the far edge of the couch. Her house is nowhere near the store, is not between any store and Sister Hilary's place. "What about it? You hated it, didn't you?"

"No. Of course not. I didn't hate it at all. Claire, it was mar-velous. It was just what we were looking for. It was perfect." Sister Hilary is wearing jeans and an oversized T-shirt. It's wrinkled and pours onto her lap like milk. "I just wanted to thank you for all your hard work. We really appreciate it."

Claire peers over at the clock beside her bed. "You came here at two a.m. to tell me how much you like my movie?"

"Mmm hmm."

"Anything else?"

"No. That was it."

"I see." Claire gulps a spoonful of yogurt. It's cold and decent. Her head—still muddled, getting clearer—crowds with questions. But what to ask? The wrong words could ruin it. "It's weird that you're here," she says.

Sister Hilary looks at her lap. "I know it is."

Claire watches her—the hesitation, the daring. *Why are*

240

you here, Hilary? What changed your mind? Claire tries to push the thoughts into Hilary's lap, where maybe, probably, she would answer them, but it doesn't happen. The questions remain in Claire's mind, safe there.

"I was just dreaming about you," she says. "That's what I meant. That's why it's weird to see you."

Sister Hilary tilts toward the table. She scans the stack of bills like this is what she came for—an emergency cash flow intervention. "Mmm," she says.

"Though the dream wasn't about you, exactly. I was looking for you but you weren't around. It was in El Salvador."

"Let's not," Sister Hilary plucks a bill off the pile, examines it, sets it back, "talk about that, shall we?"

Claire downs another mouthful of yogurt. This one is bitter and smooth. Her courage flares. "You mean El Salvador or you and me?"

"Claire, please. You think you understand it, but you don't. You couldn't. Seeing a painting doesn't even remotely begin to qualify you to—"

"What are you talking about? I don't—"

"I showed our president my paintings, you know. She liked them all except those. The ones about El Salvador. She said they were too graphic for her taste. That they might not represent our order in an appropriate fashion. If I were to exhibit them, that is. The Church can only go so far, you see. In what they can allow. There's what actually happens and then there's the face we show the world. A body removed from its face. That's our Church."

Claire, suddenly not at all hungry, sets the remains of her yogurt on the floor. "But it's good, right? For you to get it out there? To show people what happened?"

Sister Hilary stashes her hands in her lap, folds them inside the big white shirt. "Perhaps."

"You could talk to me about it, you know. You don't have to push me away every time I try to—"

241

"And how would that help?" Sister Hilary's hands spring out of her lap, opening themselves to the air. Her face twists, tightens. "How would talking to you be any different than talking to Sister Maria? Or the counselor who told me to write down my dreams, which only made it worse. Or the understanding, sympathetic Church folks who don't understand a damn thing and whose sympathy is based on their own sense of guilt for having done nothing—absolutely nothing—to help. Is that what you had in mind?"

"No." Claire digs her teeth into her lower lip. "I know it was horrible. Or I don't know, like you say. But, and this is going to sound wrong, but it's like I came up with a strategy. Of how to ease it a little."

"No you didn't."

"But I did. It's like I'm building this awful place inside of me—in my dreams, partly, but in the daytime too—so it can live there. So all that stuff can have someplace else to go. And then maybe it won't have to be as bad for you."

Sister Hilary holds her breath. For a long time, like it's a contest. When she starts to breathe again, she does so with great care, as though she's afraid of making a mistake. "I showed her the other painting, you know. The one of you."

Claire sits up, flattens her shoulders against the couch. "You did?"

"Of course. I showed her everything I've produced so far. I had to be honest with her. If I'm to receive permission to paint, then she needs to know what I'm painting."

"And?"

Sister Hilary shoves the pile of bills toward the center of headquarters. She skims the table with unsteady hands and stares at the surface as if in a mirror. "She didn't say anything about it. Nothing. I suspect she knew it was more than a simple portrait. But if you don't name something, it doesn't exist. It's worked for the Church for centuries. Why should this be any different?"

Claire's knees start to tingle. She bumps them against each other to erase the sensation, but this just makes it worse. "You're pissed. I don't think I've ever seen you this pissed before. Maybe that one time when that kid poured the whole jar of paint on that other kid's head. You looked pretty angry then, though I could tell you were trying to hide it. And then at me, you've been pissed at me before, but this is different. You seem—"

"Claire," Sister Hilary dislodges from her bill-paying post and eases herself slowly, then quickly, over to Claire on the couch, "do you have any idea how difficult it was for me to paint that picture of you?"

"No?" Claire shivers. She had forgotten about Sister Hilary's eyes, how big they are. Up close, they're like large lamps seeking larger spots to illumine, as if this will help somehow.

"You weren't there with me, so I had to do it all by memory. I didn't think it would work. The slope of your temples and the tone of your chin, the weight of your cheek. I had to pull it all out of my head and scratch it onto the canvas. It was like painting a thought. Somehow you made it through."

"Or a better version of me," Claire sputters. "You made me look really good."

"You do look really good."

"Stop it."

"All right." Sister Hilary balls her hands like a child would, before a spatter of tears. "I think I can do that."

"It's just that, I don't want to fuck it up for you. Or maybe I do. I don't know." Claire's mouth feels like a wound, a hole punched in her head by a fist. "I'm sorry," she says.

"For what?"

"You know for what."

Sister Hilary swallows. "Claire—"

"You know what I don't get, though? What doesn't make sense to me?" Claire's mouth fills with heat and soft, tangible reason. "I don't see how God, or the Universe, or whatever you're going to call it, could create a face like yours, like the one you're wearing, and no one's supposed to touch it. That doesn't make any sense."

Sister Hilary's bunched-up hands flatten out and slip underneath her legs. "I'd agree with you, but I'd sound vain."

"That's okay. I won't tell."

"You won't, will you?" Sister Hilary's mouth crooks upward like she's smiling, though it's not quite what she's doing. Her face is a maze of competing expressions—fear, delight, bewilderment. She sighs and, as she does so, picks a hand from under her leg and places it on Claire's knee. Then her thigh. "I was going to break in your house, you know. To get you back."

"You were?" Claire laughs. Being this close to Sister Hilary, having Hilary's hand on her thigh, is making her giddy. The edges of her awareness are fuzzy and relaxed and her center is a ball of bliss. "You should have. That would have been great." She shifts her body so her knees are touching Sister Hilary's. She's too elated to do anything else. "I had it coming."

"You did." The multiple expressions have whittled down to just one—hunger.

"Come here," Claire says.

Hilary does. Her face moves so close to Claire's that it disappears into a new kind of face. It's skin, mostly, and a gentle heat that lifts off the surface and licks Claire's elation. Though she knows she will kiss her—in a second, a splinter of time that is as patient and as unmanageable as the warmth off Hilary's skin—Claire sees that it is this nearness, this joy of proximity, she really wants.

"Closer," she says.

And, as if Hilary knows what Claire means, knows it's not possible to get any closer than they are in this moment, merely smiles, her lips pushing her cheeks away from the center of her face.

Which ends it. Claire can't wait any longer. She falls forward, her lips into Hilary's—sweet, flush, impossible. It's both too much and not nearly enough.

"Okay?" Claire speaks through joined mouths.

"Mmm," Hilary says. The sound flows into Claire like wine and she pulls Hilary in so there is nothing between them: no air, no caution, not even a molecule of doubt. Hilary meets this impulse by giving way, leaning back so they are flat on the couch, both of them, Claire's body above her own.

The horizontal situation is enough to drive Claire out of her haze. She's fixed, pointed. The buzz between her legs sprouts wings and sets her in motion: knees pin her to the couch; hands slide along Hilary's waist, peek under her shirt; lips taste Hilary's face and mouth and the slip of skin at the base of her neck that smells like stillness. Though it's not enough to stop her. Claire knows she could come right now, her shorts still on, hands and feet trembling with the weight of what they're doing.

So she stops. Props herself up on delirious hands and glances down at the face that has branched into a blurry fugue.

"What's wrong?" Hilary's eyes are open, but it's like they're not. Like she doesn't see Claire, but a picture of Claire that's trapped in her head. Claire knows this look—it's lust, pure and unreigned—and it's not what she wants for them. Or it's not all she wants.

"Nothing. Nothing's wrong." Claire adjusts her hips on Hilary's and matches—for a second, she can feel the click of affinity—the blunted gaze of the woman beneath her. Yet it's so much more. Claire loves this woman. She wants her, she will (she now sees this is true) die if she doesn't have her, but it needs to be, somehow, connected to her heart. Which is tricky. She's never done such a thing before.

Hilary's arms wrap around Claire and pull her back in. "Sweet Claire," she says. "You're so beautiful."

Claire thinks to deny it, but she won't. To do so would be to take something from a person she intends never to take from again. "Not nearly like you," she says. She draws her palm along the rim of Hilary's cheek. "Not even close."

Hilary hums into the motion, her eyes truly closed now, her breath drifting to shallow and waiting. She says something that Claire can't make out at first, thick as it is with want. She says it again and the word shatters Claire's confusion, synchronizes love and desire in a sound.

"Please." She said "Please."

"I love you," Claire says. Not just because she means it, which she does, but because everything that happens will spring from that place. She slips her lips back onto Hilary's and kisses her again, soothes the question harbored there. Their mouths moan, mesh, latch together. Claire is fearful at first, but remembering the request, the word like a mandate out of Hilary's throat, she slides her tongue gently between her own teeth, then lips, then Hilary's.

Hilary yields, pulling Claire's head forward. Claire's hands, which were planted at Hilary's waist, holding on, spread like starfish and start to explore, one on Hilary's rear, the other edging higher.

Their lips and tongues quicken, pulse and relax to a burgeoning pace, and Claire mimics their mouths with her emerging hands. There is nothing under Hilary's shirt but Hilary and when Claire finds her breast, plump and alive, with a nipple that curls against Claire's palm like currency, Hilary pulls her mouth from Claire's and gasps a little.

"This," she says. "This is so ..."

"Do you want me to stop?" Claire's hands twitch and pause. She'll do whatever Hilary wants. It doesn't matter.

"No." Hilary's eyes are still open and closed. "No. Not at all." Her thumb drags against Claire's lower lip. "You can't."

Claire's palm shifts on Hilary's breast, a friction that causes Hilary's pelvis to rise in a kind of panic.

"Can I take off your shirt?" Claire asks. It's what needs to happen, but only she would know this.

Hilary nods and her arms lift above her head—like a child, but nothing like a child. Claire peels off the shirt and wants to stare, just to take in the new skin and ready breasts and unraveling that awaits, but Hilary won't have it. Her pelvis rises again and Claire's head dips down, onto her breast. She rounds it with her tongue, then starts to suck. Hilary's voice turns deep, garbled. Her hips grind into Claire and her fingers, on Claire's back, dig in.

Claire could explode, with the wonder and tumult and certainty of it all, but that would be an indulgence. Instead she leads her hand to Hilary's stomach and, after that, to the top lip of her jeans.

"Can I—"

"Yes." Hilary stills her hips for an instant so that Claire, both hands now, can unzip the pants and slide under, then in.

"Is this—"

"Yes." Hilary's face stiffens and she shoves her jeans off her hips. As though they offend her. She seems to lose something in this motion—some nerve, some sanction—and her face pulls tighter, farther in.

"Should I—"

"Yes." The sanction reemerges, Hilary's hand hooking Claire's neck and pushing her back to the breast. Claire's lips pull and suck and her fingers—two of them inside, her thumb riding the edge—glide and pull with an imperative of their own.

Hilary's body fills into itself, Claire can feel this happen. She works her hips into Claire's hand and the area inside her chest, next to her breast and Claire's mouth on this breast, swells outward to take in both their bodies. Claire is held by this expansion, encouraged by it, and she pumps her fingers deeper and faster, careening into its warmth.

This is love. The smell and the taste and the pace. The desperation. This is what it feels like to make manifest that elusive drive. Claire's mouth and fingers pin her to this spot, cradle the two of them over its infinite landscape. They deserve this. They've earned it.

Hilary's fingers twitch into Claire's back. Her throat starts to release bursts of air, as though she is falling out of herself. Her fingers dig in harder, her thrust against Claire quickening.

"I got you, babe," Claire says, then regrets the "babe," pushes deeper and faster to atone for the error, though it doesn't matter because Hilary is coming, is shuddering inside her limbs and her heart and the slick of her skin against Claire's. Her bigger heart, the one in which they both exist, shudders as well, tucking them inside its folds. They are immense. And joyous.

When she's finished, when her body has wailed against the edges of itself and all that's left is a low burr in the back of her throat, Hilary takes her hands off Claire and returns them to her own face. She sighs, then stays quiet. Then starts to cry.

"No," says Claire. "You don't have to—"

"It's not bad." Hilary presses her palms into the sockets of her eyes, traps her tears inside her hands. "I didn't know how this would be, that's all. How it would go."

"It was …" Claire hesitates to mar it with words.

"There was so much."

"Yes."

"I didn't expect that. I thought it would be more contained. Private. But it wasn't, was it?"

"No." Claire melds her body into Hilary's, lands there.

Hilary closes her eyes, eyelashes glossy with tears. She's still in the shared place, just one degree away.

Claire traces a finger down Hilary's cheek, rests it in the silent space at the base of her neck.

And waits.

Pardon

Claire burrows a foot inside the batch of blankets stowed at the bottom of the bed. If she reaches to pull them up, which she could do in a theoretically graceful leg-to-arm maneuver, she risks waking the mound of slumber to her left. More precisely, she risks staring into the residual face of what was, there can be no doubt about it, an unusually elevated evening. She finally decides, after a few meager attempts to snag the blanket result in the bedcover's complete withdrawal from the bed, that where she is—under a thin sheet, skating on the other side of a full night—is the best place to be.

"Claire?" Hilary, as proof that it doesn't matter anyway, that either action would have produced the same outcome, slips her just-roused body around Claire's. "You should have let me know you were awake."

"Why?" Claire rests against the sense and memory evoked by the cover of Hilary's limbs. She won't mention that sleep never managed to catch her.

Hilary yawns. Then sighs. For a moment, Claire thinks she's drifted back to sleep. "Well," she says finally. "I never got a chance to, you know ... please you. That's not exactly fair."

"Fair?" Claire tangles her legs into Hilary's. "Believe me, that was the most amazing night of my life. There'll be plenty of time for making it 'fair,' like you say. Though it might be tough. You're incredible when you come."

Hilary blushes, buries her face in Claire's neck.

"Sorry," Claire says. "It's true, though. It was unreal. It's like everything I did before wasn't even sex, like I might as well have been playing Parcheesi."

Hilary nips Claire's ear with her teeth. "Watch it."

"Right. Me and my uncensored mouth." Claire draws a hand to her ear, protecting it against further assault. "But, really. You don't know. It was so ..."

"Mmmm." Hilary tugs Claire's hand from her head and leans in. "Tell me a story," she says. Her breath in Claire's ear is fractured and urgent.

"A story?"

"Yes."

"What kind of story?"

"A good one."

Claire stares at the ceiling, at the crack in the plaster that resembles the state of Mississippi. Only one story comes to mind, a story she should have told Hilary a long time ago. She holds it close for a few more seconds, shelters its exuberance in the corners of her mouth. Then lets go.

"Okay," she says. "Here's a story. Once upon a time, there was someone named Claire. And she looked a lot like me. Or, she was me. And she—the Claire that's me—woke up in this room about two years ago. Wasted. Except, it was more than that. There was blood all over the bed. It was coming out of my arm. I thought maybe I'd been shot."

Hilary's fingertips, which had been initiating a leisurely inspection of the area in and around Claire's ear, halt their progress. "What are you talking about?"

"My story. This is my story." Claire leans into Hilary's hand, warm cheek against warmer palm. "I found out later what happened. It was that stupid Trish and Ellen. Shelly told me. They were the girls I used to run with in junior high. We got into all kinds of trouble back then. Stupid stuff. Like breaking into people's houses and stuff like that."

"You? I can't imagine."

"Yeah, well. This was different, though. Back then. Most

kids would have ripped off the stereo and taken all the free cash, but that's not what we were about. We just wanted to hang out. To look. Like hitching a ride on ordinary people's lives—folks with nice TVs and pictures of the family plastered all over the walls. We didn't have those types of lives, any of us. And so we poked around. Until we got caught." Claire flicks her foot against the sheet, cool weight over clammy toes. "You always get caught eventually, you know?"

"Apparently."

"It was the summer after eighth grade. We were all there, but they said it was just me. Trish and Ellen claimed it was all my idea, that they were just there because I forced them to come. So I spent the time in Juvie and they got nothing. Nothing. And then that night, when I saw them again, I guess I just went ballistic or something. I hadn't seen Trish in years and Ellen had left town to get married, but there they were, and I guess one of them said the wrong thing and I was loaded and, well ..." Claire tries to yawn but instead just flaps her mouth open.

"Shelly said it was like somebody had taken out my brain and all that was left was fists and blood. Though I didn't know any of this, when I first woke up. I thought maybe someone had tried to off me while I was sleeping. I was mostly drunk, but I'd smoked a little weed too and that had got me all paranoid. God," she laughs. "I can't believe I'm telling you all this."

Hilary edges in, next to Claire's cheek. "I can."

"But see, the thing is, it wasn't even the gash in my arm that had me worried. I was ... I don't even know if I can describe it. Something had happened to my mind, with all the booze and the weed and the bashing. It was like I didn't know who I was. Everything I'd always thought of as me, the image I carried around without even thinking about it, it suddenly fell apart. Disappeared inside me like an old meal. And all I had left was nothing, a huge wad of nothing that was

251

me on that bed all torn to bits. There was no ground. Nothing solid. It was awful."

Hilary stirs, close and warm. "It sounds awful," she says.

"I remember saying, I said it out loud too, 'Oh, this is where I'm supposed to pray to Jesus.' But I didn't, of course. I couldn't. That's not who I was back then. I just tried to fight it off as best I could, even though there was no 'me' to fight it with. I just had to wait it out, inside my body. I finally fell asleep, I guess. Slipped away inside whoever I was."

Hilary's breathing is steady again and it flops against Claire's cheek like a sideways curtain. "How did you get out of it?"

"See, that's the weird part. I didn't. It was a lot later when I woke up, I don't know how much, but the sun was out and the light in the room was vicious. It was pouring on in like it had rights, you know? Like it wasn't going to stop. But that wasn't what threw me. What threw me was that it wasn't just me this time. This time, there was someone there with me and, this is the weird part, it was Jesus. Like, I mean, I'm not even religious or anything. Why would Jesus want to visit me? But there he was, right next to my bed."

"Wow."

"Yeah," Claire says. "It was so … He made so much sense. He didn't say anything, but he still made so much sense. All he had to do was stand there, and I got it." She tries for casual, but her voice splinters into pieces. "I never knew I was okay before that. Like, really okay. Like, loved. And all the stuff before, about how I wasn't me, all of that was still true because *this* is what I was. What he was seeing."

She swallows. "I'm not sure how long he was there, but after a while he wasn't any more. And I knew right then that I was going to get sober and he was going to help me, but it took me another year before I was ready to do it."

Claire sits up in bed. She's naked and her belly is covered with knees and sheet while her back hangs suspended. Hilary

252

joins in by shuttling her hand up and around the lower regions of Claire's spine.

"You're the first person I've told," Claire says. "I didn't want to ruin it by talking about it."

"You haven't told Max?"

"No." Claire winces against the flash of sunlight sneaking into the room through the window by the door. "I wanted to tell you, though. A bunch of times. Even when I first met you, I imagined saying it. I knew you wouldn't doubt it. Or tell me I was hallucinating. You'd know I wasn't."

"That's true."

"But then I didn't. I didn't tell you. It was like I didn't want to burden you. Though that's not even really what it was. I guess I saw you as the real deal, and what happened to me wasn't like that. It wasn't in your category. And you might think I was—I don't know—like, trying to be all holy or something. When I'm not at all." Claire clasps her knees under the sheet. "Not at *all*."

A sound like wind ekes out the other side of Hilary's hand. "And my holiness is so intact." She pats Claire's back.

"Don't say that." Claire drops her knees onto the bed. She takes her body, takes all of herself, and slides on top of Hilary. "You're perfect. I have firsthand knowledge of this fact." She kisses Hilary's mouth and cheeks. "See? Perfect lips. Perfect skin. God pulled a double shift the day She made you."

Hilary's eyes sink shut. "Oh babe," she says.

The Oldsmobile is dark and boundless and parked next to Kitty's truck like its new best friend. Claire and Sister Hilary stand beside them, squinting under the sun.

"I'm surprised you could stay this long," Claire says, thumb on the Oldsmobile's door latch, jamming the button in and out to cradle her nerves. "I'd think you'd be missed at the house."

Hilary is beaming, a new species greeting her planet. Her

eyes are wrinkled and her shirt is smooth. "Sister Frances moved out last week and Sister Maria is at a conference in Chicago. I won't be missed."

"That's what you think." Claire jabs the door handle one too many times and the door snaps open. She nudges it shut with her knee. "Sister Frances. What's her story? I heard she went back to LA. What did she—"

"So this is who this car belongs to. I didn't think anyone drove these clunkers anymore." Kitty, smelling like rum and looking like death's second string, shuffles onto the driveway. "I thought I was gonna have to call the cops to come haul it off."

"She was just about to leave." Claire's chin slumps toward her feet and she slips inside the hole of herself. "Just give her a second."

"You must be one of Claire's strays. She brings home a lot of those."

"Kitty—"

"Course you can't blame her, she's got her father's looks and charm, the bastard. I never should have let that boy get a snatch—"

"Kitty, this is Hilary. *Sister* Hilary. She was just dropping something off from the Bearley Community Center and now she has to go."

"Bullshit. No offense, sister, but you ain't no nun. And that car's been here all night. I know because I was out walking Sinatra before the sun came up. He had to crap."

Hilary digs something out of her pocket, which ends up being a set of keys, and rams it into the lock on the driver's door. Her cheeks are deeply blushed, like plums. "You're Claire's mother? I wouldn't have guessed. You look nothing like her."

The Oldsmobile starts with the roar of a small plane and speeds out of the driveway with such power and precision that Claire thinks for a minute someone else has taken possession of the wheel. Then Hilary takes the corner at the end of the court by clipping off an unsuspecting mailbox and Claire sees that nothing has changed.

She turns to Kitty.

"Thanks," she says. "Thanks for that."

"Don't mention it." Kitty waves her off. "I brought your mail, by the way. Tex saved it up for you."

Claire snatches the bundle out of Kitty's wobbly grasp and falls silent. A letter from UCLA crowns the top of the heap.

Kitty draws closer, her body occupied with the set-reset stance of the chronically inebriated. "There's a school letter in there. You better open that up."

"See," Claire wipes the envelope off the top of the pile, "that just shows how clueless you are. This letter has the thickness of a potato chip. Do you know what that means?" She mashes her heel into the driveway. "Do you?"

Like it's a game, like she's just been invited to play, Kitty lifts into an approximation of readiness. "Well ..." she says.

"Well, it means I didn't get in," Claire says. "When an envelope is this thin, it means they don't want you at their school. 'Thanks, but no thanks. Good luck in your future endeavors.'"

Kitty's lifting, her gearing-up continues unabated. "I know a lot more than you think," she says. "Like, for example, I know you act like you hate me, but you don't. We're the same, you and me. We got the same stuff." She laughs, a broken babble, and wanders toward the house with a pace of her own.

Claire, standing alone in the backwash of this maternal display, attempts to hike up the lump of mail in her hands—to erase what's happened, to make it vanish—but gets it wrong and the pile shreds and splatters all over the pavement. It's junk mail and flyers, brash pleas for her time and attention. And it's something else as well: a fat envelope with her name, her Claire McMinn, in someone's else's handwriting and the name of the school, the San Francisco State Department of Cinematic Studies, stamped in the top corner. Like a grin.

255

A Story for the Crows

"What do you mean 'We can't do this anymore'?! We've barely done anything to begin with. We just got started."

"And now we're stopping. I was out of my mind. I never should have come over the other night."

"So you avoid me for a week? Pretend it never happened? That's your idea of an enlightened response to the situation?" Claire kicks aside the pile of clothes impeding her leg from stretching across the mess that is Sister Hilary's bed. Hilary, in a not-to-be-misinterpreted articulation of their lack of affiliation in matters bed-wise, is on the other side of the room, reorganizing the herd of cups on the windowsill.

"This is about Kitty, isn't it? She's a freak, for sure, but that's no reason to—"

"This has nothing to do with Kitty, and you know it."

"No, I don't. I have no idea why you would throw away something that obviously brought you so much happiness. I mean, come on," Claire starts to get wound up just thinking about it, fits one thigh over the other to simmer down, "how can you say it's a good idea for that not to happen again?"

Sister Hilary is hard at work. She bangs cup against cup in an ever-anxious quest for a satisfactory arrangement. She's like the guy at the Fair with the shells and the nickel, only her cups are facing skyward and there's no nickel.

"Because it's not a good idea for it to happen again," she says. "It would be insane if it happened again. I have a responsibility to my Church and my community that cannot be overridden by the sway of—"

"Please," Claire says. "Not *sway*. Don't make it about *sway*."

"Okay, then. Fine. It's not about that. It's about free will. I choose to be a nun and I choose not to be with you. Is that any better?"

Claire gulps. The back of her throat tastes like sand. "You could choose differently. Sister Frances did."

Sister Hilary peers beyond her cups. Her face in the early evening light is pale, almost clear. "Sister Frances did nothing of the sort. She's back in Southern California, resuming her teaching career."

"In the middle of the semester?"

Sister Hilary slips her thumb into a cup handle, crooks it inside the porcelain. "What are you talking about? The timing of Sister Frances' departure in no way implies—"

"What about William? What's her game plan with him? He is in love with her, after all. It's the least she could do. Go back down there and see what she can hash out. Pick up where they left off. She's sober now, so maybe that can help her decide what to—"

"You're making this up."

"I'm not, though."

"There is no William." Sister Hilary's rearrangement activities shift to her clothing: retucking her blouse, removing bits of tissue from the pockets of her skirt and placing them on the window ledge. "Sister Frances has no suitors. She would have told me."

Claire chews her tongue, rolls it around inside her mouth. "I thought maybe she did. I thought that was maybe one of the reasons you came over the other night." She picks up the swatch of sheet loitering under her palm, lifts it to her nose, and inhales defiantly. It's clean and smoky, like it was aired out in the woods. "It would have been a good reason."

257

"It's irrelevant, what you're saying."

"But it's not. And even if it was. There's still what happened." Claire allows the sheet to rest in her lap. Her anger and annoyance rest with it, slinking off to the edges of the bed. "Everything's different now, but that doesn't have to be a bad thing. That doesn't mean we have to do stuff without thinking about it. We can figure this out. We don't have to—"

"No." Sister Hilary closes her eyes, eases into a face caved with fatigue. "It's irrelevant what you're saying because I'm leaving. I'm going back to El Salvador. There's a mission down there that needs assistance and I've agreed to a six-month commitment. I leave next week. I'm sorry." Her eyes poke open, but they settle on the detritus at the desk—the pens and papers and the jar with brush heads popping out of its emptiness like blossoms—instead of on Claire.

"El *Salvador?*" Claire joggles on the bed but it's mostly an internal maneuver. Her legs and her torso remain locked in place. "Why would you do that? It was a nightmare. You can't even talk about it and now you want to go *back* there? You can't. You can't do that to yourself."

"I spoke with our president about you," Sister Hilary says. "I told her everything that happened between us. We both agreed that a break from this location would be well advised. Besides, I need to take what's happened and realign my commitment to this work, to the Church."

"A Church you were totally dissing the other night."

"I was upset."

"You were a lot of things." Claire bridles the pinch between her thighs. "But that doesn't mean you have to run off to El Salvador. That's crazy. And all the people you lost. Idalia. It's just going to make it worse."

Sister Hilary drops a few inches, folds into the windowsill. "No."

"I'm sorry." Claire untangles from the sheets and her own misguided language. "But that's what I mean. How hard it is to deal with." She rushes off the bed, stopping in front of the blossoming brushes and Sister Hilary's speechless stare. "I'm just saying. Maybe there's a better answer. Even if you never see me again, you could at least stay here. Keep yourself safe. And away from a place that's going to remind you of all that death. And bodies. All that stuff."

Sister Hilary won't reply. It appears as though she can't. She is solemn and unmoving and coiled tight around herself.

Claire picks a brush off the desk and enfolds it in her fist. "It's me, I know. I always say the wrong thing. I'm an idiot. Really. Though I guess you already knew that. I should have—"

"Idalia was my first." Sister Hilary's words are flat, fractured. "There shouldn't have been a first, but there was. And it was her. We didn't even know what we were doing. It never would have occurred to us to call ourselves 'gay.' Or 'lesbian.' It was just between the two of us. It didn't exist anywhere else. And when she died, it was just … It was just God's way of answering a question I didn't even know I was asking. Until you showed up." She tries to smile. "And then I had to ask it again."

"But I thought that you, that we—"

"You thought you were my first." Sister Hilary's face is a warning, a reignited flare. "That my responsiveness to you was a function of your unending prowess and not my own familiarity with the act. Of course you did. Did you ever see *me*, Claire? Past your visions of conquest and vanity?"

"That's *all* I saw." Claire's own affront remains at bay, pressed aside by the remembrance of love in action. "That's all there was. Why are you trying to will that away?"

"Because I have to. What did you think? I'd leave the order to forge a relationship with someone I barely know? Or I'd ask you to—that I'd put you through that? That kind of responsibility?"

"You have to ask. To get an answer to something like that, you at least have to ask."

259

"But I won't." Sister Hilary shakes her head, heavy inside its pit of effort. "It's not your fault, Claire. I knew what I was doing. From the start. I wanted you and I got you. And then I had to take a hard look at what, exactly, I had gained. Which was nothing."

"Nothing?" Claire takes a step toward the window, toward Hilary and the cups and the thick Source that surrounds them. "C'mon. You're lying. What about the other night? What about when we were together and your heart grew like that? So big like that."

Sister Hilary stands, hands limp at her sides. "That was you. That was your heart, Claire. Not mine."

"No."

"This was never going to work. Couldn't you see that? Couldn't you see from the beginning where this would end up?"

And suddenly, she can. Now that she's standing closer to Sister Hilary, Claire can see it even better.

Max was right. Her dalliance with Sister Hilary was both more of the same and something entirely new. And a trick, of sorts. Wooing the first-timer who turned out to be anything but. And yet still remote. Impossible. Proving to Claire that she is, as she always suspected, unlovable.

Except it's not true. Sister Hilary may be leaving, but the shape of her departure is such that Claire is left holding a trinket. Barely formed, fashioned by unwitting hands, this tiny gem of a thing survives to remind her of what was gained. Remind her that caring isn't a disease, but an option. A necessary one. One that she might be—God willing—good at.

Claire trips backward, onto the bed. She gazes at Hilary, who has managed to remove herself from the room even as her body stays behind. The image pulls tears from Claire's eyes, shoving her further into the new world that gathers itself around her. She is both wrecked and pleased, devastated and elated. For here, in this still-tenuous, trinket of a place, she can see what's next. That she'll do this again. Not with Sister Hilary, probably not with Sister Hilary, but with someone. Someone excellent. And it will go better. Or it won't explode quite so quickly. And then that time, or maybe the next time (or the time after), Claire will settle in. Bask in the deep pace and steady horizons of reciprocal love. Love that will never end. Or maybe it will snag and tangle and need to inch apart to breathe, but that's beside the point. She'll let it catch her, this love. She'll learn to bear it.

It's just this scratch of time in which she can see it; Claire knows that in ten seconds the vision will be gone and she'll be back to begging for the thin slice of All She Has. And yet, now that it's arrived, she suspects she won't forget the truth. And where it came from.

"You're wrong," she says. "I had no idea where this would end up."

Bunny's got a hold of Reynold, the across-the-court neighbor's cat. Reynold is approximately the size of a human toddler and, as such, pours off Bunny's arms and down her legs like an overwhelming guest.

"Play a game?" She hikes Reynold, who appears to be enduring captivity with a patience unavailable to most cats, up past her armpits. "Play a game with us, Claire?"

Claire halts in front of her relatives. Sadness thumps inside her and her mouth is worn and dry. "What game?"

Bunny swings the cat from side to side and his hind paws, bulbous and matted with fur, scrape against the tops of her feet. "Hide and Go Seek. We take turns hiding Reynold in different places and then you gotta go find him."

Claire sighs, assessing the scene. Bunny, besides the cat, is wearing a dress five sizes too big for her and six shades too bright—a color in an arena that gives "purple" a bad name.

Walt, for his part, is barely wearing a thing: no shirt, no shoes, and, from what Claire can see of the shorts defaulting to gravity and edging past his bony hips, no underwear.

"Oh, yeah," she says. "This game. I heard about this game. This is the one that ends when Reynold claws the hell out of one or both of you and Tex has to go buy more Band-Aids."

Walt beats a stick, coated with a substance Claire hopes is mud, against the pavement. "That ain't true," he says. "Reynold don't mind."

"I don't know," Claire says. "Sounds too scary for me."

"Kitty said you're moving to L.A." Walt whacks the stick extra hard and his shorts dive down another inch. Claire resists the urge to reset them.

"Not exactly," she says. "I'm going to San Francisco. The school in Los Angeles didn't let me in."

"Why not?"

"Because one of my teachers never sent his recommendation. I did something bad to him and he got me back by messing up my application. So now we're even, me and him."

Walt freezes, his eyes a gleam. "So it's okay to get people back?"

Claire kicks his stick, checks her shoe for residue. "Not like you do, bucko. Your idea of getting back always seems to involve instruments of destruction and bodily orifices."

"Orfis?"

"Never mind."

Bunny wanders over to the sidewalk and sinks down, Reynold obliterating her lap and portions of surrounding curb. "We could put dirt in the mailbox," she says. "That was boss."

Claire waits. She can stay or she can go. It's a decision she made a long time ago. She just didn't know it until now.

"Or I could tell you guys a story," she says. "I know a game that's about telling stories."

Walt scratches the ring of dirt around his neck. "How come I never heard of it?"

"It's new. It's a new game." Claire scouts a spot next to Bunny and plops down, Reynold's tail silently lashing her thigh. "We each pick a thing. A person or an animal or anything you want."

"Like a turd?" Walt says.

"Not like that, bozo. You have to pick a regular thing."

"A turd is a regular thing."

Claire laughs in spite of herself. "You know what I mean."

"Okay." Walt relinquishes his stick and crawls into Claire's lap. He smells like bubblegum and little boy sweat. "I pick a man who sells encylopeedas."

"Regular or door to door?" Claire adjusts her legs so Walt is level and flush against her stomach.

He wriggles deeper into place. "Door and door."

"I pick Reynold," Bunny says.

"You can't pick him." Walt bops against Claire's belly. "Claire, tell her she can't pick him."

"Sure she can. There's nothing wrong with Reynold being in the story." Claire cracks her knuckles, one at a time. The sound pings into the court. "And me, let's see ..." She pretends to think. "I pick ... I pick a nun."

Bunny slams her knees against the curb and Reynold droops to her ankles. She squints. "A nun? Why you wanna pick a nun?"

"It's all right." Claire plucks a fleck of dirt from behind Walt's ear. It's sharp and warm, a tiny chunk of the planet. "I'll make it good. You'll see."

There's a crowd of crows in the trees across the court and, past them, a sky that's as simple and complicated as Claire's ever seen. She opens her mouth and lets it happen.

Z Egloff was born in California, raised in the Midwest, and schooled (academically and otherwise) on the East Coast. She currently resides in Northern California. *Verge* is her first novel. For more information, visit www.zegloff.com.